Dishes dried and put away, they returned to the bedroom. "Would you like more to eat, dessert perhaps?" he asked.

"No, thank you." The only dessert Ebony wanted was Richard. Wanting to leave before she embarrassed herself, she looked for her shoes.

He came up from behind and began massaging her shoulders. "Are you relaxed from the long day?"

She dropped her head to the side, exposing her neck to his feather kisses. She wanted to give in, but they had just met. It was too soon.

He turned her around to face him. "Did you enjoy the entertainment?" He gestured toward the Loony Toons playing on the television and returned to her neck.

"Excellent entertainment and food." This was a dangerous game, but she wasn't ready to quit—not yet.

He held her close. "Have I met all of your needs thus far?"

His acceptance of her, his warm whisper, his loving caress, his masculine scent all weakened her self-control. "You have been a most gracious host."

He lightly kissed her nose, then rested his forehead on hers. "Can I continue meeting your needs?" His mouth lowered to hers.

EBONY ANGEL

DEATRI KING-BEY

Genesis Press, Inc.

Indigo Love Spectrum

An imprint of Genesis Press, Inc.
Publishing Company

Genesis Press, Inc.
P.O. Box 101
Columbus, MS 39703

ISBN-13: 978-1-58571-239-7
ISBN-10: 1-58571-239-6
Manufactured in the United States of America

First Edition

Visit us at www.genesis-press.com
or call at 1-888-Indigo-1

DEDICATION

To those making the best out of an impossible situation.

ACKNOWLEDGMENTS

I thank...
God for the many blessings he bestows on me.
My family for the overwhelming support they give to me.
Angelique Justin, for taking a chance on a romance with very
    non-traditional characters and plot.
Doris Innis, my editor, for keeping me from going overboard.
Last, but not least, my readers. I truly appreciate you.

CHAPTER ONE

The cold slap of an early-morning Chicago winter greeted Ebony as she stepped onto the snow-covered porch. She adjusted her scarf and hat, then gingerly made her way down the icy steps and on the sidewalk.

"You got class dis early?" drawled Meechie, one of the neighborhood lookouts. He stepped from behind a parked van and blocked her path. "It's still black outside, girl."

"I can't talk today. I'm late." She observed her self-appointed protector in his ragged field jacket and filthy gloves. Drugs had claimed him long ago. Now he spent his days looking out for the police. In exchange for shouting warnings to the drug dealers operating down the block, he received his daily dose.

She inched around him. "Go inside before you freeze your tail off."

He pulled one of her book bag straps, stopping her in her tracks. "Trae know you out here?" He pointed a bony, gloved finger in the direction of the alley she was headed. "It's too damn dark for you ta be alone. He ain't gonna like me lettin' you go down there. You better get in the house. It can't be five yet. He ain't gonna like—"

"I'm not worried about Trae," she cut in. "Thanks for your concern, but I'm late." Easing away, she said, "Don't worry. I've lived here my whole life. I'm safe."

"Maybe I should walk with you?"

An amused smile touched her lips. Meechie moved slower than the line at the bank on the first of the month. How could he protect her? She'd seen dried twigs that weighed more and were stronger. "Thanks, but you'd better stay at your post." She trudged through the snow-covered lot into the alley with a heavy heart. Meechie was deteriorating

so quickly, she wasn't sure if she'd be able to convince him to go to rehabilitation before it was too late.

As usual, most of the lights were out. She made a mental note to
complain to the alderman, again. Someone appeared from between two
garages, startling her.

"You got a smoke?" a crackly female voice asked.

Ebony stood under one of the few working streetlights. "Sorry, I
don't smoke."

The bag lady cocked her head to the side as she crept into the light
with Ebony. "Oh." She leaned forward, squinting. "You a good girl."
She pulled the scarf down from her mouth and raised her ashy fingers,
chastising, "Don't walk down no alley. All these nasty perverts 'round."
She stuffed her hands under her armpits and bounced in place. "Don't
do that no mo'." She pulled down on her hat and shuffled away.

"Wait a second." Ebony rushed to the woman. "Take these." She
took off her gloves and handed them to her. "It's too cold to be outside
without gloves."

The woman's eyes shot wide open. "Ooo, these dem good insulated
ones." She slipped on one of the gloves. "Oh, there's fur inside." She
held her hand down and out as she opened and closed her fist. "Warm,
and looks good." Black eyes bright with gratitude, she shook her head.
"No one ever gave me such nice finery. Bless you, chile'."

The woman's joy at receiving the unexpected gift warmed Ebony's
heart. She smiled. Even if she missed the train, her day wouldn't be
ruined. She resituated her book bag, stuffed her hands into her pockets
and ran down the ally, then cut across the park.

Half out of breath, Ebony looked up at the long metal stairway
leading to the platform of the Laramie Street el station. Taking the steps
two at a time, she suddenly remembered her monthly pass was in her
other purse. Praying she wouldn't break her neck, she ran faster. When
she reached the platform, to her surprise, someone was at the transit
card machine.

She stood behind and to the side of the man, wondering why anyone would leave home in an expensive cashmere trench coat without hat or gloves in sub-zero weather.

He kicked at the machine. "What is wrong with this stupid thing? It won't take my cards! It won't take my money!" He drew the bill back, flattened it and tried to force it into the slot.

His wavy black hair half covered his reddened ears. *Probably frost-bitten,* thought Ebony. *And why is a white guy in this neighborhood anyway?* She heard the train approaching. She stepped in front of the man with a $5 bill in hand. "Excuse me."

"Hey!"

"We'll freeze to death waiting for you." She purchased the transit card, then turned to him. "Here you go." She handed the card over.

Their eyes locked. She had never seen such beautiful smoky blue eyes in her life, and his sexy crooked grin raised her temperature high enough to need central air. The clickety-clack of the train pulling in snapped her out of her trance. "Get going."

Handing her the card, he shook his head. "I can't take this."

The rich timbre of his voice sent her heart racing. She crossed her arms over her chest. "If you don't move, we'll both miss the train." She pretended to tune him out while she dug through her purse for $5. "You still there?"

Richard Pacini swiped the transit card, then pushed through the turnstile and ran along the platform. At first, he wanted to curse out the long-nailed, rude woman in the warm-looking parka. Then she set her stunning sepia eyes on him, and he melted. Memories of her sweet smell lingered; he inhaled deeply. The cold air burned his lungs, jolting him out of his daydream. He hopped on the train and stood in the doorway.

The conductor stuck his head out of his cubicle's small window. "Step fully into the train, sir."

Richard looked back at the turnstile for the young woman. She was still at the transit fare machine. He worried the machine was now giving her as much trouble as it had given him. "Can we please wait a few more seconds?"

"I'm on a time schedule. Step inside."

"I'm changing cars." Taking a risk that the man would leave him, Richard hurried along the platform to the conductor's car and hopped on.

"Next time you pull a trick like that, I'll close the door and pull off." The conductor poked his head out the small window, looked both ways, then closed the doors.

"I'm sorry. I was waiting for someone." Richard chose a seat near the front of the car and watched the streetlights as the train moved down the tracks. He hoped he hadn't caused her to miss the train. The way she crossed her arms over her chest and the determination in her eyes, told him she wouldn't accept the transit card. His only choice was to make the train and stall. He would lay odds his great-grandmother had the same fire. His grandfather, Nonno, often reminisced about her beauty, intelligence, kind heart and fire.

"Where do I get on the Red Line?" he asked the conductor.

"Get off at the State Street station. There are signs. You can't miss it."

It was only 5:22. Already feeling the long day stretch before him, Richard yawned, leaned forward and dropped his face into his hands.

The automated message announced the next stop. He heard the doors sliding open, and then closing.

"*Hola, Oscar.*" Ebony untied her hood, unwrapped her scarf.

"*¿Cómo está*, Ebony?"

She walked to the conductor's compartment, nodded slightly. "*Bien gracias, pero muy frío.*" She held up her hands.

Richard heard bright joking and sat up straight. No matter what language, he would recognize her deep, confident voice and her plush charcoal parka anywhere.

"Where the heck are your gloves?" Oscar asked in English. "Don't make me call your mother." The train stopped and doors opened. Oscar leaned out the window and did a visual check both ways.

"If you want to dog me out, dog me out in Spanish, please. I want to be fluent." She held onto the edge of a seat as the train lurched forward and moved down the tracks. "For a minute there, I thought I had missed you today." She heaved her book bag around, then plopped it on the seat. "I'm writing down our number. If I had of known giving away my gloves would get you to call, I would have given them away eons ago."

Richard watched her rummage through the bag for a pen. If she turned, he could see those exquisite eyes again. Oscar seemed a little short and old for her. Richard's eyes traveled from her boots to her jeans, then stopped at the end of her coat. He used his imagination to fill in the blanks for what lay beneath the parka. He guessed she was slightly over six feet tall.

"I have the number."

"So why haven't you called? I've told Mom all about you. I even showed her your picture."

Richard didn't realize he was smiling until Oscar shot him a knowing look. He stopped smiling instantly, but he couldn't stop the blood from rushing to his face. He pretended to study the advertisements along the walls of the train.

"I'll call. I promise. So why were you late?"

"Trolls reset my alarm clock for 4 P.M."

Oscar laughed. "Trolls?"

"We have a really bad troll problem. I think I need to call an exterminator." She unzipped her coat. "Thanks for holding the train for me. I had to switch cars, but I made it."

He shook his graying head. "You know I love you, but I didn't hold the train. Some maniac stood in the doorway talking about waiting for his friend." The automated system announced the next stop. "I need to get back to work. *Adiós.*"

"*Adiós.*" She turned and saw Richard. "Well hello there. I see you made it safely." She sat in the seat beside him.

His pulse raced. The contrast between her smooth dark skin and dazzling white smile was as captivating as her sepia eyes. He found himself staring.

She frowned. "Is something wrong? I can sit somewhere else."

"Oh no, no. Cat got my tongue for a second there. I apologize. I didn't mean to stare. You're just so beautiful."

Ebony covered her face with her hands, displaying at least two gold rings on each finger and long acrylic nails.

He gently pulled her soft hands from her face. He'd swear she was blushing. "Much better. I'm Richard, Richard Pacini."

"Ebony Washington."

He reached inside his coat pocket, took out his wallet and searched for a small bill. "Let me repay you now."

"No need."

He held out a $50 bill. "This is all I have." She laughed lightly and shook her head. He knew he'd never seen a brighter day. "What's so funny?" He brushed his hand over his dark, wavy hair.

"You tried to put a fifty in the machine. No wonder it was confused. You don't ride the train much, do you? And I'm not taking your money."

To keep from insulting her, he put the money away. "This is my first time. My car had not one—but two flats."

"I'm not trying to get into your business, but people like you don't usually come on this side of the tracks unless they're looking for drugs or a cheap trick."

"Like me?" He grinned. "You mean white."

Her lips tipped up at the corners. "Yes, white." She took off her charcoal fleece hat, allowing her blonde microbraids to fall freely. "It's getting hot in here."

"Whoa, now that's a shock. Amazing contrast." He started to reach for a few strands to examine, but thought better of it. He didn't want to insult her. "This had to take hours to do. Extensions right?"

"About twenty to be exact, and, yes, I wear weave. Do you always get so personal with strangers?" The next stop was announced over the speaker system.

Expecting to see annoyance, he was relieved to see amusement dancing in her eyes instead. "It works for me." The doors slid open, a few passengers stepped on, then the door closed. "I'm not here *trolling* for women or drugs." A slight breeze brought a hint of her sweet scent. Like her, the scent made him wish for more.

"You've been eavesdropping." She wrapped the scarf around her hands.

"Who, me? I'd never. What happened to your gloves?"

"I gave them away." She unrolled the end of the scarf, offering it to him. "So how did you end up at the Laramie Street station?"

"A semi was stuck under the Austin viaduct, so I continued down to Central."

"Oh, I bet I know what happened. A water main broke on Central last night. I'll bet Central is still closed."

"So that's it! I continued down the road when my car started to lean. I drove down to the next street. For a second I thought the power was off in the neighborhood. You should call your alderman or someone and have the lights fixed. Anyway, I drove around the corner and parked under a streetlight to change my tire."

"Didn't you have a spa—" she stopped abruptly. "Wait a second. You said two flats."

"I should have known there was something wrong with the spot I parked in. The few other empty spaces had chairs and other furniture in them." The whole placing chairs in the street to reserve a parking space was new to him. Born and raised in Texas, he'd moved to Chicago in December. He was still waiting on a call from his sister to welcome him to her city.

"Well, if you had spent all that time shoveling, you wouldn't want anyone taking your space either. Even the mayor says to respect others' parking spots."

"Yeah, I guess that's why the spot I parked in was filled with nails. I didn't see them until I got out of my car."

"Ouch."

"Yep, ouch. I saw the train station on Laramie and went for it. I'll call AAA from work. No offense, but I didn't want to be sitting in that area any longer than needed."

"Smart move."

The automated message announced the approach to the State Street station. He had meant to ask for her number before they separated, but time flew by too quickly.

She stood slowly, zipping her coat. "I'm afraid this is my stop. I have to catch the Red Line."

The tinge of sorrow that colored her voice encouraged him. "You're not losing me that easily."

"You're transferring also?"

"I am today."

CHAPTER TWO

Richard handed Ebony his cell phone. "Program your number in." Their fellow passengers ignored them, except for two young black males who had entered the Red Line train with them: one was snarling, the other looked as if he might explode any minute.

"Here you go." She returned his phone. "But you won't call."

"Why would you say that?"

"Right now you're cold, and it might be affecting your brain," she teased. "Wait until you've had time to thaw."

"You think I'm prejudiced? Or are you subtly telling me you would never date a white guy?"

She studied him a long while. "Neither. I really like you, but I'm a single mother and don't have time for games. What would your family say if you took me home for dinner? No sense traveling down a dead end when I'm on a long journey."

He checked the time on his cell phone, flipped it open and made a call. "Good morning, Nonno." He loved the way she cocked her head to the side as if to say, "What the heck are you up to?" If he could convince her to take those awful blonde extensions out of her hair, she would move from an eleven to a twelve on the beauty scale, which maxed out at ten.

He winked at Ebony. "Yeah, I know it's early, but I knew you'd be awake. Would you do me a favor?"

Ebony lowered her face into her hands. "I can't believe you're doing this. Tell whomever goodbye and hang up."

"It's alright, this is my grandpapà." He removed his finger. "I'm sitting here with the most beautiful woman I've ever seen. She won't go out with me because I'm white." He laughed at her mortified expression. "Of course I brushed my teeth."

"You're a dead man, Richard." She looked out the window. "Isn't this your stop?"

He watched a few passengers board. "Nope…Sorry, Nonno, Ebony was trying to distract me…" He frowned. "What do you mean she's probably too good for me? You're supposed to be on my side." His hearty laugh drew stares. "Just tell her I'm the greatest thing since pasta." He held out the phone. "He wants to speak with you."

"Are you serious? You don't really have anyone on the line do you?"

He held the phone to her ear, then watched her closely. After a few seconds, she relaxed, held the phone for herself, then laughed and joked with Nonno. He knew his grandfather would win her over. He hadn't met a woman who could resist the man's charm. Even his ice queen of a mother melted when Nonno was around.

She disconnected and handed him the phone. "Your grandfather's a mess. He said if you don't treat me right, I should look him up."

"Note to self: Stay away from Nonno when Ebony's around. Now tell me about your child." He dropped the phone into his inside coat pocket.

"Crystal's seven, and the light of my life."

His face scrunched up. "How old are you?"

"Twenty-four."

"That old? I thought you were eighteen, and I was getting me a young chick." He flashed a sly grin, his eyebrows bouncing. "Do you have any pictures?"

"Not on me. I haven't carried pictures since my wallet was stolen a few years ago." The the 87th Street station was announced. "Now, I know this is your stop."

"I'll ride to 95th with you, then double back. Are you trying to get rid of me?" he teased, suddenly worried his questions had become too persistent, too personal. He wasn't usually this forward, but he wanted to know everything about her.

"Of course not. So you're opening an office on the south side? Folks out here need financial planning, too."

"My thinking exactly. If everything goes according to plan, I'll be the CFO of a Fortune 500 company by the time I'm forty." He moved to Chicago to take a regional manager position in his investment firm. Only thirty years old, he was the youngest regional manager in the company's history.

"I have a few financial connections if you're interested."

"Thank you. I'll take all the help I can get. So what about you? What are your plans after college?"

She made a praying motion with her hands. "I'm so glad this is my last semester. I thought graduation would never come. My short-term plan is finding a job with a consulting firm and moving. My long-term goal is to own a consulting firm someday."

The excitement and pride in her voice warmed his heart. She was living proof that the economically depressed parts of the city produced more than criminals, drug addicts and welfare queens. "So you want to be the boss lady?" The train stopped at the 95th Street station. "I'll walk you out."

They walked onto the platform together and went to a secluded but well lit corner. "Thanks for everything," he said. "I don't know how to show my appreciation." She bit her bottom lip, and he thought he would overheat. He longed to kiss her luscious lips, but feared spooking her. "I'll call you." He could tell by her stiff stance that she didn't quite believe him.

She took off her scarf and handed it to him. "Wrap your ears and face with this. You'll have to walk a few blocks from the station, and there's nothing to block the wind."

"I'm not taking your wrap. You need it."

Slowly spinning with her arms held out, she said, "Look at me. An Eskimo called just the other day wanting to borrow this coat." She flipped the front flap, then shook the hood. "My scarf and hat are a fashion statement."

He hadn't intended on being outside for longer than the time it took him to run from his parking space to his office. He allowed her to tie the scarf loosely around his neck, grateful she didn't sign on to the stereotype that white people don't get cold. Her sweet aroma called to him. "What perfume are you wearing? It's been driving me crazy all morning."

"I'm allergic to perfume. I use lotions and shower gels. This one's called sweet pea. I bought it at Bath and Body Works."

He stroked the scarf, wishing it were Ebony. His instant attraction to her surprised him. He had always been level headed about women. "I think I'll buy stock in Bath and Body today. They have a winner." He lifted her perfectly manicured fingers to his lips, then pulled her hand back slightly, staring open mouthed. "Tell me this isn't a ring on the end of your nail." He touched the tiny gold ring on the tip of her index fingernail.

She laughed. "You're just noticing it?"

"You are one beautiful—yet strange—woman." He gently kissed her knuckles. "I'm pleased to have met you, Miss Ebony Washington."

"You are one handsome—yet impulsive—man. I think you need to head on to work and warm up, Mr. Richard Pacini."

Ignoring curious stares from bystanders, he took her by the hand and escorted her to the exit stairway. "I'll call you tonight. Is nine too late?"

"No. I'll be around. Here comes your ride, and I need to get on before I have to wait for the next bus. Bye."

He watched her walk up the steps, wave over her shoulder, then disappear around the corner. He almost convinced himself that if she hadn't of smiled when she waved, he would have gotten on the train. He laughed at himself. He had never acted this rashly in his life. He could only pray she didn't think him a scatterbrain. There was something about her that kept him wanting to see more of her.

He checked his Tag Heuer watch—slightly past 6:30. He took out his cell phone and dialed one of his business associates as he went up the exit steps. Someone had to open the office; he didn't have to be the one. He finished his call while running to catch up with Ebony at the bus stop.

Richard and Ebony sat on a bench in the rotunda of the student union. Early on, barely a soul was in sight, but as the morning wore on, the place came to life. People were everywhere talking, joking, laughing and hurrying to class. It reminded Richard of his student days at Howard University.

The hours with Ebony passed like minutes. He wondered if she hadn't checked the time or moved seats for the same reason as he. He didn't want to do anything that might ruin the moment and bring their time to an end. Slightly winded from their jog from the bus stop, they had sat on the first bench they came to. Unfortunately, it was next to the revolving door. With each rotation came a gust of freezing air.

The patch of bright yellow sweater that peeked through the opening of Ebony's coat was a lovely contrast with her dark skin. He appreciated contrast in everything from color to personalities. The often unexpected beauty resulting from combining the differences intrigued him. "You're one contrast after another," he said to Ebony.

"Don't you mean contradiction?"

"Granted, it's not everyday someone from your neighborhood earns an undergraduate degree from a school like the University of Chicago. But I don't consider that a contradiction. I think of contradictions as things that shouldn't be but are. The contrast between your upbringing and your college experience will give you an advantage over others."

"Is that why you went to a historically black university?"

He held his coat closed as the revolving door spun around. "That and the incredibly beautiful women." They both laughed.

"I'll bet your parents had a fit."

"And you would be right. At least my mother did." He sat tall in his seat, tilted his head slightly upward, cleared his throat and imitated his mother's clipped tones. "This simply will not do, Richard. Harvard. Yale. Now those are real universities. Somewhere you can be proud to be a graduate of."

"My friends and mother weren't supportive of my going to the U of C. I had a full scholarship, but they didn't understand the opportunity. I don't think they were trying to hold me back on purpose. A lot of people are afraid to try something different, and they become afraid for you, too."

"Why didn't you go there for your graduate school?"

"To be honest, I didn't want to go to graduate school. You don't know how bad I want to move out of my neighborhood. The only type of job I could find would have paid enough to move me from one bad area to another."

"Oh yeah, we were in a serious recession."

"The market was filled with experienced computer science professionals who had been laid off and were willing to take any position. So I decided to continue in school to give the market time to recover. By the time I graduated, I had already resigned myself that the U of C part of my life was over. Don't get me wrong. They have great programs, but I was ready for a change."

"Is Chicago State a historically black college?" Over ninety percent of the students he had seen so far were black.

"It's not considered one."

"Ebony?"

They turned toward a chubby young woman walking toward them. She stopped a few feet short of the two. "Oh, so this is why you skipped class today. You'd better not miss artificial intelligence." She continued on her way.

Ebony pulled her coat sleeve back and checked her Timex. "Oh my goodness! It's almost three." Grabbing her book bag and purse, she stood. "Where did the time go?"

He took her book bag from her. "I'll walk with you."

They waited outside the classroom the few minutes before her class started. "Sorry I made you miss class."

"I had a great time. Thanks for making me miss class. I'm sorry for making you miss work."

He wanted to kiss her, but settled for taking her soft hands into his. "I'll call tonight." She didn't pull away or seem to care that students were watching them. He didn't care, either, but knew to test the waters before dipping in. "I have more contrast to discover about you."

"Sounds like fun."

"It will be." He handed her book bag over. "Tonight." He brushed his lips over her ear, then touched his lips to her cheek.

"Tonight." She nodded a goodbye.

Tonight would be different for him, he thought. After the day they had shared, he saw his whole life changing.

Ebony sat against the wall of the aerobics room at the school gym with her friend, Jessica Moore. She had missed her morning workout, but made up for it after her artificial intelligence class. "He had the sexiest grin you'll ever see. It's crooked." She felt herself flushing, so lowered her head to her knees. "When he called his grandfather, I thought I'd die."

Jessica took off her ponytail holder, letting her black microbraids fall to her shoulders. "I can't believe you're interested in some white guy. Trae's gonna snap."

"He really needs to get a grip." She leaned against the wall.

"He's Crystal's father. He has a right to be concerned."

"There is a tremendous difference between concerned and controlling. I'm not playing his games. I date whomever I please."

"All right. You gonna get that white boy shot." She pointed her chubby finger at Ebony. "He's only after you for sex. Once he gets a taste of dark chocolate, he'll be on his way. You need to marry Trae. He loves you, girl. What do you see in that white boy, anyway?"

Ebony closed her eyes, wondering why her friends kept pushing her toward marrying Trae. It all seemed so simple to her: She didn't approve of his lifestyle, she wanted things out of life he could never offer and she wasn't in love with him.

Her heart sang with joy as images of Richard entered her mind: His curiosity intrigued her, his openness freed her, his goofy humor tickled her. But there was more. Something she couldn't quite pinpoint drew her to him, but this much she knew: He understood and wanted the same security she longed for. Praying he would call, she sighed.

"Are you listening to me, Ebony?"

"I'm tired of this." She shrugged and shook her head. "I don't know. You're supposed to be my best friend."

"I am."

"This is unbelievable. If you're my friend, why would you want me to marry a man you think would shoot someone? Trae is a drug-dealing gang-banger. His life isn't a secret. He doesn't even have enough sense to be ashamed of his criminal activity or try to change his life."

"He's not that bad," Jessica protested. "If you would marry him, he would change, but you won't give him a chance."

"I'm not so arrogant as to think I can change people, and I shouldn't have to. Don't get me wrong. I love Trae. He gave me Crystal. I'll always have a special place in my heart for him. But I don't want the life he has to offer. I want—need—a security Trae doesn't understand." She also resented him for forcing her to remain a part of the drug world—a world she detested. The lives she'd seen lost to addiction weighed heavily on her soul. She wasn't sure how much more she could take.

"Trae wouldn't let anyone hurt you, girl."

"I'm not talking about physical security. I don't approve of his lifestyle. How long until he's arrested? How long before the cops search my home because of his activities? How long before he's killed? How long before Crystal discovers what he is? How long before she loses her father?" She trailed off.

Voicing some of her greatest fears spiked a chill of reality along her spine. She had lost her father to the drug life, and couldn't bear the thought of Crystal losing hers, couldn't bear the thought of her baby seeking to fill a void that could never be filled. She had been trying for years to convince Trae to give up the drug life so they could all be free.

She thought about the arrangement she had made with Trae when Crystal first came into her life. She thought he would change. Prayed he would change. Thought she could change him. But reality finally slapped sense into her. Changing had to start in Trae's heart.

"I don't want what he has to offer." She had also worked for years to provide the security her child deserved; soon, it would be hers. She could picture living in a nice quiet neighborhood where it was safe for Crystal to play hopscotch on the sidewalk, make friends with the neighborhood children and have a normal life.

Ebony didn't need a large home, just a home of her own in a safer neighborhood. Earning her master's degree was the road to her dream, not dating a drug dealer, not counting on others to provide for her child. Now that the economy had finally turned around, her day was coming.

Jessica stared at Ebony a long while. "You really like this white boy, don't you?"

"Stop calling him white boy. His name is Richard. And, yes, I really like him." Talking about Richard sent excitement pulsing through her body. "Besides being fine as hell, we connected on an emotional level from the moment we met. He didn't bat an eye when I told him about Crystal. We talked for nine hours, and it was like nine minutes. I can't find the words to explain."

Jessica sucked air through her teeth as she rolled her chubby neck. "You know I got your back, girl. If you want this wh…Richard, I'll help you." She took Ebony's hands into hers. "Just do me one favor. If Richard ever hurts you, don't let Trae find out."

"Oh, my goodness. Aren't you being a tad bit dramatic? I've dated other men, and guess what? Trae didn't hurt any of them. We grew up on the streets. He's only surviving. I just found a better way to survive." Years ago, her uncle Dan used to be a drug dealer, but he turned his life around and was now a role model for the young men in the community. Many a night she wished Dan were her father. She didn't see any reason Trae couldn't do the same as Dan. Trae was an excellent father to their child, so she knew he had the potential in him to change. She silently prayed Trae's time for change would come soon.

"I've never seen you so worked up over a man before. This isn't like you." She held Ebony's chin with her fingers, examining her closely. "You're glowing, girl. You could actually fall in love with this guy. Trae didn't have anything to worry about with the others."

"Trae knows I'll never be *his woman*. Someday I'll marry. I don't know who, but you better believe it won't be a drug dealer. I need to shower before I head downtown." They walked along the hallway toward the locker room.

Jessica looked up at Ebony. "So when you gonna hook me up with Skeet?"

"He's a playa. I'm not hooking up my best friend with a playa. That's final."

"I'm grown. I can handle him."

Ebony opened the locker room door. "You're not blaming me for his playing you. Nope. This ain't that kind of party. Ask him out on your own. You need to stop thinking you have the power to change people."

Jessica *tsked*. "Why do you insist on playing this tired, old record?" She spun the combination on her lock.

"Because I don't want you hurt—again."

"Instead of saving me, you need to worry about Richie Rich hurting you. Hook me up. We can double date."

"You have issues."

CHAPTER THREE

Richard glared at Clark, his work associate and longtime friend. "Don't ever call her ghetto-fabulous again." He spun his chair around and looked out the window at the plaza parking lot.

"We didn't move to this God-forsaken tundra for you to ruin everything for a *ghetto-fabulous* piece of ass." Clark snatched Richard's cell phone off the desk and scrolled through to Ebony's number. "How could you show me this crap? How could you get so serious about any woman so fast?"

Richard regretted telling Clark about Ebony. In his excitement, he hadn't thought clearly. He wanted to announce to the world that he had found Miss Right. He vowed to be more careful in the future. "Ebony won't ruin what we've set out to do." He understood Clark's confusion. Before today, Richard had appeared to be all business. In reality, Richard worked so hard to keep loneliness from consuming him.

Clark walked around the desk to face Richard. "You know I'm not prejudiced. Some of my best friends are black. But you also know the old white men who run businesses have different beliefs. They want a certain image for their company. A CFO with Slamquesha for a wife doesn't fit the bill. Yes, you need to find a wife, but she needs to at least be white. If you must go slumming, pick a trailer-park tramp and clean her up. Make her look the part." He pressed the delete button then, handed the phone to Richard. "Bye, bye Slamquesha."

"What have you done?" Richard snapped, scrolling through the numbers.

"I'm saving you from yourself."

Richard stood quickly and grabbed Clark by the collar. "I suggest you get out of my office before I kick the tar out of you." He pushed him away. "You better pray she has a listed number."

Straightening his suit, Clark retreated to the opposite side of the office. "Can you take her to business dinners? Okay, so I shouldn't have erased the number. We've worked to hard for this. Keep her on the side. Or, if you must have a black woman, find one who comes a hell of a lot closer to fitting into corporate America."

"Goodbye, Clark." He sat at his oak desk. "If you ever cross me again, you're fired. Close the door on your way out."

Clark stood in the doorway, glaring at Richard, then left.

Richard hit speed dial on the speakerphone.

Nonno's deep voice and thick Italian accent filled the office. "Boy, why you keep calling me? I'm trying to get a woman of my own. What do you want?"

Richard drew his jittery hands through his wavy, black hair. "I'm so angry, my hands are actually shaking."

"What happened?"

Richard related his argument with Clark.

"I've never known you to care one iota about these women. This girl must be the one. You get your butt on that train every morning until you find her if the number isn't listed."

A smile replaced the frown on Richard's face. His grandfather always cheered him up. "You're a hopeless romantic."

"I'm not romantic; I'm Italian. You want me to call some of my people and have Clark taken care of?" Nonno joked.

Richard laughed at the offer. "Okay, Nonno. We won't be putting any hits out on people, yet."

"Times have changed for the better. Follow your heart."

Richard leaned back in his chair. "I don't know how this happened. There's just something about her that goes beyond the superficial. We connected. I saw it in her eyes. I feel it in my heart. She's smart, funny, drop-dead gorgeous, knows when to be serious, has a kind heart…"

Nonno chuckled. "Sounds like you've got it bad. You're the romantic."

"I'm not romantic; I'm Italian."

"I liked her, too. It's about time we shook the family up a little."

"What are you talking about? Shake up the family?"

"Don't mind your grandpapà. I'm old and talking out of my head."

Richard reached for the picture of his grandfather setting on his desk. "You're a troublemaker."

"And you take after me. Find Ebony."

"I will."

Richard disconnected his call to the taxi company, dropped the cell phone into his coat pocket and stared at the now-empty space in which he had parked his car. "I can't believe this." Someone had stolen his car.

The few people out in the bitter cold seemed amused by his situation. He tugged his hat over his ears, scarf over his nose, flipped up his coat collar, jammed his hands into his pockets and hurried down the street toward the food shop where he told the taxi to meet him. AAA had left a message that they had changed the tires of his car so it was ready. He chastised himself for not leaving immediately to pick up it up.

He had caught up on work, then taken the train from the south side in hopes of bumping into Ebony. He knew his chances were slim to none, but he had to give it a try.

"Y-you g-got twenty-five cents?" asked a scrawny, bearded man wearing holey gloves and a worn-out bomber jacket.

Wondering what one could buy with a quarter besides a gumball, Richard felt around his pocket for loose change, then handed the coins to the man. "This is all I have," he lied.

The man squinted. "Y-you got a sm-smoke?"

"I don't smoke." He stepped around the man and continued walking. When he told Nonno Ebony had an unlisted number, Nonno jokingly told him to scour the neighborhood yelling her name. Thinking Ebony had Nonno pegged when she said he was a mess, he smiled.

He entered the packed submarine-sandwich shop and stood at the window, looking out. Ignoring his growling stomach, he concentrated on warming up and praying for a taxi to get there quickly.

Forty-five minutes passed, and no taxi. He called a different taxi service. This one guaranteed it would be there within ten minutes. A half-hour later, still no taxi.

His spirits lifted when he spotted a charcoal parka with fur trim around the hood heading for the sub shop.

He backed into a corner behind several people. Ebony entered the shop and stood in line. It was a little past nine. They both had had a long day. After she placed her order, she turned as if she sensed him there.

"Richard." Her face lit up, warming him with her smile. "Are you stalking me?" She weaved her way through customers to reach him.

"The thought crossed my mind." He took her book bag. "This thing is getting heavier."

She flexed a muscle that was hidden by the bulk of her parka. "I can handle it. Couldn't resist our cuisine, huh?"

"Well, actually..." he explained that his car had been stolen, and that he was waiting for a taxi to take him to the police station.

Her face blank, she asked, "You're joking, right?"

"Six seven three," called the cashier.

"Wait a second." She paid for her sub, then pulled Richard outside. "Come with me." Disgust had hardened her voice. "I can't believe the cops told you to call a taxi. You'll be waiting the rest of your life, and then some."

"I was starting to think the same thing." He held his coat closed tightly, hoping to buffer the full force of the bitter chill.

"Hey, Stam." She ran across the street, said something to a scrawny man coming out of the convenience store, then trotted back to Richard.

Richard strained to get a better view of the man. It was the same man he had given the change to. "Who's that?"

"I asked him for help. Let's get to the house. I live on the other side of the park, several blocks away." She pointed at his shoes. "I think we should walk around instead of cutting through the park. Less snow."

"If my feet could speak, they would thank you." His handcrafted leather shoes were beyond repair thanks to the salt, slush and scuffs. He was worried about what was inside the shoes. He had lost feeling in his toes on his walk to the sub shop.

They walked briskly, not speaking until they reached her two-flat. "Here at last. Meechie, come here a second." She motioned for the lookout to come across the street.

Richard stood in the shoveled parking space with his hands stuffed in his pockets. "Why isn't there any furniture or appliances to save this spot?"

"This is Mom's spot. No one will park here."

"Who dis?" Meechie asked. "He work for Dan?"

"Nah, this is my friend Richard. Richard, this is Meechie. Have you seen anyone cruising the neighborhood in a silver Mercedes?"

"No. I ain't seen no Mercedes. I saw a silver beamer a bit ago."

"If you see anything, let me know." She looped her arm around Richard's and led him up the porch stairs. "Go inside, Meechie."

He sauntered across the street. "I just came out a few minutes ago. Carry your butt in the house an' let me makes my money."

"Yeah, yeah, yeah." She took out her key.

"I'm not trying to down your friend, but Meechie looked like crap."

"Talk about understatements. He's a crackhead from way back. I dropped a few flyers in his place about a rehab on the north side. He needs to get away from the west side to have a chance at staying clean. He knows too many people around here."

He followed her up the inside stairway and into the flat. A half wall, which had been converted into a bar, separated the kitchen from the dining and living rooms. The wood-paneled walls and earth tones of the furniture gave the flat a homey feeling. He could see that one of the bedrooms led off the dining room. He assumed a second bedroom led off the kitchen.

"This is a nice place. Awfully clean. Are you sure a child lives here?"

"I'm pretty sure. We all have a bit of neat freak in us. Hand me your coat, and put your shoes on the rack."

He glanced over his shoulder at Ebony and overheated instantly. Her jeans and yellow sweater outlined every curve. If he hadn't been afraid her daughter would walk in, he would have asked for a tour of her bedroom.

"You have the cutest grin."

Pushing his thoughts aside, he flushed. "I didn't realize I was smiling." He took off his coat and shoes. His toes were killing him, which was an improvement from no feeling at all.

"Make yourself comfortable. The remotes are on the end table." She took the cordless phone off the bar.

"Where's your daughter?"

"Mom took her grocery shopping. They'll be back pretty soon." She dialed, then held the phone to her ear. "I'll have us something to eat in thirty seconds." She headed into the kitchen with her sub and the phone. He followed.

"Hey, Dan. I need some help." She propped the phone between her ear and shoulder and took two plates out of the cabinet.

Richard leaned against the counter. The burnt orange wallpaper extended the warmth from the front of the house into the kitchen. He spied a second bedroom on the opposite side of the refrigerator. He sat at the kitchen table, telling himself to be a good boy. Her child would be home soon, and he didn't want to chase Ebony off.

"My friend's Mercedes was stolen off Long today, and some jerk-off cop had the nerve to tell him to take a taxi to the station to file a report." She cut the sandwich in half. "I brought him home with me. Can you do something?...I already asked Stam...Thanks, Dan." She disconnected, then opened the refrigerator and grabbed the lonely can of cream soda.

"We'll have to share." She closed the refrigerator, handed him the soda, then set two plates on the table. "It's not much, but until Mom gets back, it's the best I can do. My uncle is sending a cop." She set the phone on the table.

He pulled out her chair. "It's more than enough. Is your uncle a cop?" He politely pushed the chair in as she sat. "Meechie thought I worked for him. You'll have to add that to your list of why a white guy would be in the neighborhood." He took his seat.

"Got jokes, huh. Let's say the blessing. I haven't eaten all day." She bowed her head in prayer.

"Mama!" Crystal yelled as she burst into the flat.

"Girl, you scared me to death." She hugged her daughter.

Crystal jumped up and down. "Can I go to Auntie Genevieve's and spend the night? Please, please, please. I don't have school."

"It seems like you all have more in-service days than school days lately. And there's someone else in the room, Crystal." She motioned toward Richard.

The child looked over her shoulder, reddened and covered her mouth with her hands. "I'm sorry." She turned fully and curtsied. "Hello, I'm Crystal Washington." She held out her tiny hand.

Crystal's charm doused the shock Richard felt when he saw the child. Unlike Ebony, Crystal had the same olive complexion as his. People would think she was his child before Ebony's. She also seemed short for a seven-year-old. He shook her hand and bowed his head slightly. "I'm Richard Pacini. Pleased to meet you." His eyes traveled from the child's crystal-clear blue eyes to Ebony's sexy sepia eyes.

"The pleasure is all mine." She spun around. "Can I go to Auntie Genevieve's now?"

"Go pack a bag." Ebony smiled with pride as her child trotted off, frizzy, sandy-brown ponytail bouncing.

He waited until Crystal was out of earshot, then asked, "How did you have such a light-skinned child?"

"I love your directness. More people need to be like that."

"It works for me."

Ebony's mother, Marissa, entered the flat with a bag of groceries before Ebony could answer. "Hello, sweetie. How was your day?" She asked, then noticed Richard. "Sorry, I didn't see you sitting there."

Ebony made the introductions. Richard saw the family resemblance immediately. Both women had exquisite dark-brown eyes, high cheekbones, oval-shaped faces; both were tall and slender, yet curvaceous, and both had horrible taste in hair color. Marissa sported burgundy twists that reached her shoulders. He figured Ebony must have her father's complexion, because her mother's was a creamy caramel. He smiled, thinking he preferred dark chocolate any day.

"I'll put away the groceries." Ebony took the bag from her mother. "Would you please go call Oscar? I promised you would call today."

"I'm not sure I'm ready to start dating again." She cut a small portion off Ebony's sandwich.

"I love you, Mom, but Dad's been dead well over ten years. I think it's time for you to test the waters."

Richard was amazed she spoke about such personal things in front of him. His family didn't talk about personal things in front of each other, let alone strangers. Ebony's mother didn't miss a beat.

"I'm too old to start dating again."

"Nonsense. You're beautiful and full of life. Isn't she, Richard?"

"Most definitely. If I weren't chasing after your daughter, I'd be after you."

Marissa flushed, giggling. "I like him. Nice meeting you, Richard." She nodded on her way to her room.

"You, too." Relief washed over Richard; he had passed the Mom test. After seeing Crystal and Marissa's unconcerned reaction to him, he suspected he wasn't Ebony's first white date.

The sound of the front door slamming against the inside wall startled Ebony and Richard. He spun around quickly, ready to protect Ebony. Two tall black men stepped through the door looking as if they had just come from a photo shoot for *Thugs 'R Us*.

CHAPTER FOUR

Richard stood in front of Ebony, quickly assessing the situation.

"Trae, Skeet!" Marissa chastised as she stormed out of her room. "How many times I gotta tell you not to kick my damn door? Do it again," she warned, "and I'll cut your braids off." She returned to her bedroom, shutting the door.

"Mom's gonna kick y'all's tails for abusing her door."

Richard relaxed slightly but continued watching the two men carefully: They were both tall, had intricate cornrows, looked as if they had seen their share of street wars, wore baggy jean outfits and had parkas similar to Ebony's. The taller one had broad shoulders, and his complexion matched Ebony's. The one Richard's height had a much lighter complexion.

They set the bags they carried on the counter next to the kitchen sink. Ebony made introductions and went to put away the groceries.

Trae appraised Richard from head to toe. "That's a sharp Valenti. I have a few of his suits. You work for Dan?"

"Leave him alone, Trae," Ebony warned before Richard could speak. "He's my friend."

Skeet's low-rumble laugh filled the room. "Looks like baby girl here wants to explore her options." He took a banana, and her portion of the submarine sandwich. "You didn't want this, did you?" He ignored her murderous glare and bit into the sandwich.

Though they were the same height and size, Richard felt slightly intimidated by Trae. He shook it off.

Crystal ran into the room and hopped into Trae's arms, breaking the tension. She held his face between her small hands. "Baby needs a new pair of shoes." She looked over at Skeet, winked, flipped in Trae's arms and threw up her stockinged feet.

"Dang, girl." Skeet chuckled, finishing the sandwich. "I told you to use that line when I'm *not* around. Come here." He held his arms out for her.

"I forgot." She clung to Skeet, taking his banana in the process. "Will you ride me to Auntie Genevieve's? Mama said I could go."

"Go get your bag." He set her on the floor. "I'll catch y'all later. Can you braid my hair tomorrow, Ebony?"

"I just braided it Saturday, Skeet. I'm back in school now."

He pulled her over to him. "You don't have class on Tuesdays. You have time to fix my hair."

"Tuesday and Thursday are my study days." She took the coffee out of the sack and placed it on the counter.

"You only been in class two weeks. You can't have that much to do. Hell, you even wrote that thesis junk before the semester started."

Hands on her hips, she reminded him, "My GPA is 4.0. I'd like to keep it that way."

Ebony's fire attracted Richard. He liked a woman who wasn't afraid to stand up for herself. He looked at Trae, who was still sizing him up. He hadn't noticed his green eyes before.

"So you gonna have a brotha walkin' around with frizzy braids. You ain't right."

"My braids stay longer than three days. I'll hook you up on Saturday, or you can have someone else do it."

"Stop talkin' crazy. You know I don't let anyone else touch my hair." Crystal ran out of the bedroom. "Dang, girl. Do you eva walk?" He took her bag, picked the child up and hugged Ebony. "Saturday."

He tapped fists with Trae, then nodded at Richard. "Catch you later, Smoke."

Richard frowned. He liked Skeet instantly, but didn't understand why he called him Smoke. "Catch you later, Skeet."

Trae stood at the counter, watching Ebony put away the groceries. He and Richard both smiled when she bent to open the fruit tray at the bottom of the refrigerator. Richard, sitting at the kitchen table, had a better view.

As if reading Richard's mind, Trae stepped forward, obstructing his view. "If you don't work for Dan, where did you meet Ebony? We don't see people," he paused, "dressed like you around these parts very often."

Richard examined his designer tie, white dress shirt and dark gray Leonardo Valenti trousers. He had already taken off his suit jacket. "Dan's not a cop, is he?"

Trae laughed. "Hell naw! He's allergic to 'em."

"We met on the train this morning," Richard answered.

"What you doing taking the train?"

"Stop, Trae," Ebony interrupted, as she unpacked the third sack of groceries.

Trae chewed on his inner jaw. A spark ignited his eyes. He reached into his parka pocket and pulled out a CD. "Guess what I have?" He placed the CD in the boom box on the counter. Marvin Gaye's "Sexual Healing" filled the kitchen.

Ebony's face lit up. "You finally cut my oldies disc."

"Sure thang." He pulled her close, dancing and singing softly.

Feeling jealousy stirring, Richard longed to knock the stupid grin off Trae's face.

Ebony calmly pulled away. "I need to finish putting these groceries away. Thanks for the music."

"Come on. One dance." He tried to kiss the back of her neck, but she moved.

"Stop or leave," she warned. "How many times must we go through this?" She turned the player off.

The disgust on Trae's face brought a smile to Richard's. Trae reached into his pocket again, this time pulling out a form and a pen.

Richard shook his head and wondered what his bag of tricks had yielded this time.

"Sign here." Trae handed Ebony the pen. She signed on the document without reading a word, then continued putting groceries away.

Richard couldn't believe his eyes.

With a triumphant smirk, Trae leaned against the counter. "When we goin' out, Ebony?"

"Have you seen the weather report, Richard?" Ebony asked.

He frowned. "There's supposed to be another snow storm the day after tomorrow."

Her lips tipped up at the corners, and devilment danced in her eyes. "So there was nothing about hell freezing over?" She winked.

"Checkmate!" Richard laughed.

Trae quickly stepped forward, setting off Richard's danger alert. "That shit ain't funny." Trae grabbed Ebony's arm. Richard hopped out of his chair.

Trae released her, then trained his enraged green eyes on Richard. "Oh, you stupid enough to think you can take me, Opie? This ain't Mayberry. I'll light yo' ass up. This here is my woman."

Ebony stood between the two. "It's time for you to leave, Trae," she said through clinched teeth.

"You pickin' this limp-dicked mother over the father of your child. Hell naw!"

Richard began to intercede, but Ebony cut him off. "First, I am not your woman. Second, I know you *think* you are the Father, Son and Holy Ghost, but you are not my master. Third…"

Their verbal sparring allowed Richard to get a closer look at Trae, who had fine-textured hair, the same as Crystal's. *Involvement with Ebony means dealing with Trae*, thought Richard.

"…And you may run the streets, but this is my turf—"

"Ebony, stop," Trae interrupted.

"No, you stop! I'm sick of this." She turned away, bumping into Richard.

Richard wanted to hold her, tell her everything would be all right, but he wasn't sure they would be. He wasn't sure if he wanted to deal with Trae, or why she didn't take Crystal and run.

She lowered her head into her hands, massaging her temples. "I'm tired of this."

Trae mouthed an expletive, then turned Ebony to face him. His gruff manner gone as he caressed her face. "You're cheating." He pressed her head to his shoulder.

Richard could now see Trae would never hurt Ebony. He loved her. He presumed they had Crystal as teens and were making the best of the situation.

"All's fair in love and war," she murmured.

"Okay, you win. I'll back off."

She hugged him tightly. "Thanks, Trae."

"Lookie here, Smoke. You gonna hang around my girls, you gotta deal with me." He released Ebony. "I won't interfere in y'all's game, but Crystal's my daughter. You hear what I'm sayin'?"

"I hear you," Richard answered, bracing himself for another surprise from Trae's bag of tricks.

Trae then pulled out a wad of hundreds from his inner coat pocket. "Don't have your nose stuck in them books all day." He counted out a thousand. "Take Crystal shoe-shopping and buy yourself a little somethin'." He nodded toward Richard. "And get Smoke a real coat while you're out."

"What are you talking about?" Ebony asked.

"They said some white dude was walkin' around in a trench coat this morning without a hat or anything. The only reason he wasn't jacked was they knew he must be crazy."

"Great. First my car is stolen, now everyone thinks I'm a lunatic. Why do you and Skeet call me Smoke?"

"Oh, lawd, Ebony, you better school this boy if he's gonna hang around here. I gotta go." He handed her the money. "I'll be out of town for a few days. I'll be back in time for you to braid my hair."

She tossed the money in a drawer. "Be safe, Trae."

The two men nodded at each other as Trae left. Richard knew he hadn't seen the last of Trae.

Gripped by apprehension, Ebony leaned against the bar that divided the kitchen from the dining room. "I'll understand if you don't call me once I get you home safely." She chewed her bottom lip. "I have a lot of extra baggage." She fidgeted, shifting her weight from one foot to the other.

He wasn't one to cut and run at the first sign of trouble. Anything worth having was worth fighting for. He held her soft hands. "I lost your phone number." He pulled her close, savoring their first embrace. "People may think I'm crazy now, but I was ready to walk up the streets yelling your name."

"You're lying."

She rested her head on his shoulder, and he knew he would never let her go. "Yeah, I'm lying. But what were the chances of us meeting—again? You saving me—again? And Nonno would disown me if I don't at least give it a try." He could feel her smiling on his shoulder. "Note to self: Keep Ebony and Nonno separated."

"You're a mess."

"They say I'm just like him."

"I love Trae," she said as if she were trying to convince herself. "He's a good father, but I'm not in love with him. I don't want what he has to offer."

He just saw her take money from the man, but he felt there was more to the story, that things couldn't be as they appeared. Since she obviously wasn't ready to open up completely, he would give her time to learn she could trust him, confide in him. "Yeah, I know," he whispered. "He's Crystal's father. I wouldn't expect any less."

"It's not just Crystal," she continued. "Trae's loyal, protective, loving," she hunched her shoulders, "and a jerk. But he's my friend. We grew up out there." She motioned toward the window. "After my dad died, Trae helped me survive. I can't just abandon him."

He cut his portion of the sandwich in half, then they went into the living room and sat on the couch together. He knew Trae's wad of cash wasn't from a traditional nine to five. Instead of peppering her with questions, he decided to let her to tell all in her own time.

"After Dad died, Trae was the only one around for me. Our first winter alone, Mom had to choose between starving or freezing. I told Trae about our situation. He gave me the money. I tricked Mom into thinking I'd earned it running errands for the corner store. He taught me how to survive on the streets."

Marissa had blamed Dan for her husband's murder, so refused to allow him to help pay their expenses or have any contact. At the same time she fought to win over her drug addiction. It looked shaky for a while, but she came out triumphant, then worked two minimum wage paying jobs to keep a roof over Ebony's head and save for beauty school.

"How old were you when your father passed?"

"I was twelve. Trae was fourteen, and not involved in the drug trade, but was a mean poker player. He taught me, and we made a few hundred every week easily. We basically became the man and woman of the house since Mom was having issues of her own and always gone."

He gasped. "She let him move in?"

"At first Mom was too drugged out to realize what was happening, then she was hardly ever home and always exhausted. I was scared and alone, so I never asked. I just moved him in. And no, we weren't having sex. I was only twelve."

"You would be shocked at what some twelve-year-olds do." He winked, trying to lighten the mood. "So why aren't you and Trae married?"

"The cards could lead to so much more. In my teens I grew away from the street life, but Trae embraced it. But I'll always have his back, and he'll always have mine. I owe him."

He would have preferred to hear her say she tolerated Trae for the sake of their child, yet still respected her honesty and loyalty. "Thanks for explaining. Now I understand why he's so protective."

The doorbell rang. "I'll be right back."

He took a bite of the turkey sub to ease his hunger headache.

"Come in, Stam. Sit on the couch with Richard."

Richard hoped she wouldn't have allowed the strange man into her home if he weren't there. He took another bite of his sub. Stam stared at the sub.

"You want mine?" she asked, holding out her piece.

"N-no, Miss E-ebony. I just ain't ate all day."

"I'll be right back." She went into the kitchen.

"You the guy who g-got his car st-stole?"

"I'm afraid so." He thought it odd Stam would ask a stranger for a quarter, but wouldn't accept a free sandwich from an acquaintance.

"You Miss Ebony's friend?"

"Yes, sir."

Stam eyed him from head to toe. "You work for Dan?"

"Why does everyone think I work for Dan?"

Ebony returned with a ham and cheese sandwich wrapped in a paper towel on a plate and handed it to Stam. "So what did you find out?" She sat in the recliner.

"Thank you, Miss Ebony. Th-them Collins boys t-took his car for a joy ride, then b-burned it out. It's in the alley behind Lockwood, r-right off Ferdinand." He stuffed half of the sandwich into his mouth, practically choking himself. "This is good."

"Is it drivable?" Richard asked.

"N-nope," Stam said, spitting out food as he spoke. "They burnt it out."

"You mean they literally torched my car?"

"These k-kids these days some bad-assed kids." He finished his sandwich.

Ebony took the plate from Stam. "Thanks for the information. Do you have ten you can loan me, Smoke?"

"Sure." Glad he had broken his fifty and she had Stam thinking she was broke, Richard handed her ten dollars.

"I can't take your money, Miss Ebony. I told D-dan I'd do this for free."

"I guess you better not tell him." She stuffed the money into his hand. "Do you want a cream soda for the road?"

"I'm gonna have to pass." He stood. "Thanks for the dinner." He bowed slightly and left.

Ebony sat on the couch next to Richard. "Thanks for the loan. I'll pay you back after I braid a few heads on Saturday."

"No need. What's Stam's story, and why does he call you Miss?"

"He calls me Miss as his sign of respect. He's a good man, just down on his luck. Last summer his wife lost her battle with breast cancer, and he hasn't been the same since. He went into a depression and eventually was fired from his job. Now he pretty much roams the streets begging. I'm just glad he didn't start drugs or drinking. He'll make it. He just needs time to grieve. I've already made Dan promise to give him a job."

"What are you, some sort of guardian angel or something?" he teased.

"Silly."

"Seriously, though, I think it's great. You don't find many compassionate people these days."

"Thanks."

"Why am I being called Smoke, and why does everyone think I work for Dan?" He finished the last bite of the sandwich as she explained.

"I think there's some sort of unwritten rule that says males of playa age can't use their real names."

Sarcasm noted, he asked, "But why Smoke?"

She lightly brushed her hand along his five o'clock shadow, sending his mind to places it shouldn't venture. At least not with her mother in the next room.

"Because your smoky blue eyes are the first thing Skeet noticed about you. Besides your being white," she added. "Would you rather him call you Whitey?"

They both laughed. "I like Smoke," he said. "What about Dan?"

"Wait until you meet him. You'll see. He must have seen Stam out on the street since Stam didn't want to accept payment. He'll be here soon." The doorknob turned. "Speak of the devil."

CHAPTER FIVE

Dan stepped into the flat, shaking off his trench-style cashmere coat. "It's cold as hell out there." He kicked off his Italian leather tap-toe shoes and placed them on the rack. "What the?" He picked up one of Richard's oxfords. "You ruined $400 shoes. Didn't your mama teach you to walk *around* the puddle?"

Richard flashed a lopsided, sheepish grin.

"Hello, Dan." Ebony hugged Dan, then introduced him to Richard.

"Did the cops show yet?"

"No, sir, but Stam said the Collins boys stole and torched my car." Richard immediately saw the family resemblance. Dan was at least 6'5" and dark–skinned. He also carried his size well. He resembled an older, more sophisticated version of Skeet.

"You didn't pay him, did you?"

Richard could swear he saw a halo appear above Ebony's head when she said, "I'm broke."

"Like you would tell me. Did she pay him, Richard?"

"Nope."

"Good. This girl thinks she can save the world."

"Can you float me a loan until I can braid a few heads? Crystal needs a new pair of shoes."

Richard hoped his confusion didn't show on his face. He glanced toward the kitchen where she'd left the money Trae had given her, wondering what she intended to do with it.

"Where's my baby sister?" He reached into his pocket and pulled out his money clip.

"I'm praying she's on the phone with Oscar. Don't interrupt her." She picked up her sandwich.

Dan took the small piece from her in exchange for a few hundred dollars. "I'm starving. Call me out when the cops arrive." He walked into Marissa's room with the last piece of Ebony's sandwich.

It occurred to Richard that Ebony hadn't eaten a bite, though he knew she must be starving. Instead, she had allowed everyone to take from her. In the midst of a prolific moment, he wondered if this symbolized how others took advantage of her charitable heart.

"Dammit, Dan!" Marissa screamed. "What if I was naked?" Dan closed the door.

Ebony laughed. "She hates it when he does that."

"What does Dan do for a living?"

"I guess you could say he was one of the original gangstas. He gave up the drug life years ago and turned his life around. Now he's an entrepreneur, real estate mostly. He's an icon around here." She paused. "Well maybe not an icon, but he's my hero." She rubbed her belly. "He's one of the business connections I was talking about." The doorbell rang. "This house is entirely too busy." She answered the door and let in the police.

Dan chastised them for taking so long and also for the initial desk officer telling Richard to file a report at the station. He stood watch until the report was finished and the police left. "I'll be ready to leave in a few minutes, Richard. I'll drop you home."

"I'll take him," Ebony volunteered.

Richard stood in front of a spotless black sports utility vehicle. "You and your mom have the only two clean cars in the city."

Ebony handed him the keys, motioning across the street at the lookout. "Trae has the fellas keep them clean and the walk shoveled. All I do is toss out salt. I've told them a million times it isn't necessary, but they ignore me. Some battles just aren't worth the fight."

Apprehension had replaced the cheer in her tone. In an attempt to lighten her mood and figure out just who "the fellas" were, he said, "Trae is overprotective. I know this isn't the best neighborhood, but I don't think he needs to have *undercover* security posted outside your house."

Ebony's smile didn't reach her eyes. Shoulders hunched, she bit her bottom lip. "They aren't here just for me. Let's get in the truck. I'm cold."

Richard rounded the truck and hopped in. "Nice license plate." It read EBONY1.

"Thank you." She looked down and away. "I need to tell you about Trae and Skeet," she said softly but clearly.

"Go for it." He started the engine and turned on the heat. He had prepared himself for the worst, but still didn't look forward to her full disclosures. "You only have six hundred miles on this. Is it new?" he asked, stalling.

"Dan gave it to me for my birthday last year. He always gives me humongous gifts."

"When was your birthday, last month?"

"August. I just hate driving."

The man from across the street unnerved Richard. "You really don't have very many white folks around here do you? I think Trae should give him a raise. He's staring so hard he could tell you the number of whiskers on my five o'clock shadow."

"He's one of Trae's lookouts." She explained what a lookout does, and that Trae was responsible for the drug trafficking on the west side and a few neighboring suburbs.

She seemed terrified, sitting there fidgeting with her new gloves. He pulled the SUV away from the curb. He felt Ebony watching him as he drove, but he couldn't speak, not yet. He needed time to absorb what she had said, sort through his feelings and decide if he wanted to be associated with anyone who had drug ties; no matter how indirect.

He didn't want to punish Ebony for Trae's wrongdoing, but why would she allow him around her child? He knew firsthand what happened when parents didn't protect their children. He smoothed his hand over his mouth. At a loss, he sighed.

Nonno's grin appeared in his mind's eye. He knew what Nonno would do. He could see the part of his grandfather in himself saying it was time to stir up trouble. He felt strength in knowing he was so much like Nonno, his hero.

Ebony stared out the passenger-side window. "I'll understand if you don't contact me…honestly…no bad feelings."

"Are you involved in the drug trade? What did you sign back there?"

She glanced over her shoulder at him barely long enough for him to see a sad smile tip her lips and her eyes filled with unshed tears. "A parent consent form for Crystal to go with her class to the Museum of Science and Industry. She'd left it in his car when he picked her up from school Friday." Now he felt like a complete heel.

"And, no, I don't know anything about the drug trade except the destruction I see when I walk down the street," she said, now facing the passenger window. "I try to help where I can, but it hurts knowing Trae's partly responsible, and there's nothing I can do to stop it."

"The father of your child." He stopped at a red light. The sub-zero temperatures didn't keep customers away from the corner liquor store. Hearing about Trae had him wanting a drink. He thought back to how she'd given her gloves away, mentioned trying to convince Meechie to enter rehab, found employment for Stam and even how she'd rescued him. And this was all in the course of a day. Dan had a point; she tried to be everyone's angel, including Trae's.

"Yes," she answered. "I'd love to shut him out, but I can't."

He continued watching her. She had a kind heart, was smart and responsible, but her actions didn't add up in his mind. It was as if she had taken her angel role too far.

The light turned green. He continued down the road. "I know Trae is Crystal's father, but he's a drug dealer. How can you allow him access to her?"

She leaned against the headrest with her eyes closed. "Dan has always been my real father figure. He tucked me in at night, read me stories, played with me." She laughed lightly. "Punished me when I was bad. Helped me with my homework. I love him in my heart as my father."

"What about your real father?" He waited at a stop sign, then glanced over at her. Their gazes locked. He fought the urge to pull her into his arms and make promises he had no clue how to keep.

"Mom loved him to death, but he was more interested in the drugs than me. I wanted a relationship with him so bad…"

He turned on his street and continued toward his condo. "So Dan took over."

"I can't articulate how devastated I was when Mom cut Dan out of our lives. I know she was trying to protect me from the drug trade, but at the time I felt like she was punishing me and she was a hypocrite. Here she was getting high, yet telling me Dan couldn't be a part of our lives anymore because he sold drugs."

"But your mom eventually quit."

"Not before my faith and security were shattered. In all honesty, I don't think they can ever be repaired. All I knew was I had a loving father figure who protected me, then the next day I was in an empty apartment hungry, cold, scared and lonely."

Inside the truck was warm and toasty. He saw her shiver, fighting to control her emotions. Her wounds were deep. Her fears and pain were what kept Trae in Crystal's life. Her emotions had won over logic. He thought about his own childhood wounds. How they affected his decisions. In this case he saw the angel was the one who needed saving.

"We've kept Crystal in ignorant bliss. To her Trae and Skeet are her loving cousins." She released a drawn-out sigh. "Don't get me wrong. I hate what Trae does. I'm sickened by it. I've been begging him to change for years. He's an excellent father, just as Dan was. This shows me he has some goodness in him. He will change, just as Dan did." She peered out the window.

"I'm a legitimate businessman. I can't..." But, his heart never led him wrong before. He chose Ebony.

"I understand." She patted his thigh. "I truly understand."

He continued down the road. "Sometimes I think Nonno can tell the future." He expected her to comment, but she remained silent. "Ebony, please face me."

She looked over her shoulder at him. His heart stopped. Tears were streaming down her face. He instantly knew why Trae changed his mind. Richard would do anything to keep from seeing her so broken.

He parked on the side of the road and pulled her into his arms. "I'm sorry, Ebony."

"It's not you. I'm just tired and hungry."

He didn't believe her. "Nonno instructed me to stir up the family. He's a troublemaker." He lifted her chin with his fingertip and peered into her eyes. "I'm just like him." He bent, brushing his lips over hers. "I've wanted to do this all day." The faint scent of sweet pea warmed him, the softness of her full lips teased him, her proximity aroused him.

He kissed her lightly. "You are tempting me to do things I shouldn't do." He felt one corner of his mouth tip up higher than the other. "At least not outside. Make that outside in the winter."

He continued driving down the road, happy he had brought a smile to her face.

Ebony stood in the foyer of Richard's condo, thinking *antiseptic*. The polished hardwood floors did nothing to warm the large open space he called the living, dining and kitchen areas. The bare white walls begged for decorative covering.

"Nice couch," Ebony commented, as she took the two steps down into the living room. She ran her hand along the black leather sofa, searching for something else to compliment. Finding nothing, she said, "I think Dan has one like this in his office."

"I'll fix us something to eat after I change. Make yourself at home." He went off to his bedroom. "Two minutes."

She walked around the practically bare condo. Its aura was lonely, cold. The kitchen surprised her. Expecting to find the room without cooking equipment and a garbage can filled with take out bags, she found, instead, a fully stocked, obviously used gourmet kitchen.

She returned to the living area. She would have turned on the television or radio, but saw none. She sorted through the books on the end table, all Isaac Asimov and Octavia Butler. She loved science fiction, too.

Crystal would love to have a sliding contest on the polished hardwood floor. She closed her eyes, wondering how she could explain her arrangement with Trae. She swore she would never tell anyone, and Trae held all the cards. Even though Trae and Skeet never showed their darker sides in front of Crystal, she didn't want to raise her child anywhere near their world.

She looked toward Richard's room. She had told him everything she could. Surely, he could see she wanted what was best for her child.

Once she graduated and got some money together, she could at least move out of the neighborhood. That would be a step in the right direction.

The evening's events had aroused an uneasy stirring in Ebony. In her heart of hearts, she had known Trae would give her more trouble about dating Richard. His backing off didn't compute. Shame quickly washed over her.

She recognized her growing unease as ego and pride. It was hard to admit, but knowing Trae would fight for her had given her a rush. She wasn't in love with him, and had no desire to pursue a relationship with him, yet she felt power in knowing he cared so much for her. She bit her lip, convincing herself that had to be the reason he backed off.

She lightly laughed at herself for being so arrogant. Trae bursting her bubble was just the kick she needed. Yes, he'd given Richard a hard time, but his backing off so easily showed he wasn't fighting for her affection, but control.

She prided herself for moving on and looked down on Trae for being stuck in the past. She now realized she was the one who had not truly moved on.

Richard stepped out of the bedroom wearing a Bulls T-shirt and black shorts. Her eyes traveled over his athletic build, eating him up. Like Trae, he was only an inch taller than her.

"Do you play basketball?" she asked.

He knelt before her, sending her heart racing. "I haven't since I left Texas last month." He stroked the outside of her legs, gently kissed her lips. "I hear your stomach growling. Let me show you the kitchen." He stood, pulling her along. "I'm the master of stir-fry."

"You'd better stop teasing me."

"What?" he asked over his shoulder.

"That little brush of the lips thing you do. You're a tease."

He took the cutting board out and set it on the kitchen island. "You've been teasing me since you took off your scarf this morning. I know my limits. You only get a brush of the lips." He pointed to the glass containers on the counter. "Do you want rice or noodles with your stir-fry?"

She laughed at his change of subject. "Can I do something to help?" She reached for the jar of linguine. "I know how to boil water. Give me a touch of olive oil. I make a mean pasta."

He pulled a saucepan out of one of the lower cabinets. "Let me feed you, then I'll ravage you. I promise." He set the pan in the sink, took the pasta from her, then brought a stool around. "Sit here and look pretty."

Images of ways he could fulfill his promise to ravage had her hotter than the fire on the stove. Embarrassed by her thoughts, she forced herself to focus on something else.

She watched him work his magic in the kitchen. He maneuvered the knives like a pro, glancing up occasionally from the chopping and flashing a quick half-grin that sent her heart racing.

"You love cooking, don't you?"

"Nonno was a chef. I grew up running around the kitchen. I guess I picked up his love of cooking." He rubbed his washboard stomach. "And eating."

He tried to cover the pain behind his words, but she caught it. She watched him fill several small bowls with carrot shavings, pea pods, bean sprouts, peas, spinach, mushrooms, cabbage, onions and a mound of minced garlic.

He set the garlic and onions aside. "I think we'll skip these."

"Your closeness with your grandfather is beautiful. That's rare to see these days."

He took the marinated chicken strips out of the refrigerator. "Nonno understands me. I think he felt sorry for me, so he took me under his wings."

"Both of your parents are alive, right?"

He washed and dried his hands, then stood between her legs, resting his hands on her lap. "What do you want to know, Ebony?"

"I'm sorry. I'm prying."

He pulled around a second stool and sat knee to knee with her. "You're not prying. Nonno took me to live with him when I was five. I lived with him until he had a stroke when I was eight. Then I went to boarding school while Nonno recovered. I still call him every day."

"Why did you move in with him?"

"Honestly, I'm not sure. It's one of many buried secrets in our family. All I know is Mother wanted daughters. My sisters were...are the world to her. I think Nonno felt sorry for me, so picked up the slack."

She caressed his face. "That's so sad. What about your dad?"

"He was working his way up the corporate ladder at the time. Now he's CEO of Tex Federal," he boasted. She bit her bottom lip. "What do you want to know? We already have enough working against us. I won't lie. My family dynamics are a mess, but I'm trying to be open."

"I don't understand why they gave you up so easily."

"I'm sure it wasn't easily. Nonno is extremely hard headed if he wants something. He told me he battled my mother for years before she let him keep me." He took her hands into his. "I guess we both grew up without our parents."

"But you were only a baby," she said softly, afraid to ask if he felt unwanted by his parents. The pain on his face said *yes*, the same *yes* she felt about her father. She was thankful Crystal would never have to feel this type of rejection.

He returned to the stove. "Your stomach's growling again. I'll be done in ten minutes."

She didn't hear or feel her stomach growl, this time. "If you ever want to talk about your relationship with your family, I'm here for you." It was too late for her to heal the relationship with her father, but he still had a chance with his family.

"Thanks, but I'm fine with how things are."

He continued cooking their dinner. Ebony saw him battling demons with every sprinkle of seasoning, touch of oil and flip of the wrist. For someone who liked to speak his mind, he wasn't ready to speak about or fight his own demons. She knew everyone had his limit, and she had found his.

She watched him toss the stir-fry about the wok. Instead of forcing the issue, she would wait until he was ready.

"Time to eat," he announced a short time later.

CHAPTER SIX

His bedroom surprised Ebony. Unlike the rest of the condo, it felt inviting. She could smell the light scent of vanilla candles burning. The king sized bamboo bed and chest of drawers fit perfectly into the nook built into the wall. The wood floors, forest green walls and burgundy ceiling had a warm, cozy atmosphere. "This is great."

He set their plates on the oak desk beside his door. "Your reaction when you saw the front was priceless." He chuckled. "You were trying to be so polite." He handed her the remote control and pointed to the chaise lounge. "Have a seat. The bedroom and kitchen were easy to fix up. I ran out of creativity by the time I finished them."

"You've done a great job in here."

"I liked your place. Maybe you can help me out."

"Maybe." Dark rooms can produce a boxed-in feeling; however, this room was spacious enough to offset that feeling. A built-in book-shelf and combo entertainment unit took up the wall opposite the bed. "Huge television."

"Wait until you hear the surround sound." He searched through his DVD collection for something she might like.

"I can help."

"No, no. I'll take care of everything. Just sit and look pretty. You'll get the full effect of the speakers if you sit against the headboard of the bed."

Her brows rose.

"I'm not trying to seduce you—yet." A half grin slipped out along with bouncing eyebrows. "Surround sound is something you need to experience."

She kicked off her shoes and moved to the bed, curious to see what he meant by yet. He brought a her plate of food and a glass of wine on a serving tray. "Thank you, kind sir."

"The pleasure is all mine." He kissed her lightly.

"Tease."

They ate while enjoying the large-screen television and surround sound. She couldn't remember the last time she'd had such a relaxing evening. It was as if the stress of the world was on the opposite side of Richard's front door. She found a comforting sense of security being with him.

She followed him to the kitchen with the empty plates and helped him clean up. The sight of him at the kitchen sink busting suds actually turned her on. It had been too long since her last sexual encounter, but she repressed an urge to approach Richard from behind and slip her hands under his shirt.

Dishes dried and put away, they returned to the bedroom. "Would you like more to eat, dessert perhaps?" he asked.

"No, thank you." The only dessert she wanted was Richard. Wanting to leave before she embarrassed herself, she looked for her shoes.

He came up from behind and began massaging her shoulders. "Are you relaxed from the long day?"

She dropped her head to the side, exposing her neck to his feather kisses. She wanted to give in, but they had just met. It was too soon.

He turned her around to face him. "Did you enjoy the entertainment?" He gestured toward the Loony Toons playing on the television and returned to her neck.

"Excellent entertainment and food." This was a dangerous game, but she wasn't ready to quit—not yet.

He held her close. "Have I met all of your needs thus far?"

His acceptance of her, his warm whisper, his loving caress, his masculine scent all weakened her self-control. "You have been a most gracious host."

He lightly kissed her nose, then rested his forehead on hers. "Can I continue meeting your needs?" His mouth lowered to hers.

Ebony always strived for as much control as she could have over a situation, but kiss after succulent kiss forced her to face reality. She combed her fingers through his hair. She had lost all control and fallen in love with Richard. *This is impossible.* She turned away from him and the truth.

"Is something wrong?" He held her from behind, grinding gently.

"No," she whispered, rotating in his arms.

They delved into each other's eyes with an unspoken understanding. He moved his hands up from her hips, tracing her torso and lifting her sweater along the way. She kissed the edge of his grin. No holding back, no fear. She would give their relationship an honest try.

He tossed her sweater to the side, then took off his T-shirt and threw it. Their lips met and tongues probed, claiming the passion they felt for each other. She had never felt like this before. He was meant for her, perfect in every way.

He turned her, closely fitting his arousal into her rear. He held her around the waist as they ground to their own music. Lightly brushing her neck as he moved her microbraids from around her ear, he nibbled, licked, tasted.

Ebony loved the feel of his teasing on her neck. She pushed her body into him harder, wanting to be closer, wanting to be one.

His hands traveled lower to her thighs, rubbing them, causing him to deepen the grind. They both moaned as passion's storm continued to surge.

She didn't know how he did it, but one second she was riding the storm, the next they were completely undressed. The subdued lighting did not hide his powerful physique.

Once in bed, he ran his hands along her luscious body. "You are the most beautiful woman in the world." He kissed her, and she knew he meant it. She had never considered herself beautiful, but that was how Richard made her feel.

He cupped one of her breasts in his hand, kissing, kneading and teasing until she begged for relief. He relieved her sweet agony by slipping his fingers into her, slowly fondling and exploring while showing her other breast due consideration.

Ebony whirled in bliss and sought to share the pleasure he gave her. She wrapped her hand around his hardness, slowly stroking, working him into the frenzy he had put her in.

She enjoyed watching him fight to maintain control. Her grabbing him so intimately must have been a wondrous surprise.

He reached into the nightstand and took out a foil wrapper. She kissed him gently, then helped him protect them both.

As he entered her, she felt the same feeling of "ah" seen on his face. Their rhythm matched perfectly, and the glorious sensations grew as they journeyed together on their adventure to oneness.

Richard lay watching his ebony angel sleep. She had asked him to wake her at four. He glanced at the clock. Two minutes to go. He took a foil wrapper from the nightstand and prepared to wake her. He slid the covers off and admired her body. He wondered how long it would take her to wake if he started licking her heat and if she would kill him for it. Thinking how she had called him the devil tickled him.

She cracked open an eye. "Why are you staring at me?"

He cuddled close. "I've fallen in love with a madwoman."

"You're so fickle."

"Me?"

"Yes you, Mr. Pacini. Last I heard, you were in love with an ebony angel. Now you're in love with a madwoman. I'm jealous."

He smiled, truly in love with her. Trae would need more than a bag of tricks to keep him away from Ebony. "Why would you be jealous? There's enough of *the master* to go around."

"I'm not in love with *the master* anymore. I'll call him when I'm hungry."

He covered her body with his, kissing her neck. "And who are you in love with now?" he whispered softly as he entered her, savoring the ecstasy her face showed.

When she could speak again, she replied, "I'm in love with a fallen angel that has smoky blue eyes and a sexy crooked grin."

He propped himself on his elbows, and they slowly moved together. He wanted to reply, but all he could manage was a low, guttural moan. Soon they spiraled into the heavens together.

Ebony mixed scrambled eggs into her grits. "I'll gain a hundred pounds messing with you." She reached across the breakfast bar for a glass of orange juice.

Richard set a stool beside hers. "My spare room is empty."

"Most of your condo is empty." She blew over the spoonful of grits and eggs to cool them. "I don't usually eat breakfast."

"I love you, Ebony."

Every time he said he loved her, her heart jumped for joy. "How did this happen to us, Richard?" She brushed her lips over his. "I love you."

"I've taught you well, Grasshoppa." He kissed her lightly. "I want you and Crystal to move in."

The grits stuck in her throat, causing her to choke. He held her hands above her head and patted her back. "You like how I've done the bedroom and kitchen. You can design the rest however you want. Crystal will have her own room."

"Are you serious?" she asked breathlessly. "I mean, we just met." Her heart floated above the clouds, but her mind snapped her back to reality.

"I follow my instinct, my heart. They haven't led me wrong yet." He fed her a spoonful of grits and eggs. "You would have your own master chef. No one makes grits like I do." He brushed his lips over hers.

She twisted a few braids around her fingers. "If it were just me, I'd say yes, but I have to think about Crystal. I can't just uproot her from everything and everyone she knows to move in with a stranger."

He stiffened, frowned. "So now I'm a stranger?"

"To Crystal, yes."

He took her plate. "Eggs and grits are horrible cold." He dumped the remains in the trash and began fixing a fresh breakfast.

Still thinking about the offer he had made, she watched him chop green peppers, onions and mushrooms. She wanted out of her neighborhood so bad she wanted to scream *yes*, but she couldn't use him like that. And then there was Trae. She glanced over her shoulder at the spare bedroom. She didn't want to lose Richard, but Crystal was her number one priority. She made a deal with the devil to save Crystal, and would give up on true love for her child. She stopped her train of thought. Over the years, she had learned to refocus her anger on the positive. Trae had given her Crystal.

"Ebony." He held his hand out to her. "I want to teach you how to make omelets." He positioned her in front of him and wrapped his arms around her.

Placing her faith in him to understand, she leaned against his chest.

"I've never had responsibility for anyone but myself. Except for Nonno, I've never had anyone to look out for me, then you came into my life." He kissed the tip of her ear. "You're right about Crystal. I'll get this right. Give me time."

She turned in his arms. "Can I keep you?"

"You're stuck with me now." The phone rang. "Hold that thought." He answered, "Hello Nonno…caller ID, and who else would call at five in the morning?"

Ebony took eggs, cheese and milk from the refrigerator to finish making omelets. Richard told Nonno he had fallen in love with Ebony and planned to get to know Crystal.

"All done," she whispered.

"I'll speak to you tomorrow…No, she isn't here. Me, lie? Never…I'm not romantic; I'm Italian…" He laughed and hung up. "Nonno said to tell you good morning, and he still doesn't think I'm good enough for you."

"He's a mess. Do you have any pictures?"

"One. Wait a second." He got a large manila envelope from his room and handed it to her. "I had this enlarged but haven't had time to find a frame." He sat at the breakfast bar and pulled up his plate. "This smells delicious. You trying to take my place as master?"

"Silly." She opened the envelope and examined the photo. Dumbfounded, she said the second thing that came to her mind. "You two look alike."

"Nah, I'm the cute one with the crooked grin."

"Why didn't you tell me your grandfather is mixed?" Nonno's light-toffee complexion matched Trae's.

"He's Italian. Born and raised in Italy. There are black Italians, you know. My great-grandmother happened to be one of them." He took another bite of his omelet. "You're on egg detail from now on."

"So this is how you knew your family wouldn't care about me being black?" She'd raked her mind over that question.

"My mother wouldn't like you if you were blonde." He continued eating.

"I am a blonde."

"A *natural* blonde," he amended with a wink. "She thinks I don't make good decisions in anything. She won't like you on general principle."

"What about your dad?"

"He follows my mother around like a puppy, and both of my sisters are brats. You thought you had baggage. They should change their name from Dubois to Samsonite."

His last name was Pacini, so why was the rest of his family named Dubois? She watched him finish his omelet, then devour hers. Speaking about his family brought pain and distance into his voice. "They can't be that bad."

"I grew up in a fake family. When I'm at my parents' home, I feel like we're in a Broadway production."

Most adults she knew called the place they grew up in home. Richard said "parents' home" as if he weren't part of the family. "What role do you play?"

"I'm the black sheep."

Her brows arched. "Black sheep?"

"Pun intended." He fed her a bite of omelet. "I don't act like them. I don't look like them." Rambling between bites, he continued. "Heck, I haven't played ball outside since I left college, so you can't really tell now. The one time I visited my parents during college, my mother did a triple take."

He laughed at himself. "I went through my finding-my-black-self stage and tanned extra dark on purpose. I soon learned that it takes a hell of a lot more than a tan and having black friends to be black. It's safe to say I was a bit confused for a while. Looking back, I was trying to distance myself from my parents any way I could."

"Why?"

"Just a phase, I guess. My way of rebelling against what I felt they represented."

Ebony mulled over his words. Was she his way of rebelling against his parents?

"The contrast between you and Crystal is beautiful." He smiled. "Kind of like you and me. Does Trae play basketball?" She didn't answer. "Ebony."

"Oh, I'm sorry." She pushed her insecurities aside. "Yes, he plays ball. There's a gym close by. You should come to my mom's salon on Saturday. After I fix Skeet and Trae's hair, they head to the gym." She combed his hair with her fingers. "Three fingers. You need a haircut."

He took her hand, kissing it. "It's cold outside. I grew my hair longer than usual to help keep warm."

She picked up their plates. "That's what winter wraps are for. I have studying to do. You can use my truck today if you like."

CHAPTER SEVEN

Richard parked in front of Ebony's flat. "I'll walk you in." The lookout's stare annoyed him. He had thought about how to handle the Trae situation all night, and came up with only one possible solution: become the man's friend—of sorts—until he could convince Ebony to move in with him. Ebony had insisted Trae would change someday, but she thought she could save the world. He loved her fight, but didn't think she'd win this one.

"Oh, no, you don't. I have studying to do, and you need to go to work. What did the insurance company say?"

"Are you putting me off?" He cupped her face in his hands and kissed her lightly. He wanted everyone in the neighborhood to know she was his ebony angel now. "I can help you study. Biology is my favorite subject."

Pulling away, she laughed. "My major is computer science, Mr. Pacini. Now stop seducing me and go to work. Buy a car or something."

"Hand me your phone." She passed it over. He programmed his numbers into it. "I've branded your number on my brain. How about I pick you and Crystal up at five? We can go out to eat, then catch a movie or something."

"I'd like that."

He kissed her one last time. "Since you won't let me seduce you, get out. Go study or something."

"Okay, okay." She slipped her hands into her gloves.

"I love you, Ebony."

"Now you're not playing fair."

"I never claimed to play fair. Call if you need anything." He watched her walk up the stairs, wave and enter the flat. A knock drew his attention.

"What?" Richard asked as he lowered the window.

"Trae done told us to leave you alone." Meechie's eyes shifted left, right, left, right. "But, I just wanna shake yo' hand. I couldn't stand dem Collins boys. Someone should of smoked 'em a long time ago."

"I don't know what you're talking about."

Meechie held his hands up slightly and smiled, revealing severely decayed teeth. "That's all right, Smoke. I'll keep it on the low-low." He moseyed back to his post. "I bet they won't be stealing no mo' cars."

Deep in thought, Richard drove to the new office location. Two and two kept adding up to five in his head. Why did Trae tell everyone that he worked for him? Why would Trae tell Meechie that Richard had smoked the Collins boys? It didn't make sense for Trae to back off while he pursued Ebony. It didn't make sense for Ebony to allow the likes of Trae around her child. None of this made sense.

He pulled into the parking lot. *Is this what I have to look forward to?* Images of Ebony standing up for him against Trae flashed before him. Besides Nonno, he'd never felt anyone was on his side. Though they'd just met, he knew in his heart of hearts she'd always be in his corner, and he'd always be in hers. They may not be able to save the world, but they could save each other.

Forcing himself to think rationally, Richard cleared his mind of the nonsense. *There is no benefit for Trae in killing the Collins boys. Meechie must have mixed things up.*

Ebony glared at the answering machine. Trae didn't want her, so why was he calling harassing her? She loved it when he left town, because she had a few days of freedom.

"Pick up the damn phone, Ebony. I know you're there," Trae's voice boomed through the speaker.

She snatched the cordless phone from its cradle. "And how do you know, Trae? Stop spying on me!" Man, how she wished she could be rid of Trae forever.

"A key ingredient for spying is secrecy. Now what the hell you doin' comin' in at eight in the morning?"

"You make me sick." She lit a lavender tranquility candle and set it on the coffee table. Two chapters worth of index cards and a ton of research promised to fill the majority of her day. She inhaled deeply, counted to four, exhaled. "When and where I come and go isn't your business. Aren't you supposed to be in St. Louis?" It was clear he needed to play the protective role to save face, but there was only so much she would tolerate.

"I am in St. Louis. So what's going on with you and Smoke?"

"Don't start trouble, Trae." Universal remote in hand, she turned the stereo channel to a smooth jazz station, wondering how many heads she'd have to braid to buy a surround sound system like Richard's.

"I'm not. I said I'd back off. I always keep my word, don't I?"

She kept her anger in check. He had given her Crystal and was a good father, she reminded herself. The reason he wanted the arrangement was to keep her from taking Crystal from him. And he was right. If not for the arrangement, she would have taken Crystal away long ago. She had to stop being angry with him for wanting to be a father. *Dan changed. Trae will change.* "Yes."

"I don't want you hurt. His type goes slumming for sex. After he gets his fill, he'll move on, and I'll be left to pick up the pieces."

"Richard isn't like that. All I'm asking is that you get to know him. I—"

"Yes, he is! They all are!"

"Don't go projecting your feelings for your father onto Richard." She covered her mouth. "I'm sorry, Trae. I didn't mean…I crossed the line." He was silent. "Please, Trae. I know it's fast, but I love Richard.

Give me a chance to be happy." Still no reply. "We'll talk when you come home."

"Ebony, wait." His heavy sigh came over the line. "I know his type better than you. Won't you trust my judgment on this one? I haven't led you wrong yet."

"Your judgment is clouded with racism."

"And yours is clouded with love."

"I'm a big girl. I survived a broken heart before and will survive *if* it happens again. You two have a lot of common interests. Give him a chance." She should have known Trae wouldn't get over the color issue so easily. Taking second seat to a white man had to be hard for him.

"You're in love with him?"

"Yes. I'm in love with Richard." The long silence worried Ebony. Jessica had a point. The other men Ebony had dated posed no competition for Trae. She shrugged it off. Trae wasn't a complete monster. He loved their child, and someday would choose life instead of death. He had moved on relationship-wise, and was just protecting her from the *big bad white boogieman.*

"Smoke. If he's hanging out with us, he has to be called Smoke."

"I think we can manage that." She curled her feet up on the couch and reached for her artificial intelligence book. Dealing with Trae's racist eruptions would be easier than dealing with jealousy *and* racism. Maybe half the battle had already been won.

"I've already told everyone to leave him alone, but don't get your hopes up. I know he'll break your heart."

"Yes, Daddy. I have studying to do. When are you coming home?"

"Thursday. Someone smoked the Collins boys last night."

Her index cards fell to the floor. "That's horrible. Who did it?"

"Wasn't me. I'm just glad they're gone. We already have enough heat in the neighborhood without all of the stupid stuff they would stir up. I owe someone a dinner."

"You need to seek professional help. We'll talk later."

She knew he was joking, but him saying something so cold and callous still bothered her. She set the phone down, then walked over to the window and waved for Meechie to come inside for breakfast. Maybe today would be the day their little talks would sway him to the side of rehab. Meechie wasn't the first person she guided toward rehabilitation, but he was sure proving to be the most difficult.

A tiny elbow jabbing his gut woke Richard. Crystal had taken over his right side; Ebony, his left side.

After shopping and dinner, they watched a video at Ebony's. He gently moved Ebony over then carried Crystal to her bedroom. The faint glow of the nightlight kept him from bumping into anything.

Ebony had told him she didn't allow men to stay at her place overnight. She also never introduced Crystal to her dates.

Crystal woke when he put her on the bed. "Smoke?"

"Yes, baby," he whispered.

"This isn't my bed." She pointed to a barely visible door. "That's my room. Where's Mama?"

"On the couch. She's a little too big for me to carry. I'm sure she won't mind if you sleep in her bed tonight." He and Crystal had hit it off instantly.

Trae's gang ties were unknown to her. All she knew was he owned a few car washes and barbershops. She called Trae by his name, yet by the way she had talked about him over dinner, Richard could tell she loved and respected him.

He thought about his own father, Phillip Dubois. Phillip didn't even object when Richard announced he was going to legally change his last name to his grandfather's last name, Pacini, as a graduation gift to himself.

Phillip was too busy climbing the corporate ladder to take any role in Richard's life, let alone care he needed protecting. He shook off the feelings of woe. Those days were over. Now he had a chance at building a family of his own.

"I had fun today. Are you taking us out again?"

"Of course I am." He covered her with the comforter. "But you have school in the morning, so tonight you need to sleep, and I need to head home." He kissed her forehead.

"I wish you, Mama, Trae and Skeet could get married and we could all live here."

"Don't you think it would be a tad bit crowded? And I'm pretty sure that's illegal in just about every country in the world."

She looked upon him, her face scrunched in thought. "It doesn't matter anyway. Mama says she doesn't love Skeet and Trae in the marrying way."

"How old are you? You sound grown."

She giggled. "I turned seven last month."

"Well, my Christmas baby," he tapped her nose with his finger, "go to sleep. Goodnight."

"Goodnight, Smoke." She rolled over.

Richard brushed his lips over Ebony's until she woke.

"Tease," she whispered.

"Who, me? You seduce me and kick me out, then have the nerve to call me a tease."

"Where's the baby?"

"I put her in your bed." He stroked her braids behind her ear. "Thank you."

"For what?"

"For giving me a chance with Crystal. She's great. You have done a wonderful job."

"You don't know how relieved I am she likes you."

"That makes two of us." He kissed her gently. "I'd better go before we end up naked. What time should I pick you up?"

"Six should be early enough. That way I can chat with Nonno."

"You trying to make a move on my grandpapà? Note to self: Change calling time with Nonno."

CHAPTER EIGHT

Ebony sat on the locker room bench lacing her shoes. "He didn't shoot anyone, Jessica. You heard wrong. And I don't appreciate the way you made me sound like some sort of thug groupie. What if he believed you?" When Richard dropped Ebony at school, Jessica made it her business to stress that Ebony "loved her some thugs."

She waved Ebony off. "I didn't tell him anything he didn't already know. Go ahead. Protect your man. He's a cutie. *Almost* makes me want to cross over. Why didn't you tell me he's one of Trae's boys?"

"Because he isn't. He's the regional manager of an investment firm."

"Yeah, right, and I won the lottery last night."

"What made you think he works for Trae? And lower your voice. I don't want the whole world hearing my business."

Jessica rolled her eyes. "Come off it, girl. Trae wouldn't let some white boy have his woman. I love you, but everyone knows this is a business deal. Trae needs a clean-up man for his money. Smoke is the perfect man for the job."

Ebony fell off the bench, laughing. "My God, you're making my stomach hurt. Whew. Where do you get this stuff?" She remained on the floor, holding her stomach.

"No one believes you just bumped into this perfect white guy on the train. You all could have put a little thought into your story."

"This has got to be the stupidest thing I've ever heard." Ebony grabbed her towel and headed for the aerobics room. "Richard doesn't work for Trae. I'm not discussing this further." She giggled. "Wait until I tell him."

"How do you keep attracting these high rollers?"

"What are you talking about? I broke up with Trae years ago. I grew up, and he became a drug dealer. Maybe it's time for you to grow up." Frustrated with this rerun of their previous arguments, she increased her pace. "Never mind. I'm past sick of this line of questioning, officer. Move on." It had taken Ebony years to convince Jessica to try for her bachelors. It was looking as if it would take another few years to convince her drug dealers don't make good relationship material.

Richard couldn't believe what Ebony was telling him. "You all's grapevine on the west side is out of control. First I am a crazy white guy, next I am working for Dan, then I smoked the Collins brothers, now I'm laundering money for Trae?" He laughed. "I've been a very busy boy since meeting you." The rumors were bad enough, and he hated to think what realities lay before them. This was the only life she knew, but shortly he would show her a better way. He would save the angel.

His cell phone beeped, indicating the battery was extremely low. "I'm not trying to rush you, but I want to buy Crystal a bedroom set for my place. The next date may end at my condo. I don't want you driving late at night. Purple's her favorite color. Maybe we can paint her room this weekend." He searched his drawers for the charger, then remembered he wasn't in his downtown office or using his own car.

Clark cleared his throat. Richard spun around in his chair to face him. "Duty calls. I'm ready whenever you are...Love you, too." He disconnected. "What's up?"

"With her two days and already talking street," Clark cracked, his voice thick with sarcasm. "What next? We all have to take a crash course in Ebonics?"

"Don't start with me," Richard warned. "You can go back to Texas if you don't like how I'm running things here. Otherwise, you have an invitation to butt out of my private life."

"Do your parents know you're shacking up with Miss Ghetto-fabulous USA?"

"Do you have business with me, or did you want to see how far you can push me before I leap over this desk and put my foot up your ass? If it's the latter, you've just about reached my limit."

Clark tossed a folder on the desk then backed away. "Why did we open a site out here? Read the demographics report. People in this income bracket don't invest."

"The days of our customers coming to us have passed." Richard rounded the desk and hung his suit coat in the closet, dropping the dead cell phone in the pocket. "We must be aggressive and find new markets. Yes, these people do invest. These are the working-class people. You know, the people whose buying stimulates our economy."

He crossed the room, pointing at the busy shopping plaza through the window. "Check out the cars, clothes, jewelry, hair. We're an investment option with higher returns. Chicago's a gold mine, Clark. Think outside the box." He walked back to his desk. "We want everyone to come in out of the cold and invest with us."

"Nickels and dimes won't help us." Clark rolled a chair from the conference table. "We need to focus on the Gold Coast, the Magnificent Mile. Downtown has money. The suburbs have money. Even the north side has money." He leaned his lanky body forward. "If you want oil, drill where there's oil."

Richard stared into Clark's murky green eyes. "You're being lazy. Yes, we'll have to put in all of the front-end work, but with bigger risk come bigger returns."

"Or losses. Mark my words. In this case, it'll be a loss."

"Can I count on you to give it your all? If not, I'll assign you to a different project."

"You honestly believe this'll work?" He ran his hands over his short red hair.

"I know it will."

Clark rocked in the chair, looking around the room. "You haven't led me wrong yet. I'm in." He released a nervous laugh. "Now it all makes sense. You're with Ebony to appeal to our new demographic. You'd better hope this works. The Austin office won't tolerate your smudging the company name."

Another rumor making its rounds was the last thing he needed. "Let me make something perfectly clear to you. I am with Ebony because I love her. Some day I'll bring her and her child to the office. I expect you to show them the utmost respect. If I ever catch you disrespecting them, I'll fire you. And the main office is as welcome to my private life as you are." The one lesson his father had taught him well was what happened when you put your career before your family.

"But, Richard…"

"No buts. Are we clear on this?"

"Yes. Have you told your parents about Ebony?"

"I didn't tell my parents about my other girlfriends. Why would I tell them about Ebony?" He sorted through the file Clark had tossed on his desk. "Did you need anything else?"

"I guess not." He headed out. "I've known you a long time. You've changed." He leaned against the doorframe. "I don't know if you're in love or lust with Ebony."

"Love."

Clark held up his hands slightly. "Okay, let's say you love her. Can you take her to business dinners? She can be the most eloquent-speaking woman in the world, but if she walks in looking like Bonequesha, no one will hear a word she says, and you'll lose credibility. Business is business. We both know the real reason you haven't told your mother you've found *the love of your life*." He left, closing the door behind him.

Richard leaned back in his chair, placed his hands behind his head and put his feet on the desk. He dreaded telling his mother about Ebony.

Stephanie Dubois never liked his female friends. Even in high school, she hounded him about his choice in women. She wanted him to date daughters of CEOs, CFOs or at least presidents within corporations. He wanted to date girls he liked. By the time he entered college, he had quit introducing his female friends to his mother.

Thinking about how his mother would react to him dating a beautician's daughter brought a wicked smile to his face. Humor of the situation lost, he closed his eyes. Telling her about Ebony would force him to make a choice and face realities he wasn't ready to face. Tired of the unending battle, he faded into sleep.

Eight-year-old Richard crouched behind the sofa in the study of his parents' home. In a few days, Nonno would be out of the hospital, and they could go home. He dug the Sixlets candy out of his pocket. If he ate one pack a day, his grandfather would have four days to recover from this mysterious stroke thing his parents claimed he had.

He sat on the floor, and then leaned against the wall. Once everyone fell asleep, he planned to sneak out to the boathouse. No one would find him there.

"I can't find him anywhere, Phillip."

Richard heard his mother's frustrated voice. He crawled to the other side of the couch, and then peeked from under the end table. He wondered if Sophia Loren, his grandfather's favorite actress, was her cousin, since they looked so much alike.

"He doesn't listen." Standing in front of the bookshelf, she brushed the dust off her sky-blue silk pantsuit. "I've checked every nook and cranny. I'm filthy." She stood with her hands on her narrow hips. "I don't know what to do with him," she said in the clipped tone Richard had grown accustomed to.

"He's scared, Stephanie." Phillip sat in one of the French walnut armchairs and rested his elbows on his knees. "What were we thinking?

We should have never sent him to live with Papà." He passed his hands over his short, black hair. "Now our son doesn't feel welcome in his own home."

"Of course he does. He's always been a little…I don't know. He isn't like the girls. He's wild. That's why Papà took him. We did the right thing." She settled in the matching armchair across from Phillip and crossed her legs.

"Richard isn't wild. He's a boy. You can't expect him to sit around the house all day playing with Barbie dolls."

"Every time he visits, he terrorizes the girls." She stroked her hair, smoothing strays that had escaped her French knot. "I don't know how to handle him. He was happy with Papà. We are good parents. We did what was best for our son."

"Have you seen how the girls taunt him? They're lucky all he's done is cut their dolls' hair. It's not as if they actually play with them anymore."

Richard stifled a laugh. If he weren't running away, he would tape the pages of their diaries all over the grand hall. That would teach them to call him filthy little lost boy.

"Now that Papà's taken ill, we don't have a choice. I've already sent someone to gather his belongings. We'll just have to make the best of the situation."

"Stephanie," Phillip snapped.

"What?" She waved him off. "Oh, you know what I mean."

Richard's eyes narrowed. He knew exactly what she meant. He was no one's charity case. He remembered an expensive-looking vase on the end table. He flashed a perfect smile.

Bianca, his oldest sister, had said the Octagonal Satsuma vase was more valuable than he was. His mother had probably taken days choosing it. He scooted forward, resituated himself and tilted the edge of the table. The antique vase fell to the floor, shattering.

"If I had a choice, I wouldn't live here, either!" he yelled as he stomped the pieces into the floor, making sure to scratch and scrape the marble as much as possible. "I hate this place!" He ran to the bookshelf, pulled books down and tossed them around the room.

His father, a large man, grabbed and held him close to his body. He fought in Phillip's arms. "I want to go back to Nonno!"

"Stop fighting and look at me, Richard," Phillip commanded.

Richard shut his eyes and closed his heart to the truth. He knew why his mother never wanted him. "I don't hear you. I don't want you. I don't love you. I don't need you," he chanted.

Stephanie knelt beside Richard and Phillip. "Please." She gently placed her shaking hand on Richard's shoulder. "Listen to me."

The unfamiliar crack of his mother's voice stopped him. He slowly peeked out of one eye. The tears streaming down her face made him feel guilty for breaking her vase. He dug in his pocket and pulled out his candy. "This is all I have," he whispered. "You can have it."

She gently closed his hand. She had the most beautiful sepia eyes. He didn't think he would ever see any quite like them. The contrast between her creamy white skin and dark eyes amazed him. She didn't allow any of her children to play in the sun, especially Richard. She had explained that the sun's rays cause some disease that makes your skin fall off. Her reasoning didn't make any sense to him. Nonno was always in the sun, and his skin hadn't fallen off.

She took his hands into hers. He was amazed by the contrast between his olive complexion and her alabaster complexion. He turned away from her and the feelings stirring within him.

He could practically hear his sisters singing their favorite *Sesame Street* song. He frowned.

"I don't belong here. You don't want me, and I don't want you." He folded his arms over his chest. "I want to go to the hospital and stay with Nonno."

She hugged him from behind. "But I do want you. I love you, Richard." He stood stiff in her arms. "Please, baby, forgive me. I can explain." She rocked him. "You're my baby. I do love you."

Phillip sat on the floor in front of Richard. "We love you and want you to live here with us."

"No, you don't!" He glared over his shoulder at his mother. "You don't have a *choice* but take me in. I'm the filthy little lost boy." He marched to the middle of the room, crying more than singing, "Guess which one does not belong here." He pointed at his parents. "Guess which one is not the same."

Stephanie crossed over to him. "Stop!"

"Can you guess which one does not belong here?"

She grabbed him by his shoulders, pulling him to her body. "You belong here." She wiped his tears away. "You belong with me. I want you with me." She rocked him. "I'll never let you go again. Never again. Please forgive me, baby, please." Exhausted, he leaned against his mother. She kissed the top of his head. "I love you, Richard."

Phillip joined in the embrace. "We love you, son."

Then why did you give me away?

Ebony saw her black SUV in the parking lot of the plaza, but the investment firm was dark. The other stores on the strip had also closed. She lifted her book bag onto her shoulder and ran to the office's front door.

The closed sign was in the window. She tried the handle. The door was unlocked. She entered the office. The silence and darkness troubled her almost as much as Richard not answering the phone. She stared at the front door. If there were a robber inside, he would be making noise, so she locked the door. She felt along the wall, but couldn't find the light switch. She dropped her book bag to the floor and got the tiny flashlight at the end of her key chain from her purse.

She followed along the dark hallway until she found the office with Richard's nameplate on it. She slowly crept into his office. The parking lot lights provided enough light for her to see into the room. She heaved a big sigh of relief upon seeing Richard lying back in his chair asleep, his feet on the desk. He had kicked the phone off the hook. She placed her purse and keys to the side.

"Richard," she whispered. "Richard." She smoothed the worry lines on his face. "Time to go home." His disoriented and scared look sent her into worry mode. "What's wrong?"

His face softened. "You've come to save me again," he whispered hoarsely.

"What am I saving you from?" She was failing with Trae and Skeet, but wouldn't fail with Richard.

He kissed her lightly. "Childhood memories. Oh, shoot!" He jumped up. "I was supposed to pick you up. Where is Crystal?" He helped her stand. "I'm sorry."

Ebony hugged him. His fast-beating heart thumped against her chest. "Mom has her. I'm worried about you." She ran the back of her hand along his five o'clock shadow. "Tell your people to lock the office at the end of the day, even if you're here working. This is the south side of Chicago, not an upper-class suburb of Austin."

"Yes, ma'am," he said with a crooked grin. "I'm sorry. I must have gone to dreamland. I need to charge my cell phone."

"What are the dreams about?"

"Crystal feels loved. It's hard on kids…" he rambled on. "I'm glad Crystal has you. Your family isn't conventional, but you make sure she feels loved, wanted."

They'd both grown up knowing the pain of feeling unwanted, and wouldn't wish it on any child. She thanked God for sending her someone who understood her. "I'm glad I have you."

"Well you're stuck with me." He tilted his arm toward the light coming in from the window to see his watch. "It's almost ten. I need to feed and put you to bed."

She wanted to know more, but let him change the subject. She had pressed too hard with Trae and Skeet, and they had fought against her. She didn't want to repeat mistakes. "If you're planning on fattening me up, it's only fair to let me cut your hair. I do hair every weekend."

CHAPTER NINE

Dressed in a royal blue sweat suit, Richard entered the finished basement of the salon. If Trae wanted to play basketball, he'd be ready.

Crystal ran across the room yelling, "Smoke!" and jumped into Richard's arms. "I didn't think you were coming."

By the end of the week, Richard felt comfortable answering to Smoke, which scared him. He wanted nothing to do with his mother's world, but this sure wasn't the life he wanted. He kissed her forehead. "I had to pick up my new car." He quickly looked around the game room: a combo washer-dryer and linen shelves took one wall, a mural of four dogs playing poker covered the back wall, and a large-screen television on the front wall.

"Stop running inside," Trae said from the pool table.

"You get another silver Mercedes?" Skeet asked.

Ebony repositioned Skeet's head. "Stop turning. You're messing up my braid." She stood to the side of the barber's chair and leaned over to curve the braid.

"It's opal." Richard put Crystal down and kissed Ebony on the cheek.

Skeet turned in the chair. "Opal! That sounds sweet."

Ebony whacked Skeet on the shoulder. "You just screwed up the braid."

He stood, brushing back his thick, black hair. "Well, since it's messed up anyway, I'll go see this car." He started up the stairs. "Hand me the keys, Smoke."

Richard tossed the keys to him, then sat in the barber's chair. "He's a big kid."

"Would you hand me the clippers, Trae?" Ebony asked.

Richard spun around in the chair. "I hope you aren't planning to use those on me."

Trae laughed. "Yeah, cut that mess. He looks like the sixth Beatle." He handed over the clippers. "You should have spinners put on your ride. Skeet owns a detail shop."

"What's that?" Richard remained still while Ebony placed a large white towel over his shoulders.

"Double rims where the inner rim spins, like Ebony's."

Crystal jumped up and down. "Yeah, and tinted windows. Can I go see the new car, Mama?"

"Stay close to Skeet."

Crystal darted up the stairs as fast as her little legs would carry her.

"How's business goin', Smoke?" Trae grabbed his bottle of beer, sat on the couch and propped his feet on the coffee table.

Something in Trae's grin told Richard he was about to pull another trick out of the bag. "I'm blown away that we're doing so well this early." His eyes shifted to the left as the clippers buzzed by his ear. "We advertised in the *Chicago Defender, Sun-Times* and a few other places, but these past two days have brought in two accounts worth a hundred thousand. This is unbelievable." His firm often worked with accounts worth millions, but this was a new office, so he was grateful for the early show of support from the community.

"Sounds great to me." Ebony switched the guard on the clippers. "The sides and back are gone. Now I'll make the top lay down." She drew her fingers through what was left of his hair. "You have a really nice wave to your hair."

He shifted in the chair. Her playing in his hair, her sweet pea scent and her soft voice all worked on his libido.

"When are you opening an office on the west and north sides? I hate the south side and don't want to keep sending people down there."

Trae's words worked better than an ice-cold shower. Richard's head fell back onto the headrest. "Oh, God, please tell me you haven't invested drug money into my firm."

"Drug money? Ebony, what you been telling him? I'm a legitimate businessman. I specialize in the service industries." He tipped his beer. "Don't have time to worry about inventory accountability."

"I told him everything, Trae." She pointed the clippers at him. "Now, what have you done?"

Richard stepped forward. This was one battle he wouldn't allow Ebony to fight. "Are both accounts yours?"

"Damn, Smoke. Loosen up. Get a beer and chill out. Nice haircut." The Cheshire cat from *Alice in Wonderland* had nothing on Trae's grin.

Crystal skipped down the stairs into the basement. "Your car is so pretty, Smoke. It would be extra pretty if it was purple."

Richard forced himself to replace the scowl on his face with a half grin. "Would you hang out with your granny in the shop for a little bit, honey?"

She went up the stairs, brushing by Skeet as he entered.

"What's wrong with y'all? Frozen in time or somethin'?" Skeet retook his seat in the barber's chair. "Damn, Smoke, why you let her jack your hair up like that?"

Richard and Trae stood in the center of the room staring each other down. Trae sucked air through his teeth. "So what you gonna do?"

"Are these your businesses?" Richard demanded. Unfortunately, when they acquired new clients, conducting a background check was not standard operating procedure. Not that a check would help. Illegal money and true owners of businesses were easier to hide than most real- ized.

"Hot damn!" Skeet interrupted. "Smoke figured out we're his new investors. Show time!" He tapped on the arm of the barber's chair. "Move out of the line of fire, Ebony." He held his hand out to her.

She waited on Richard. He nodded to indicate he wanted to handle this. She stood beside Skeet.

Richard eyeballed Trae, from his freshly braided hair, to his designer sweats; from his stockinged feet to his green eyes. "I won't allow you to corrupt my business, Trae. I'll drop your accounts."

"Humph. Won't your bosses have something to say about your turning away big money from a poor neighborhood?" He crossed his arms over his chest. "If you're gonna bluff, come with somethin' bigger. I believe you'd call this checkmate."

"I'd quit first. Keep your drug money." He stalked over to the barber's chair. "Do you mind?" he asked Skeet.

"Hell naw! Your head is jacked up." He moved to the couch.

Richard caressed Ebony's face. She looked so defeated, hurt. He loved her kind heart, but the same heart blinded her to one truth: not everyone can be saved. "Try not to worry, my little angel."

He kissed her lightly, then put on his poker face. "I'm disappointed, Trae. Because you chose your *profession* over Ebony, you actually thought I would. I know what's important." He patted her hand. His father had chosen business over family. Richard had no intention of making the same mistake. "I'll start my own firm." When he chose Ebony, he knew it was an all or nothing deal.

After a long, awkward pause, Skeet clapped. "Bravo, Smoke. You passed."

"Passed what?"

Trae crossed the room toward Richard. "Those accounts are completely legit. I wanted to see if you'd choose Ebony, the money or your career." He shook his head. "I thought you'd take the money or cut and run." He held his hand out. "You're in."

Richard hesitated before shaking hands. "No more games, Trae. Ebony and Crystal are my life now."

"No more games," Trae answered a tad bit too quickly for Richard's liking. "Give the man a beer, Skeet. He's earned it. I'll spread the word about your firm. Legit channels, of course. You need to support Ebony in style."

"There's no need. I'll manage." He sensed that Trae was still playing games, but chose to drop the matter until he could get Trae alone.

Skeet handed Richard a bottle of beer. "Listen, Smoke. When you're in, you're in. We take care of our own. Your bringing the firm into the hood is a great idea. Use the connections you have."

Richard looked over his shoulder at Ebony.

"No offense, Trae, but I think he should go through Dan to build his network. He's been totally legit for years."

Trae sucked his teeth. "Fine. Go through Dan."

"Truce," Richard said, making a mental note to keep an eye out for more of Trae's games.

"I still don't like you with Ebony, but you're what she wants. I made my choice and have to live with it. Don't cross Ebony, and we'll be cool."

Skeet spent the rest of the afternoon entertaining everyone with wild stories.

"You playing ball with us, Smoke?" Skeet asked. "Can you dispel the rumor?"

"What rumor?"

"White men can't jump," Trae chimed in.

Richard laughed. "Got jokes, huh? Talk all the trash you want. When we're out on the court, this white boy's gonna show you how it's done." This would give him a chance to be alone with Skeet and Trae to discuss them taking their business elsewhere without Ebony trying to ride in and save the day.

Trae passed the ball across the court. Richard caught the ball, balanced his footing, lined up his elbow and eye with the basket and shot from the top of the key. Skeet leaped into the air, caught the ball and slam-dunked it.

Crystal and Ebony jumped up from the sidelines cheering. "We won. We won!" They high fived each other, singing, "We bad. We know it." Crystal ran onto the court and jumped into Trae's arms.

"See why I don't bring them? They're too emotional."

Feigning indignation, Ebony huffed, "Come on, Crystal. I know when I'm not wanted." She kissed Richard on the cheek, then took Crystal to the opposite side of the gym to play hopscotch.

Trae nodded at their three-on-three opponents. "Good game."

"Good game, homes." Jose motioned toward Richard. "How long you been with Trae, Smoke?"

The men sat along the wall of the gymnasium, drinking bottles of water. Trae had arranged to rent the gymnasium every Saturday afternoon for his private games. Ebony didn't usually attend the games, but insisted on going this time. Richard was sure to watch over him.

Richard was surprised when three Puerto Ricans joined the game. "I don't go that way," Richard joked. "Ebony's my girl."

Skeet laughed. "Damn, Jose, I didn't know you were sweet."

One of the lookouts ran into the gym and pulled Trae to the side. Richard watched Trae pace, obviously agitated by what the man said.

"Smoke," Trae called.

"Yeah." He ran over.

"Take the girls to your place for a while. I'll contact you later. Ebony, Crystal, grab your things. You've got to go."

"What's going on?" Richard asked.

"The cops are about three minutes away. You need to leave."

"Okay, I'm out." In his head, Richard knew what Trae was, but now it was finally registering what Trae *was*. This was not a game, or make-believe. He looked at the Puerto Rican males. They were most likely drug associates. Fear, anxiety and anger rushed through Richard. How could he have allowed himself to be caught in the company of men like these? He had to get his girls away from this lifestyle.

"Smoke." Trae paused. "I don't want this life for Ebony and Crystal. I'm stepping to the side to give them a chance. I can't step out. You understand what I'm saying?"

"I do," he answered, but was not entirely convinced.

Trae walked toward Skeet, still speaking to Richard. "Get them out of here, Smoke. You only have two minutes left."

CHAPTER TEN

Ebony's silence worried Richard. She had remained quiet the entire drive to his home, staring out the window, seemingly on the verge of tears.

He unlocked his condo door. "Why don't you take your rope and jump in the dining room, Crystal?"

Crystal tore off her coat. "I actually get to jump *in* the house?"

"Until we get downstairs neighbors, yes."

She flashed a broad, happy smile. "I love your place." She took off her boots and ran, sliding to the center of the dining room with her rope.

He hung their coats in the closet. "We need to talk." The arrival of their first argument traveled with dread. Why she chose to live in Trae's shadow instead of moving to a suitable environment to raise Crystal confused and angered him. It was as if she wanted out of the drug life on one hand, but still wanted to hold on as a security blanket on the other.

She nodded, then headed for the bedroom. He followed, wondering why she tried to save everyone except herself. She purposely surrounded herself with people in need. Things had changed for her, whether she knew it or not. Now she had someone to watch out for her best interests.

He searched his mind for reasons. She had the kindest heart he had ever known. There was no way she would *choose* to raise her child in a drug-infested environment. She was too close to the situation to see that she had alternatives. That had to be it. He loved her, and planned on showing her she had choices.

Ebony slumped on the chaise lounge. Richard sat on the edge of the bed, reached forward and took her hand into his. "I can't stand by and watch you die."

Her head tilted to the side.

"When you heard Trae had funneled money into my business, I saw the light in your eyes dim." She stiffened. "When we had to leave the gym abruptly…" his throat tightened and voice trailed off. "I love you too much to watch you sacrifice yourself."

"I'm not sacrificing myself, I'm helping my family," she said softly.

"By carrying their burdens, their guilt, forgiving sins? By running around passing out rehab pamphlets, gloves, sandwiches?"

Overwhelmed by frustration, a part of him wanted to bolt. But he couldn't. Though they had only known each other a short time, his love for her was genuine, and he owed her the chance to explain herself. He also refused to be like his father. Phillip had stood by while his wife and daughters ostracized and made Richard feel less than worthy. In his book, Phillip was just as guilty of emotional abuse as the rest. No, he wouldn't turn a blind eye while Ebony was taken advantage of. He ran his hands over his freshly cut hair. He couldn't help her if he lost control. He took several deep breaths, releasing them slowly until he felt calm enough to continue.

"You can't save someone who refuses to be saved."

"I know," she whispered. "I can't ignore what's happening on our streets. I can't pretend that Trae isn't causing misery. But it's my fault. I can't desert him."

Confused, he asked, "Your fault?"

Tears streamed down her face. "He started selling drugs so we would have more money. I knew he was a card shark, but…" She wiped her face. "He wanted me to have everything. He didn't think hustling at cards brought in enough. I didn't find out about the drugs until Crystal came along."

"You can't blame yourself for his choices. You can't keep punishing yourself for the bad decisions he's still making. You can't atone for his sins."

"I keep telling myself the same thing, but my heart doesn't listen." She laughed nervously. "How can my heart hear over the noise of destruction in our streets?"

"Then you need to move your heart away from the noise," he whispered. "You have to move out of the neighborhood."

Thinking he was pushing too hard and she would quit listening, he quickly added, "I'm not saying to totally cut Trae and Skeet off from Crystal. She would be devastated, but you have to minimize exposure to that environment." He thought about the way Crystal always ran around the house. "She can't even go outside and play, Ebony." Before he moved in with his grandfather, his mother used to make him stay in the house while the girls played under the shade of the trees. He felt trapped, and he lived in a mansion, not a small flat.

Childhood memories beat at his subconscious—fought for recognition. Stephanie never said it, but he always knew she was ashamed of him. It was as if she didn't want people to know he existed. He stopped his train of thought. The past was the past and couldn't hurt him. Ebony was the here and now, his love, his angel. He had to save her.

She remained silent.

"I'll help you find a place."

Sitting up, she asked, "And how do I pay for this place? Hit Trae up for some drug money, or maybe beg Dan for a handout. I'm not a charity case. I'm a full-time student. The grant money I have after I pay for tuition and books I give to Mom for rent. I earn about $200 a week braiding hair, Crystal's tuition is $400 a month. With the rest I have to clothe, feed and pay for anything else that comes up."

"I saw you accept money from Trae."

"Yes I accepted Trae's money," she snapped. "How did you think Meechie would pay for rehab? Trae doesn't offer medical benefits. I use Trae's drug money to repair some of the damage he causes. I don't want his dirty money or charity. Everything me and my child have," she pointed a multi-ringed finger at herself, "I paid for with money I earned, or Mom or Dan gave as a gift."

"You're splitting hairs, Ebony."

"And your point?"

"I know you're using the money for a good cause. I truly admire what you're trying to do, but you're going about it the wrong way. By accepting tainted money, you become tainted."

"What do the police do with drug money they seize? Why do they sell the property of drug dealers? What do they do with the money?"

He had no idea. "That's totally different, Ebony. It's their job."

"Oh, so I shouldn't help people because it isn't my *job*?"

"You know that's not what I mean."

"Using your philosophy, aren't the police just as tainted? I know of at least a hundred grand of tainted money your company has accepted. How many other clients with tainted money do you have?" She folded her arms over her chest.

"We didn't know."

"And why is that?" she asked rhetorically, with an attitude-filled roll of the neck. "The drug money and property seized by officials is used for everything from beefing up their budget to community projects to lining pockets. I'm just cutting out the middle man and helping those who need help."

He could see they would go in circles on this issue until Bill Gates ran out of money. It was time for solutions. "I'll give you the money for Meechie."

Her facial features softened, and she lowered her hands to her lap. "You'd do that for Meechie?"

"I'm doing it because I love you, but I can't afford to put all of Chicago into rehab. Maybe you can obtain grants, or find company sponsors to help pay for the good works you do."

"You're the greatest." She reached over and took his hand into hers. "Thank you for doing instead of just standing in judgment. I've tried for grants and to find a sponsor, but I think no one wants to give me funding because I don't represent a non-profit organization."

"Well, for now you concentrate on Meechie, and I'll worry about future funding. You're not in this alone any more." He prayed the gratitude and love in her eyes remained after they tackled the next subject.

"You need to move out of the neighborhood. You can't allow your pride to interfere with what's best for you and your child. If you still think it's too soon to move in with me, I'll help you move somewhere else. I know Dan would help you out."

"I appreciate what you're trying to do, but you don't understand."

"Explain it to me."

"Mom made mistakes raising me, but I'm proud of her. I didn't know Dan paid our bills. My parents had become dependent on him. After my father was murdered, Mom wanted nothing further to do with the drug world. Instead of taking money from Dan, she cleaned herself up, then worked two jobs to support me the best she could. She saved enough to put herself through beauty school and eventually bought her own shop. The flat we live in is hers."

She held her hands to her chest. "I'm proud of my mom, and I've learned from her mistakes. I'm not about to be dependent on anyone to provide for me and my child. I love Dan, but I needed him. Leaving the drugs alone wasn't easy for Mom, and I know she banned him from coming around, but he should have done something. My aunt Genevieve should have done something. I don't know." She leaned against the backing of the chaise. "I guess that's why I can't stand by and do nothing when I see something is wrong. I graduate in a few months. Don't worry. I'll find a good job and be able to move shortly."

The sad tone of her voice alerted him to delve deeper. "Don't you want to move?"

"Of course I want to move. But, that doesn't ease my guilt for abandoning people in need. The neighborhood needs good role models, like Mom and Dan, who have turned their lives around, but I choose saving my child over saving the neighborhood."

"I know you want what's best for Crystal." He hesitated, then said, "Trae isn't best for Crystal. As long as Trae is in the picture…" Her explanations for why she allowed Trae to stay in her life always flowed so easily. As if she'd convinced herself these were the reasons, and was now just repeating them.

"And what do you suggest I do? Are you so naive that you believe Trae will just walk out of our lives because I ask?"

Holding in his frustration, he stated the obvious. "Ebony, he's a drug dealer. Call the cops."

Ebony laughed. This certainly wasn't what he expected.

"And what do I tell them?" she asked after she calmed. "I have no evidence, no proof. All I have is what I see when I walk through the streets. The cops know more than I do, and haven't been able to convict him of anything. I'm making the best of an impossible situation. Give me a viable solution, and I'm more than willing to jump at it."

She was right. There was no way Trae would allow her and Crystal to walk out of his life. Now that he understood where she was coming from, he needed time to find the viable solutions. "We'll make it through together." He caressed her face. "You look exhausted."

"I'm so tired of all of this. Will it ever end?" She lazily glanced toward the pillows lining the head of the bed.

"Lie on the bed. It's more comfortable." He watched her switch places. "I'll shower, then fix dinner." He covered her with a light blanket. "Try to rest." He kissed her gently on the lips. "I love you."

Richard inhaled deeply. The scent of corned beef and potatoes had filled his condo. He took the steamer from the cabinet and placed it on the kitchen island.

Crystal jumped rope in the dining room until she ran out of extra energy and found a video to watch.

He took out the cutting board and a head of cabbage, setting them on the end of the island. The comfort he usually found in cooking seemed lost today. He couldn't stand seeing Ebony so distraught.

He chopped the cabbage into strips. Crystal and Ebony would be devastated if anything happened to Trae and Skeet, but Richard knew that *when* something happened was a more likely scenario. Ebony would blame herself for not being able to save them and Crystal would lose two people she loved dearly. He threw the cut cabbage into a colander and rinsed it.

He understood Ebony's anger and helplessness about the situation, but there had to be another way. Trae and Skeet were always so careful with what they said around Ebony and Crystal, but maybe if he could "befriend" them, he could find the evidence the police needed.

He nervously chuckled. He was scared as hell, but someone had to stand up and do the right thing. He wouldn't stop being the good "friend" until he found proof that would lead to a conviction.

The entry buzzer sounded. He glanced at the monitor mounted in the back wall of the kitchen and buzzed Trae and Skeet in. "Come on up. The door's unlocked."

He poured broth from the cooked corned beef into the steamer.

Skeet's tall, dark figure walked through the door. "Damn, Smoke, who stole your furniture?" He leapt off the foyer into the living room, disturbing the peace. "I own a furniture store. I can hook you up." He tapped the lonely leather couch as he approached the kitchen.

Trae stood in the doorway with his hands out. "What's the deal, Smoke?" He closed the door. "You need some furniture."

"Yeah, yeah, I know. Keep your voices down. Ebony and Crystal are asleep, and I don't want to wake them before dinner is done in another fifteen minutes or so." He finished preparing the cabbage. "So what happened? It's been hours." They all sat around the breakfast bar.

"Short answer—harassment," Trae replied. "This new gang task force thinks I'm *colluding* with my rivals. Makes them nervous."

"Are you?"

"Of course we are," Skeet answered. "Do you have a television?"

Richard motioned toward the bedroom. "Make yourself at home. You can turn the channel, but *do not* wake the girls." Skeet headed for the bedroom.

Just as Richard thought. Trae and Skeet didn't see him as a threat to their empire, so would speak more freely than if Ebony were around.

But he also knew it would take time before they became comfortable enough to share any useful information.

"I expect you to close those accounts your people opened, or I'll drop them."

"It's already in the works."

Richard intended on verifying the accounts were closed first thing Monday morning.

They heard bedsprings squeaking.

"Skeet!" Ebony yelled. "If you jump one mo' gin, I'm gonna kill you."

Trae and Richard laughed. "Skeet is a big kid," Richard said.

"Smoke!" Crystal yelled. "Come get Skeet. He keeps poking me."

They heard a loud thud. "Don't get back in this bed, or I'll kick your tail. Now get out!" Ebony roared.

The condo finally became quiet. "He must be finished. Why do you do this, Trae?"

"Damn, man. I have to hear this shit from Ebony. Don't you start, too."

"Just tell me why, and I'll drop it."

"I guess you can say I'm addicted to the lifestyle."

Skeet walked into the room with a picture. "Check this out." He handed the picture to Trae. "Why didn't you tell us you're passin'? Is that your father?"

Sly grin on his face, Trae looked up from the photo. "Yeah, you should have told us you're actually one of us. I knew a white boy couldn't hang. I had a feeling."

Richard frowned. "Wait a second. Are you saying I'm all right with you now that you know I'm of mixed heritage?"

"No. I'm saying you were saved by your drop of black blood."

Skeet took the framed photo from Trae. "Please don't get him started. His daddy was a no good piece of white trash. Now he blames all white men for his jacked up childhood. As Ebony would say, 'He has issues.' Is dinner done? I'm starvin'."

"Seven more minutes. This is my grandfather. He's only half-black. Am I black enough for you, Trae?"

"No, not really, but you can hoop and know how to invest, so I'll give you a pass for now."

All three men laughed.

"You're right, Skeet. He does have issues."

"Hell, how you gonna say I have issues when it's your octoroon ass who's passin' for white?"

"I ain't passing nothing but the time of day, Trae. I learned in college to be me. I've accepted all of who I am. Can you say the same?"

"Damn. That's some deep shit there," Skeet interjected.

CHAPTER ELEVEN

Richard had never seen so much purple in his life. Though he had final approval, he had allowed Crystal to design the bedroom he intended for her. The only saving grace in the room was the bamboo bedroom suit, and she had asked if they could paint it purple. She even covered the beautiful cherry wood floor with a hideous, splotched rug that was many shades of purple.

He turned off the light and went into the living room to relax before his guest arrived. His investigation had been fruitless thus far, but he wouldn't give up. But now he had conflicting feelings that were worrying him. He actually found himself wanting to save Trae and Skeet from themselves.

He longed to tell Nonno everything, but feared his grandfather would ride in to save the day and be caught up in this mess. He pushed his misgivings aside. Soon Ebony would be moving out of the neighborhood, and that would relieve some of his stress.

He thought Ebony did an excellent job on the rest of the condo. She lightened the forest and burgundy tones from the bedroom and used them throughout the living, dining and kitchen areas. He leaned back on the couch, recalling breaking it in. Unlike the leather couch he had bought, the soft suede was perfect to make love on.

The security buzzer interrupted his train of thought. "Come on up; it's unlocked."

Richard handed Trae a bottle of beer. Over the past six weeks, they'd spent a lot of time debating investment strategies, playing ball, arguing, entertaining his girls, laughing and growing mutual respect. Ebony was a mixture of intriguing contrasts, while Trae and Skeet were frustrating contradictions.

He couldn't believe how much his life had changed since he'd left Texas. Men he originally considered ruthless monsters had somehow worked their way into Richard's heart and became human. People worth saving.

Crystal's father obviously loved and taught his daughter right from wrong. This man was worth saving. The men he hung out with in the basement of the beauty shop were worth saving. He chuckled lightly. If he could find a twelve-step program for drug dealers, life would be grand. If he could only separate the good from the bad, but he couldn't. He felt as if he were betraying the male role models Crystal loved, but he had to continue. They were tainted. The love they gave was tainted.

"You should have told Crystal no on the purple thing sooner." Trae rested in the overstuffed chair. "Did the head honchos say anything else about you losing those accounts?" On Richard's request, Trae had pulled out the accounts he had originally opened.

"I thought I'd be fired for a while, but Dan's connections have been extremely lucrative. Headquarters isn't even complaining about the free investment classes we've started offering the community. This summer our west and north side offices open." Richard picked at the label on his beer. Predicting Trae's reactions where Ebony was involved proved virtually impossible.

"Good. Now why did you call me here?"

Richard set the beer on the coffee table. Like him, Trae didn't beat around the bush. "Tonight I'm asking Ebony to marry me."

Trae snarled. "So what's this? You asking my permission?"

"I don't need your permission," Richard answered calmly. "I came to you out of respect and friendship. I know how you feel about Ebony." He looked into the perplexed face of the man who loved his woman, and felt sorry for him. Trae picked a life of crime over Ebony, and just realized what he'd lost.

Trae sighed, lowering his head into his hands. "I chose you." He paused. "I've been trying to prepare myself for this but…" He thumped his fists on his thighs. "She's getting married."

"What do you mean you chose me?"

Trae took a swig of beer. "I had you checked out when Ebony first brought you around. Those first few weeks I kept testing you, and you kept passing. I want Ebony to have the life you can provide her. I just want to be the one to provide it."

"But you can't."

"I know." Trae paced the room. "I can't believe I'm doing this." He hit at the bookshelf. "I hurt Ebony once, and have been trying to make it up ever since."

Richard wanted to know what Trae had done, but didn't ask. Other ground needed covering. "I love Ebony and Crystal. I'll do right by them, and won't interfere with your relationship. We can do this."

"Those are my girls. I'd die for them."

"Let's be honest. I know you love them, but you have chosen a life of drugs and death over them. They're number one in my life."

Trae spun around. "They're my heart. They're number one!"

Richard countered Trae's hostility with calm. "Why are you still in the game? Why do you continue to put them in harm's way?" But his concerns now included Trae and Skeet. He wanted them to choose life over death; wanted them to see his way was exciting, fulfilling and challenging. He laughed at himself for falling into the same trap as Ebony.

Sobering reality washed over him. *You can't save someone who refuses to be saved.* He had said it a million times to Ebony; he needed to heed his own words.

He knew Trae was forever battling his feelings for Ebony. Richard respected him for being man enough to step aside and allow her to be free. If circumstances were reversed, he knew he couldn't do it. That was what separated him from Trae. He would never give Ebony up.

"I protect them!"

"From danger you put them in. I've learned the game. How long before one of your rivals goes after them?"

"Shit." He hit at the couch as he passed.

"I'm not telling you anything you don't already know. We need to get this out in the open. You thought I was a safe white boy you could manipulate."

"Thought is right." Trae released a nervous laugh. "You're as bad as me." He blew out an exasperated breath. "I'll never forgive myself for hurting Ebony. You make her happy and can keep her safe."

"She needs all of us, Trae," he said to encourage him to choose life.

"Humph, I can't believe I'm letting someone marry Ebony. Have you bought the ring?"

"I think she wants to pick it out herself. Can you stay with Crystal a few hours tomorrow?"

"I'll do you one better. I was supposed to go to St. Louis. Instead, I'll take my baby girl to see her granny down in Florida. We'll be back in three days."

"Your mother?"

"Yeah. Her birthday's Friday. She's been clean for years, Smoke. And don't worry, Crystal will call her Auntie."

"I'm sorry, but I'm wondering why you hate your father when your mother didn't seem much better."

"She tried to raise me for ten years before her drug addiction took over; he never claimed me. That is, until he needed money. She wouldn't win any prizes, but she tried."

Richard shook his head, puzzled. "You know, Trae, I just don't get it. I know what you do for a living. It doesn't seem to match who you are as a person. Yeah, you're rough around the edges, but I know *you*. This isn't computing."

"What? Because I'm a drug dealer, I can't love my child, my family? How can I thump heads one minute and take Crystal to the movies the next? This is a business. Not everyone has the stomach for it. Hell, think of me as a soldier."

"It's not the same."

"What do you think they do with their M-16 rifles and tanks? I'm no longer in the infantry. I've worked my way up. I'm the commander-in-chief. I don't have to pull the trigger anymore."

"It's different."

"Why, because the blood on their hands is legal and the blood on mine is illegal? Blood is blood. Death is death. The only difference is I don't stand on some platform pretending my shit don't stink. I'm in this for the money."

"There are other ways for you to make money."

"And I will someday. That someday will come when Trae is ready. Not when Ebony or Smoke is ready."

Richard could see there was no breaking through to Trae. "Okay. I'll back off."

"I need to make flight arrangements." An awkward silence stood between them. Trae broke the silence, saying, "I'm not gonna lie and say I'm all for this marriage, but I know this is how it has to be. Keep Ebony happy and we'll be cool."

"Then we'll always be cool."

Ebony's eyes shifted from Jessica to Dan. "You're not actually leaving me with her, are you? How could you desert me in my hour of need?"

Dan pushed away from the dining room table. "Genevieve expected me an hour ago. You women are running me ragged," he teased as he walked across the living room to the coat rack. "Don't listen to Jessica. Smoke's already saved me over two hundred grand. You better keep him."

"See. He's a keeper." She stuck her tongue out at Jessica, then moved to the living room couch. "Bye, Dan."

Dan nodded on his way out the door.

Jessica made herself comfortable on the recliner. "As long as Smoke's making him money, Dan wouldn't care if he's a serial killer. I'm looking out for your best interest…"

Unable to fathom why Jessica never accepted Richard, Ebony studied her best friend carefully. At first she thought Jessica was jealous or angry Richard had taken so much of the time they used to spend together. Then she thought Jessica was upset because they were moving so fast. Now she didn't know what to think.

A picture of Trae holding Crystal was on the large-screen television next to a picture of Richard teaching Crystal chess. She had expected Trae to be the one to give her the most grief about Richard.

"Are you listening to me, Ebony?"

She tucked her long legs beneath her and leaned her body against the arm of the couch. "Smoke's a good man. I don't understand why you can't see it. Why can't you be happy for me?" Over the course of the weeks since they'd met, she had joined the others in calling Richard Smoke, and he loved it. Especially when she called out "Smoke" when they made love.

"I want to be happy for you." The recliner squeaked softly as Jessica leaned forward. "I finally know what you want out of life. Smoke can't provide it."

The sincere sorrow in Jessica's voice confused Ebony even more. "But he can. I'm in love with him. Truly in love."

She held her chubby hands out to Ebony. "Listen to me." She took Ebony's hands into hers and trained her big brown eyes on Ebony. "Do you honestly think Trae would allow anyone to walk in off the street and take his woman?"

Ebony pulled away. "I'm not *his* woman. Haven't been for about eight years now. Besides, that has nothing to do with Smoke."

Jessica yanked her scrunchie off, allowing her black microbraids to drape around her shoulders. "I don't want to see you hurt." She stretched the scrunchie a few times, then rolled it onto her arm. "I don't want you hurt."

"Please, Jessica, tell me why you feel this way." Thoroughly frustrated, Ebony lifted her hands to the heavens. Numerous gold bracelets fell down her arm. Though inexpensive, her jewelry was the one luxury she lightly indulged in. "Give me something, anything, to work with." She watched her friend fidget nervously with the scrunchie. "You are working my last nerve, woman. What the heck is wrong with you and Smoke?"

Jessica threw her hands up. "Okay, okay, but let me say my piece. I have a few questions for you. They're just food for thought: How many legit people does Trae allow to get close to him?"

Ebony continued building her defensive shields. Over the past two months, they had become quite extensive.

"What are the chances of Trae stepping to the side for a complete stranger who happens to be a *legit white guy* to take *his woman*?" She pointed a perfectly manicured nail at Ebony. "Deny it all you want. You know Trae considers you his."

Ebony straightened her cream blouse and rearranged her bronze flouncey skirt to cover her bare feet. In actuality, she wasn't sure what to think about Trae. Most of the time he acted as if he didn't care about her relationship with Richard; other times, he acted like a jealous lover. In the end, she figured it didn't matter. What Trae considered his and what was reality were two totally different things in this case. "I assume you are getting to the point."

"I know you like to believe Trae would never deceive you, but you need to face facts. Smoke works for him. He's been helping him launder money."

"No, he isn't!"

She sucked air through her teeth. "Come on, Ebony. You know damn well Trae don't trust nobody but you and Skeet, and he's iffy about Dan. Now you gonna tell me he all of a sudden decided to trust some strange white guy—who wants *his* woman—to dabble in his finances, make acquaintances with his drug connections?" She rotated her thick neck. "Give me a break. He would have had Smoke dropped on that first night, and you know it."

Ebony picked at the arm of the sofa. She didn't have a comeback for Jessica. Ignoring what she didn't know, she focused on what she did know. Richard and Trae had somehow become friends, and she was grateful. With Richard's help, she may be able to convince Trae and Skeet to leave the drug life. It felt so good to finally have someone to fight alongside her instead of against her. "I have no idea why Trae accepted Smoke." She hunched her shoulders. "Maybe God answered my prayers."

"This does not add up. Smoke isn't the answer. They set you up."

"They wouldn't do that to me! You're wrong." She inhaled deeply, trying to calm herself. The scent from the vanilla candle burning reminded her of Richard's condo and his loving touch. He wouldn't deceive her.

"He tried to buy a transit card with a fifty-dollar bill. What kind of literate idiot does that? They knew what time you take the train. I would have left his butt standing on the platform, but you," she pointed at Ebony, "you would never leave anyone standing in the cold."

Ebony tried to interrupt, but Jessica cut her off. "He parked on nails? Yeah, right. Any white man in his right mind would have called AAA immediately, not leave his sixty thousand dollar car behind." She chuckled, resting her hands across her ample stomach. "He *lost* your number. His car was stolen. He *met* you at the hoagy shop. Too many coincidences. In the real world, Trae would have had him dropped because Smoke was either a suspected cop or trying to move in on *his woman*."

"You're wrong." She set her feet on the floor and crossed her arms over her chest.

"Why? Because I'm not saying what you want to hear?" She walked into the kitchen.

Ebony followed Jessica. "Because your logic is seriously flawed. If I'm Trae's woman—and I mean a capital *if*—why would he set me up with Smoke?"

"Trae's been in love with you since you were shorties." She took a glass out of the cabinet, pointing it at Ebony. "He knows he's blown it with you." She turned on the faucet, letting the water run cold. "He's a control freak. You have custody of Crystal, but you consult him on all decisions about her. How many friends do you have outside of Trae's circle?" Her brow raised. "And I'm including Smoke in that circle. Trae keeps an eye on you.

"How many years has the lower flat been empty, Ebony? I'll tell you, since you and your mom moved in. And I'll bet the condo under Smoke will remain empty as long as you're there. Hell, he knows you'll get married someday. Once you join the workforce, men will be beating down your doors. This way he is in control." She filled her glass with water. "He has chosen your husband."

Ebony's stomach churned angrily. "He wouldn't, they wouldn't." She sat at the kitchen table, searching for a logical reason behind Trae accepting Richard and vice-versa. Jessica was right. Forget that Richard was white. What man in Richard's position would have accepted her lifestyle so easily?

"The hell he wouldn't. I never could stand his manipulative butt." She pulled out a chair and sat with Ebony. "Why do you think I stopped chasing after Skeet? Because what you kept telling me finally sunk in. I do deserve better. So do you. I don't want you manipulated into marrying what you think is the perfect man. He's Trae's lackey."

Jessica's words computed perfectly in Ebony's mind, but her heart rejected them. Richard's love for her couldn't be an act. And, yes, the deal she made with Trae worked out to his advantage, but he knew she would take Crystal and run, otherwise. She couldn't hold his wanting to be a father against him. What she held against Trae was the selfishness of his love. His selfishness is what kept her and Crystal trapped in the drug world.

"He wouldn't do this to me. I believe in Trae and Smoke."

"Listen, honey," Jessica said quietly as she set her glass on the table. "I know this is hard for you. Believe me when I say it hurts to tell you, but I'm your best friend. I'm looking from the outside in. I'm not blinded by love, loyalty or a Dudley Do Right mentality."

"Maybe two plus two is actually five in this case." Richard hadn't said anything about the hundred grand Skeet and Trae had invested in his firm. She pushed thoughts of betrayal out of her mind. Richard was legit. He knew how she felt. He loved her. Jessica was just jealous.

"One more tidbit of food for thought: Why did Smoke take to his street name and your circumstances so easily?" She hunched her shoulders. "Rich, straight-laced white boy gets lost in the hood, then embraces it fully, no questions asked. I mean damn, Ebony, he knows more about Trae's business than you do. And have you seen him lately? His walk has brotha written all over it."

"I object." Feigning horror in an attempt to dissuade the line of questioning, Ebony straightened up. "Smoke has always had a confident, sexy walk."

Jessica waved her off. "He even had his ear pierced. And what has he let Skeet do to his car? Spinners and a tint so dark it can't be legal. His car is like every other high-rollin' thug's car."

"And about half the other guys on the west side. This is all new to him. Maybe he's experimenting." She played with her braids. "I'm experimenting." She dropped the braids. "Have you considered he's working to fit into the environment in ways that won't compromise his morals?

"Pretty soon I have to lose the blonde microbraids." She flashed her fingers. "My acrylic nails are so long they curve, and don't get me started on my tip ring." She toyed with the tiny ring on the tip of her nail. "I have two to three rings on every finger. All gone." She proudly displayed her twenty-four rings and numerous bracelets. "I'll need to dress the part of a business woman in corporate America. Superficial changes do not change who I am."

"Humph, you have an answer for everything, don't you? Okay, let's say you're correct, and he isn't working for Trae."

A big smile paraded across Ebony's face. "Okay, he doesn't work for Trae. Now I need to pack Crystal's bags." She stood.

Jessica stopped her from leaving. "Not so fast, missy. You have a different issue you need to work through with Smoke."

Somehow she knew Jessica would never give up. "What issue?" She plopped into her chair.

"He's ashamed to introduce you to his friends, work associates, parents."

Ebony's jaws dropped. "That's not so. Where did you get such a crazy notion? I'll have you know his grandfather is half-black."

"Yeah, so I've heard," she replied dryly. "It's apparent Smoke's family wants to lighten up and cross over. He could pass, but if he marries you…" She hunched her shoulders. "Well, let's just say you would set his family back more than a few generations."

Willing her outrage away, Ebony calmly said, "This is the twenty-first century, Jessica. There is no need for anyone to pass."

"That's easy for you to say, but what would his lily-white mama say?"

"If you must know, he hasn't introduced me to his family because he doesn't get along with them. He had been living here for a month when we met, and he hadn't called them once. They're snobs, and having a beautician's daughter as a girlfriend wouldn't sit nicely. He's already told me he expects problems."

"A dark-skinned daughter of a beautician sounds more accurate. How about his business associates? Doesn't he ever have business dinners?"

"He's only been here a few months." She knocked the ceramic kitten-shaped toothpick holder over and played pick-up sticks.

"Yeah, I know. And in that time he's turned the south side office into a high-traffic, big money-making firm."

"You're grasping for straws. Since we met, Smoke has spent almost every evening he's been in town with me. I've even been to his office a few times." She opened her eyes wide and made jazz fingers. "There's no conspiracy to hide his dark-skinned girlfriend."

"How do you know he was out of town?"

Ebony stared at Jessica, wondering why she pressed so hard. "I never realized you're a conspiracy theorist. No matter how I answer, you'll find another plot, another angle. I love you for watching my back, but I'm fine. Trae and Smoke aren't plotting against me. I need to pack a bag for Crystal and get ready for my date."

CHAPTER TWELVE

Ebony scrutinized her reflection in the full-length mirror hanging on the back of her bedroom door. The cool aqua of her long flowing tank dress contrasted well with her smooth dark-chocolate skin.

Thoughts of Richard pointing out contrasts warmed her heart. She readjusted the bobby pins in the French roll she had put her hair into. She still couldn't believe she had bleached her hair blonde. What possessed her to listen to Skeet? She chuckled.

"What's so funny?" Trae asked from Crystal's doorway.

"I can't stand my hair." She grabbed her pale aqua shawl off the computer desk.

"Humph. Welcome to the club." He crossed the room. "How many times do I have to tell you to stop ordering from Chadwick's?" He took the clearance catalog off the computer desk and tossed it into the trash, then took the shawl and dropped it on the bed. "You deserve the best."

"This is the best I can afford, plus I like the clothes." She eyed his charcoal Armani suit. "Don't throw hate my way because I can spend twenty bucks and look like a million."

He laughed, admiring himself in the mirror. "Hell, I'd look good in a used paper bag. Come here a second."

He stood behind her, wrapping his arms around her waist. "We make a handsome couple."

She stepped away. "Looks aren't everything."

"No," he paused, "they aren't. I was out of line." He stroked her cheekbone with his fingertip. "You'll always be my girl."

He hid so many things from her, yet she refused to believe he would set her up. "You'll always be my guy, but I'm Smoke's woman."

"Yeah, I know. Don't worry your pretty little head." He pushed a stray braid into her French roll. "Smoke's my dawg."

"He's been promoted to dawg? How does Skeet feel about sharing this honorable position?" She had thought her comment would lighten the mood, but it didn't work. All joking aside, she said, "Tell me what's wrong. What happened?"

"I lost something today. I never truly realized how valuable it was. Now it's too late."

The regret in his voice touched her. She hugged him.

He rocked her gently in his arms. "You don't know how much I needed this," he whispered.

"Is this why you arranged the sudden visit to your mother? You think it's too late to repair the relationship."

"I wish it was that simple." He backed away. "I'm tired. Don't pay me any never mind."

The pep in his step was missing, and he looked mind-weary. "It's me and Smoke, isn't it?"

"I honestly want you to have a happy life together." He sat on the bed.

She longed to believe him, but fear of his motivations nagged her. "Something's been bothering me about you and Smoke. I should have mentioned it sooner."

A slow, devilish grin creased his face. "No, Smoke isn't working for me. Jessica grilled me yesterday. She's lucky she's your girl."

Ebony let out a sigh of relief. "Why did you accept him so easily?"

Feet still on the floor, he lay back, patting the bed for her to lie beside him. She sat at the computer desk instead.

"It hasn't been easy. Sometimes I see you two together and want to strangle him."

"What about other times?"

"I've never seen you as happy as when you're with Smoke. You're so free with him, and I'm jealous." He stared at the ceiling fan. "I love you, Ebony. Staying out of the way of your happiness is the one selfless thing I've done in my life. It's not easy."

Doubt still crowded her mind. She sorted through the photos on her desk of Trae, Skeet and Richard playing pool in the beauty shop basement. "Given your history with white men, why did you trust Smoke so quickly?"

He sat up. "Full of questions today, aren't you? I didn't trust him at first. I just acted like I did. I had him checked out to make sure he wasn't DEA or some other type of cop. I didn't expect you and Crystal to fall for him so quickly. Damn." He shook his head. "Smoke was perfect for you, except he was white and not me." He chuckled uneasily. "He even fits in with us. He knows how to walk a tightrope as well as you."

"So you stepped aside."

"I can't give you the life you want. He can. I had to swallow my pride and push aside my jealousy. Smoke will take good care of you, and won't try to keep me out of your lives. He's a good man."

"Thanks Trae." She crossed the room and hugged him. She saw this as his way of finally letting go. Soon she'd be free. They released each other. "I'm really proud of you. We've grown up," she said.

"I shocked myself. You won't believe this, but I'm actually thinking about finding my dad."

"That's great! Why did you change your mind?"

"I've been soul-searching a lot lately. You've told me a thousand times I was using Dad's color as an excuse. I don't know. I feel like I need to try with him."

She bit her bottom lip. He wasn't the same person as a year earlier, and between his acceptance of her and Richard's relationship and this declaration, something didn't sit right with her.

"You're gonna bite that off. What do you want to know?"

"You've changed, Trae." She took his hands into hers. "Your heart isn't in your work anymore. Leave the life."

He caressed her face. "The only way out for me is death. I want more for you and Crystal."

A chill went down her spine as everything fell into place. "Dan left the life. He can help you."

"That was years ago. Times have changed."

"Yes, they have. Death isn't your only option."

His hands glided over his braids. "I'm into something—something big. I want to see it through. Once I do, the only out for me is death, jail or both. I'm not sure I can keep you safe."

Her eyes and nose stung. Her conflicting emotions for him battled. She reminded herself that everyone deserved to be saved. "Please don't do it, Trae. Stop before you start." She blinked away tears.

"I can't walk away. I've been dreaming and working toward this day for years, and soon…"

"Soon what?"

"I thought this victory would fulfill me, but I feel hollow."

"Why do it?"

"Don't get me wrong." He leaned forward. "I want this, Ebony. I want it so bad I get hard thinking about it. But what comes next?"

"I know you can't tell me what you're up to, but after this job, please leave the life. Start a new adventure, new challenges."

"If what I'm trying succeeds, they won't let me walk away. At least not for a few years." He grabbed Crystal's suitcase. "That kid's awfully quiet out there."

She allowed him to change the subject. Richard cooked to avoid talking. Trae became super dad. She had learned to give them both their space to think.

Richard leaned against Ebony's front door. After tonight there would be no turning back, and he still hadn't told his parents about her. They had never accepted him, and he wouldn't give them the chance to reject Ebony.

Admitting to himself that he still wanted his mother's acceptance, he sighed. Noríno kept telling him to stop being stubborn and call his mother, but Richard couldn't bring himself to do it. He was past tired of her treating him like a second-class citizen.

The last time he spoke to Stephanie, they argued over his move to Chicago. She insisted he move to the New York office, where his father had more business connections.

She would never approve of Ebony. He closed his eyes. Marrying Ebony meant losing his chance at winning his mother's approval.

Visions of Ebony chasing him and Crystal around the condo with a Super Soaker filled his mind. Ebony accepted and loved him as is. With her, he had already won. He turned toward the door.

Richard walked into the flat and greeted everyone.

Crystal looked around Ebony. "Smoke!" She ran and jumped into his arms. "I'm going on a plane."

Trae took her from him. "Let the man take his coat off, then pounce on him."

Richard couldn't tear his eyes away from Ebony. She hid her anxiety behind a plastic smile. "Whoa, a plane ride!" His attempt at cheerfulness failed miserably. He hung his coat, then set his loafers on the rack.

Excited and oblivious to the somber moods in the room, Crystal nodded. "We're flying to Florida to see..." She frowned. "Who are we seeing again?"

"My mother." Trae set her down.

"Oh, yeah, that's right. We're gonna stay in a hotel with a pool."

Richard sat on the couch beside Ebony. Her usual fire had faded. "I love you," he mouthed.

Crystal looked from Richard to Trae to Ebony. "What's wrong, Mama?"

Ebony patted her hand. "I'm just a little tired. Oh, shoot. I forgot to pack your swimsuit."

"I'll get it." Crystal ran off.

"Stop running in the house," the three adults said in unison.

Trae sorted through his briefcase. "I have something for you to sign before I leave." He found the forms, then set them on the coffee table.

To Richard's annoyance, Ebony reached for the papers and pen without hesitation and signed. This type of behavior had to stop. "Can I see those?" Richard asked.

"No," Trae calmly replied.

Ebony handed the papers over to Richard. Trae jumped forward, snatching the documents. "What are you doing?" Trae snapped.

"I'm in no mood for this. Let Smoke see there's nothing to be suspicious of." She held her hand out.

Richard watched her stare Trae down, and his heart filled with joy. Unlike his mother, Ebony would always be on his side.

"We've been doing fine for years. Why all a sudden we need Smoke's okay?"

"Smoke and I are one now. Hand him the stupid papers so he can see what a waste of time it is." She flashed a listless smile at Richard, then left the room to help Crystal find her swimsuit.

Worried about the cause of her depression, Richard watched her leave. This episode had cinched it. No way could he introduce her to the drama of his family. She had enough to deal with already. After they were married and settled in, they would both be better prepared to deal with his mother.

"I don't appreciate this crap. I would never hurt Ebony. This is legit." Trae tossed the papers on the table. "Go ahead. Take ten years to read every word. Hell, get a lawyer to look at them."

As Richard considered if winning this battle would contribute to his losing the war, his eyes traveled from Trae to the papers and back to Trae. "I don't need to see them." Ebony was an expert on which battles to fight where Trae was concerned. He decided to follow her example for now.

"That's more like it. For a second there I thought you didn't trust me." Trae picked up the papers and stacked them neatly on the table. "I'm trusting you with my girls. We have to trust each other."

Trae's tone sounded cryptic, but Richard didn't have the energy to figure out what he had in his bag of tricks. All he wanted was to know what upset Ebony. "You have a point."

"I found out that Crystal's school offers three different scholarships." He turned the pages so Richard could see the school's emblem. "They don't tell black folks shit. Ebony's been paying out the yang when Crystal should be going for free."

The more he listened, the angrier he became at Trae for ignoring Ebony's obvious anguish. "You know, I don't give a damn about those papers. In case you haven't noticed, something's wrong with Ebony."

"You need to keep Jessica out of your business. We came to an understanding." He leafed through the papers. "She's not to say my name again, and I won't kill her unhappy ass. That heifer came down on Ebony today."

Richard cursed under his breath. Jessica had grilled him earlier, but Ebony usually ignored her comments. There was more to the story. He understood why Jessica thought he worked for Trae. From her point of view, that was the only answer that made sense.

"You better neutralize her," Trae recommended.

Richard watched him closely. He seemed uncharacteristically nervous.

Trae glanced toward Ebony's room and leaned forward whispering, "I've been thinking and," he trailed off and leaned back on the recliner. "I can't believe this is happening."

"Jessica doesn't have this much of an effect on Ebony."

"I want for you to adopt Crystal."

"What?" Richard gasped as he jumped up.

"Sit down and be quiet," Trae snapped under his breath. "We don't have time for you to start trippin'."

Richard sat, resting his elbows on his knees. "None of this makes sense."

"It's as clear as a bell, Smoke. My mom was a whore and my father a hype. Ebony's right. How long before Crystal realizes what I actually am? Who I actually am? How long before one of my rivals takes after her? I want her to have a father she can be proud of, not some drug dealer. I want her safe."

"Quit. I'll help you."

Trae smiled. "You sound like Ebony. I need you to do this. I'm counting on you to give Ebony and Crystal the life they deserve."

Richard acknowledged the pleading in Trae's voice. "I love them. You know I'll adopt Crystal, but I won't lie. You're her father. She'll just have two that love her." He held his hand out to shake to an end to Trae's games.

Trae shook his hand. "We cool."

Ebony returned with Crystal in tow. "Did you two settle your little dispute?"

Trae stood. "What dispute?" He didn't wait for anyone to comment. "Did you pack a light jacket? It's in the seventies down there."

"Everything's ready." Ebony hugged him. "Have a safe and fun trip." She bent, kissing and hugging Crystal. "I'm expecting a daily call from you."

"Okay, Mama." Crystal hugged Richard. "I'll call you, too." She left hand-in-hand with Trae after Ebony finished signing the papers.

Ebony leaned on the windowsill, watching Trae and Crystal on the street below. "Trae's in trouble," she whispered. "I'm scared for him."

Richard embraced her from behind. "We have to help him."

She looked over her shoulder at him. "I love you." She turned in his arms, resting her head on his shoulder.

Every time he heard her heartfelt proclamation, he felt he could conquer the world. "I love you, too." He gently drew his hand along her spine.

"I figured something out today, and I don't know what to do about it."

"You're not alone. You can lean on me," he said as she relaxed against his body.

"Trae accepting you didn't make sense. I kept making excuses, but now I know the truth."

Richard continually probed his mind for answers about Trae accepting him and found none. Trae was so inconsistent: at times he acted jealous, other times he encouraged their relationship, yet at other times he tried to sabotage them.

Ebony's soft voice continued, "Trae is standing on a train track refusing to move out of the way. Instead, he's making sure someone he approves of is left behind to take care of us." She stepped away.

Richard pulled her back into his arms. She wasn't alone. This was their fight. "I know you're worried about him. I'm worried also, but he knows the game. He'll land on his feet," he said with conviction he didn't feel.

"He's into something." She looked around the living room as if searching for the right words. "Something big, something that will get him killed if he succeeds."

"What?" From his investigation, he knew something was up, but they would never give enough information. All he knew was it had something to do with St. Louis.

"This is total speculation, but I think he's about to cut the middle men out of the distribution network. He's been too friendly with other gangs and dealers lately, and traveling all over the place."

"They'll kill him," he said aloud, to himself.

"He's been priming Skeet to take over the business and you to take over watching me. He's even about to make amends with his parents."

And asking me to adopt Crystal. He didn't know what to think. "I'll talk to him. It can't be too late."

"This great guy once told me something like—you can't save someone who refuses to be saved."

Feeling powerless, he held her tightly. "I'm sorry, Ebony. I don't know what to do." He had grown to care about Trae and Skeet. Now he fully appreciated the dilemma that was her life—*their* life.

CHAPTER THIRTEEN

Eight-year-old Richard stood at the top of the stairwell with his hands over his ears. His older sisters circled him, taunting, "Guess which one does not belong here. Guess which one is not the same."

He had almost made the great escape, but his wicked sisters knew a shortcut to the stairs. He slammed his eyes shut. "I can't hear you. I can't see you. La la la la la!"

Each sister took one of his arms and forced his hands from his ears. Screaming stopped, he struggled to free himself.

"Mommy said to stop calling you lost boy," thirteen-year-old Bianca spewed. "Now we need a new pet name for our little nig—" He yanked out of Bianca's hold.

Eleven-year-old Gail could barely contain him. He was already taller than she was.

Bianca put her hands on her narrow hips and glared down at him. "Why don't you run away? Let him go, Gail. We would hate him to think we actually want him to stay." Gail released him.

Bianca fluffed her long, brunette hair. "Speaking to Richard is a waste of breath. Why don't you go ahead and leave?"

"I will leave!" Richard shouted.

"Well, don't let me keep you." She shoved him with all her might. He lost his balance. She grabbed for him, but it was too late. Instead of falling down the steps, he fell over the banister, crashing face first onto the marble-topped Victorian console table below, then falling to the floor.

His sisters ran down the stairs. "Help! Help!" They rolled his lifeless body over, exposing a face covered with blood.

"Oh, my God," Bianca cried. "I killed him. I didn't mean to."

Sudden pounding at Ebony's bedroom door roused her and Richard.

"Skeet!" Marissa yelled. "Get out of my house makin' all that damn noise!" The banging stopped.

"I'm comin' in," Skeet announced. The door hinges creaked and the smells of fresh coffee filled the room as he entered.

Ebony flopped over and covered her head with a pillow. "Make the bad man go away," she moaned.

Glad to be wakened from his dream, Richard glanced at the clock. "What's wrong with you? It's seven in the morning. Have you lost your mind?" Wearing only briefs, he covered himself with the comforter as he sat up against the headboard.

"You look like shit." Skeet snarled. "I haven't been to bed yet. Y'all got any new toothbrushes, Ebony?" He closed the door and watched himself in the full-length mirror. "Damn, I look good."

"I know you didn't come here for fashion advice. If so, your jeans are too baggy and that Lakers' throwback played out last year. Now go away." He rubbed the side of his face.

The fall had left Richard with a little nerve damage. Reconstructive surgery repaired his face, but left the crooked grin Ebony loved. Until she entered his life, he had hated it, and the memories it never allowed to fade.

After he was released from the hospital, his parents had sent him away to a boarding school. At the time, he felt he was being punished when it was his sisters that should have been. He didn't mind the separation from his parents and siblings, but he had missed Nonno terribly. Within months, Nonno's health had improved enough for him to take Richard back in. He heard that Nonno had raised seven kinds of hell to regain custody of him.

Skeet rounded the bed to shake Ebony.

"Don't even think about it," Richard warned. "What do you want?"

Skeet kicked at the bed. "You drain the fun out of every damn thing, Smoke. I knew you'd be up early to go ring shopping and didn't want you paying retail."

Richard shot Skeet an *I'm gonna kill you* look.

"Oops." He laughed. "Let the cat out of the bag, huh."

Ebony threw her pillow at Skeet. "What is this crazy man talking about?"

He tipped out of the room. "Call me when you're ready—and congratulations."

Richard lay beside Ebony. "He's a giant kid. I had this romantic evening planned, then…" His voice faded.

She laid her head next to his on the pillow. "Then we ended up sleeping here, with you consoling me."

He caressed her face. "Every second I spend with you is precious. They're my friends, too. I want them out of the life as much as you do." He paused a moment to gather his thoughts. No matter how much he cared about them, at the end of the day, they were drug dealers. It terrified him to hear himself making excuses for them. He had to find something before he became tainted. "We can't stop living our life, Ebony."

Hair all over the place, nightshirt rumpled, sleep in her eyes, dried tears on her face—she was still the most beautiful woman he had ever seen, both inside and out. "Would you do me the honor of becoming my wife?"

She didn't move or make a sound. Self-doubt hung in the air. What if she believed Jessica…He stopped this train of thought. "You're making me nervous. Say something." He flashed an anxiety-ridden half-grin. "Will you marry me?"

Her face lit up. "Yes, yes, yes," she screeched, hugging him. "I couldn't believe my ears."

He kissed her lightly. "You've just made me the happiest person in the world." He cupped her into his body. He wanted to make love, but with Skeet in the house, he would have to wait. "I'm free on Monday. We can have a small wedding. Crystal can miss a few days of class."

"You are too silly." She grinned. "I'm so happy. Wait until I tell Jessica. She's gonna have a heart attack."

"Good." He encircled her waist, gently grinding.

She tapped his hand. "Don't say that."

"She doesn't like me, and the feeling is mutual." He stroked her hair neatly behind her ear. "Do you think Skeet's gone?" He nibbled on her earlobe, eliciting a moan. "I want to make love with my fiancée," he whispered.

"You are such a tease." She turned in his arms. "I know you smell the bacon and eggs. Mom's cooking, so Skeet is still here."

"He's better than birth control." They both laughed. "I'll force myself to behave. Give me a date. When do you make me an honest man?"

"I'm thinking after graduation. That gives us plenty of time to plan."

She filled the void in his life, making him whole. He had to protect her. "I want for you and Crystal to move in with me." He covered her soft lips with his fingers before she could object. "I know how you feel about shacking up, but Trae is up to something. I don't want you or Crystal caught in the crossfire."

"What can happen in a few months? He's kept us safe this long."

"He asked me to adopt Crystal."

"What?!" She hopped out of bed.

The rage in her voice stunned and hurt him. Trae giving up his rights to Crystal meant they were free to be a real family. "Don't you want me to be Crystal's father?"

She looked at him as if he had lost his mind, and he knew he had misread her.

"Don't you know how much I love you? I want nothing more than for you to be Crystal's father, and my husband."

"I love you, too. Tell me what's wrong? We're a team now."

"I just…What are we going to do about Trae?"

Richard watched as she paced from the closet to Crystal's room. Something about the adoption had upset her. Something she wasn't ready to talk about. "I've been trying to figure out a way to help him all night," he said.

"There has to be a way to convince him to give up the drug life," she said.

"How many years have you been trying?"

She stopped pacing long enough to smile weakly. "Too many to count."

He reached out as she passed and pulled her onto the bed. "Listen up, little lady." He rolled her over, lying on top of her. "I love you and have to put you and Crystal first. I put the finishing touches on Crystal's room yesterday. We can move you in next weekend."

Ebony bit her lip.

"You're gonna bite that thing off." Her grin sent his libido soaring. He licked her bottom lip, sucked it into his mouth. "Does your door lock?" he whispered. A hint of the sweet pea shower gel on her skin brought back fond memories of their first meeting.

"You're not playing fair."

"All's fair in love and war." He locked the door and returned to bed. "Move in with me. Don't make me wait." He feather-kissed along her neckline down to her collarbone. "I'm buying you new nightclothes today." He pulled down the collar of the nightshirt. "You get nothing else from Chadwick's."

She laughed.

He tried acting indignant, but her laughter was contagious. He flashed his famous lopsided grin. "I'm trying to make love here. You could kill a guy's self-confidence laughing like that."

She rubbed against his hardness. "You feel pretty confident to me."

CHAPTER FOURTEEN

Ebony handed a bottle of beer to Skeet and a Pepsi to Mr. Loren, then sat at the dining table next to Richard. Richard had said he had something important to tell her about his family right before their uninvited guests showed up.

"This condo is sweet, Smoke. Once you two marry you should move to a larger place so I can have this one." Skeet took a swig of beer. "Anyone live in the condo downstairs?"

"You aren't moving in below us, Skeet." Ebony watched Mr. Loren closely. He wore wrinkled jeans, a red and tan checkered flannel shirt, busted down boots and carried a big ol' filthy tackle box. He resembled an ice fisherman more than a jeweler, but she kept quiet. After all, she and Richard were dressed in jeans and matching Navy Pier T-shirts. They had told Skeet that they didn't want his assistance in procuring wedding rings; as usual, he acted as if they hadn't said a thing. At least this way she would have an idea of what she wanted when they went ring shopping.

Richard caressed her hand under the table; she relaxed.

"What's the deal with that purple monstrosity back there?" Skeet motioned toward Crystal's room. "Don't ever take decorating tips from a seven-year-old."

Mr. Loren turned the tackle box to face Ebony and Richard. Ebony's mouth dropped as the tackle box turned into a display case lined with royal blue velvet. Each compartment of the top two shelves held separate diamonds of different shapes and sizes, sixteen diamonds in all.

Skeet chuckled. "I hope your bank account is fat, Smoke. Look at her."

Richard lovingly watched Ebony finger the diamonds like a child over Halloween candy.

"Wow! I can't wait to see your whole rings." She rummaged through the bottom of the tackle box, but only saw tools and miniature catalogs.

"Switch your mind off ghetto mode. You're having a ring made." Skeet took a catalog of designs from the bottom of the case and handed it to her. "If you don't see something you like in there, Loren can design something for you. You just need to give him a few ideas of what you like."

She glared at Skeet. "I'm not ghetto. Don't make me cut you. What's the price range of these, anyway?" She pointed her favorite diamond out to Richard, thinking she might as well get the price range.

"Five to ten thousand," Skeet said before Mr. Loren could answer.

Her mouth dropped wide open. "Thousand!" she complained. "I can buy two whole sets for half that, Skeet."

Richard caressed her cheekbone. "It's all right."

It never ceased to amaze her how even his slightest touch calmed and warmed her at the same time. He had already spent more than she wanted decorating Crystal's room. She couldn't allow him to sacrifice his bank account for the most beautiful diamond she would ever see in any lifetime.

"Where are the ones normal people can afford?" She rested her hand on Richard's lap, seeking reassurance he freely provided.

"Smoke can afford ten grand for this," Skeet said.

Though gold was her thing, she knew diamonds were expensive. Why he would bring the most expensive diamonds around was beyond her. She wanted a diamond like the one Skeet showed her, but didn't want Richard's male ego to feel obligated to purchase something he couldn't afford. Biting her bottom lip, she peeked into his smoky blue eyes. Love and amusement danced playfully in them.

"If you want this diamond, it's yours," Richard whispered.

She narrowed her eyes on Richard. They had agreed not to purchase anything from Skeet's connections, because they were most likely fronts for his laundering activities. There had to be a reasonable explanation for Richard veering off the path. She would have to wait until they were alone to find out what it was. Until then, she'd play along.

Skeet handed her the oval diamond she had pointed to. "This ain't cubic zirconia or that cheap, substandard crap you buy at the mall." He handed the European Gemological Laboratories certificate for the diamond to Richard to read over. "That little baby there is three and a half carats, flawless, colorless, has exquisite symmetry..." Richard choked. "Damn, dawg, get some water."

Richard abruptly stood. "My room now, Skeet!"

Ebony's brows rose. Richard looked ill, but she didn't blame him. Ten thousand was way too much to pay for a clear rock. She shook off the disappointment.

"Thumb through the catalog. Give her anything she wants, Loren." He followed Richard into the bedroom.

Richard couldn't speak, not yet. He pointed at the chaise lounge, then poured them both a brandy at the mini-bar. Seeing Ebony light up whenever she looked at her engagement ring would be worth any amount of money, but the moral price was too high. He gulped down his brandy, then poured another.

"Hey, stop being greedy." Skeet rose.

"Sit!" He pointed at the chaise.

"What's wrong with you? She loves the diamonds."

"I love Ebony with all of my heart, but I'm not made out of money. I can't afford a hundred grand for a diamond. Hell, I still have to pay for the wedding." Though the diamond was large, he didn't realize it was that large, and he thought it was a lower-quality stone. The price Skeet had given them would fit his range. Once he saw the certification, reality slapped him. The diamond was worth a heck of a lot more than ten grand. He groaned. Ebony would be disappointed that he couldn't afford a similar diamond, and this could lead to proof that Skeet was laundering.

Now that the opportunity to get evidence of illegal activity was within his grasp, he hesitated. It was so easy to stand on moral high ground when he wasn't in Ebony's shoes, so easy to pass judgment.

Skeet wrinkled his face and hunched his shoulders. "Don't tell her. Humph, I thought there was actually something wrong. I spoke to Dan this morning. He's paying for the wedding, so that's already taken care of." He took himself off time-out, crossed the room and grabbed his drink. "Did you see the way her whole face lit up?"

He'd never forget. Her look was why he had misspoken and said he would buy the diamond from Skeet. Disgusted with the situation, he asked, "How could you show her a hundred thousand dollar diamond?" but wanted to ask, "Why won't you give up the life? Why are you making me do this? Why?" The previous summer, Nonno had sent Richard diamond ring shopping for Stephanie's sixtieth birthday; Nonno always wanted the best for his daughter, thus Richard had learned a lot about diamonds.

As if the conversation at hand bored him, Skeet swirled his brandy in the glass, settled on the chaise and stretched his long legs. "For one thing, it is worth a hundred and twenty thousand dollars, and you don't have to pay retail. I'm a dealer. I'm giving it to you wholesale."

Richard's anguish was reflected in his derisive laugh. "Oh, Lord, he really is crazy. Don't play me for stupid. There isn't that much markup in the world."

Skeet chewed his inner jaw. "So I'm giving you an additional discount. What's the problem?"

"You just don't get it, do you?" He crossed the room and sat on the edge of the bamboo bed.

"You really need to loosen up." Skeet scanned the room for the remote control. "What if I told you I own a diamond mine in South Africa?"

"I would say you're lying."

Skeet flashed a million-dollar smile. "And you'd be correct." He grabbed the remote off the nightstand. "I buy directly from mines. I am all of the middlemen. I get these babies at an amazing price. You won't find better quality."

"Not that amazing." Richard lay back in bed, calculating how to raise the money to legally purchase Ebony a similar diamond without jeopardizing them financially. He still had to pay for Meechie's future rehabilitation, and now that he would be able to adopt Crystal, he was seriously contemplating opening his own firm in a different state. One night Ebony had confided in him that she had never traveled further than the suburbs of Chicago. He knew it would be difficult to convince her to leave the known for the unknown, but he also knew she would see things his way in the end.

Asking his parents for a loan was out. He liked his brother-in-law, but asking him was out. Asking Nonno had possibilities, but he wouldn't lend that much money without strings attached. He grumbled. Strings he didn't want to deal with, such as trying to make up with his parents. Strings he had foolishly considered telling Ebony about.

"Okay, you win. I won't launder any money on this deal." Richard remained silent. "I'm serious. I'll contact a totally legitimate dealer and make the arrangements."

Richard sat up. "I'll find my own dealer."

"I want Ebony to have that diamond. Ten thousand. I'll pay the difference."

"No thanks. I want to buy her ring."

"You're pissing me the hell off," Skeet snapped as he threw the remote at him.

Richard barely ducked in time. The remote crashed against the headboard and broke apart—much like Richard felt like doing. He laughed at the lunacy of it all. Never had he imagined his life could become so crazy.

"What the hell are you laughing at?"

"I've never seen you angry before. It's amusing." He picked up the batteries and backing for the remote.

"Well your goody-two-shoes ass has pissed me the hell off today, so laugh hearty."

Richard watched his big friend stalk across the room to the wet bar and take out his anger on the brandy. "Try to see this from my side, Skeet. I can't allow another man to buy my wife's engagement ring."

"I'm giving you the opportunity to buy your own damn ring!" He slammed his glass down. "This is ridiculous. Do whatever." He stormed out.

Guilt ridden, Richard sank onto the chaise. He didn't have concrete evidence yet, but was close. Now he had to find something on Trae.

Ebony poked her head into the room. "You alright?"

"Not really." He motioned for her to join him.

She sat across his lap and rested her head on his shoulder. "Why did you say you would buy the ring from Skeet?"

"I got carried away. Then when I realized what I'd said, the reality of Skeet laundering money hit, and was too much for me."

"Boy, do I understand."

"I'll buy you any ring you want, but not from Skeet."

"Agreed."

He prayed she had forgotten about the talk they were to have about his family. He needed more time to decide what exactly to tell her, to figure out how he felt, or if he would tell her anything. He stretched his long legs out. "Why don't you come to New York with me? We can give hump day a whole new meaning."

"I have my first interview Tuesday. On Wednesday I have a test."

"I'm sorry. I was thinking the interview was next week."

"The interview isn't a big deal. I thought I should test the waters before I get serious."

He felt her heart beat rapidly against his arm, heard a nervous twinge in her voice. She had mentioned the interview only once a week or so ago. She had quickly changed the subject. "I'm always interviewing. Tomorrow let's role play."

"It's no big deal…really."

"I wish I could skip this trip to New York. You need me here." He nudged several stray braids behind her ear. If she wanted to be hired in corporate America, it would take a lot more than an afternoon of role-playing. Maybe the reason she couldn't find a job after she earned her bachelor's degree had something to do with her style. The job market was so tight a few years ago companies would seize on any reason to cut potential employees. "Let's go interview-shopping tomorrow."

She could pass with the hair, but the twenty rings, huge hoop earrings, long curling nails and—he ran his fingers over her gold bracelets—at least ten bracelets on each wrist would have to go.

"I know how to dress. This is no big deal. It's practice for the real thing."

She tried to hide her case of nerves, act like she didn't care, but he knew better. "Treat every interview as if it will lead to your dream career."

"Yes, Papà Smoke." She rested her head on his shoulder. "What did you want to tell me about your family?"

He stroked her hair. "I'm sorry, angel. I need a little more time."

She caressed his face. "I'm here when you're ready."

CHAPTER FIFTEEN

Ebony sat in the waiting area of Banks Consulting, a small, minority-owned software firm located in downtown Chicago. She kept telling herself the interview was only practice.

She twisted her engagement ring around her finger. They had found the perfect ring for well under ten grand. Thoughts of Richard filled her mind, and she calmed down slightly. Role-playing removed fear of the unknown, but did nothing for her nerves. *Treat every interview as if it will lead to your dream career,* resonated in her mind.

She held her hands out for inspection. After she'd dropped Richard off at the airport, she had her long acrylic nails changed to a basic French manicure. She shook her arms. The bracelets slid down, bunching at her wrists below her sleeves.

She stood, smoothing out her navy blue skirt and blazer. She stepped up to the reception desk. "Excuse me, ma'am. Where is the restroom?"

Ebony groaned at her reflection in the mirror over the restroom sink. She wanted to appear more conservative. She removed jewelry: first the dangling, multi-hoop gold earrings; next, all of the rings except her engagement ring; last, the numerous bracelets.

She stuffed the jewelry into her purse, then took her microbraids out of the ponytail and used the scrunchie to work her hair into a bun. It wasn't the best bun, but it would have to do.

She examined herself in the mirror. Skeet was right, some dark-skinned women looked great with blonde hair. Her face soured. She wasn't one of them. She reached into her purse, found the diamond earrings her mother had given her for Christmas, and put them on.

She stepped away from the mirror and smiled at the business-woman in the navy blue suit she saw in the reflection.

The middle-aged receptionist gave Ebony an approving nod and escorted her into senior partner Darryl Beacon's office.

"Please take a seat." Darryl motioned to the chair in front of his desk.

"Thank you." Heart pounding in her ears, palms clammy, nerves on edge; Ebony tried to imagine the short, balding, pot-bellied black man across from her was Richard, and they were role-playing again. She watched him nudge his glasses up on his nose. *There's not that much imagination in the world.*

"Is something funny, Ms. Washington?"

Her eyes flew wide open in horror. "I'm sorry. I have a bad case of nerves." She willed the jumping beans in her stomach still.

His warm smile helped put her at ease. "This is your first interview, isn't it?"

"Am I that bad?" She had never made it to the interview before when she job-hunted. The economy was so bad she never stood a chance.

He chuckled. "I'll tell you what. I'll make this as painless as possible."

Ebony felt as if she had a copy of the final exam a week early. Question after question was some version of the ones she had practiced with Richard. An hour later, Darryl had shown Ebony around the office, introduced her to the other engineers, and offered her the position.

Overwhelmed by Darryl's generosity, she sat across from him, searching for right words. Turning down a job offer was one scenario she hadn't practiced. "To be honest, I don't know. I need a few days to consider my options." Though a small firm, Banks Consulting had offered her an extraordinary package. Confidence at an all-time high, she knew she could expect more from a large corporation. With the extra money, she could move out and build Crystal a sizeable college fund.

Her heart swelled with pride. It took six hard years, but she would be leaving grad school in a few months with a high-paying marketable skill. She would never have to choose between keeping her baby warm or fed. She could care for her child without anyone's help.

He nodded slowly. "I like that. Never rush into major decisions." He fumbled with the card dispenser on his desk. "Take your time. If you have any questions, call me directly. I'm sure we can work something out," he added.

Her mood darkened. The interview had gone off without a hitch. The employees seemed friendly, and she was offered a dream job. Darryl was a tad bit anxious, but nice. Yet something didn't sit right with her. "I should know in a week or so."

She took the card. Then it hit her. This was the first time Trae wouldn't be a part of her decision process. Jessica was correct when she said Trae was a control freak. That was the reason Ebony didn't tell him about the interview. It was her way of secretly rebelling. *Rebelling?* If you did something to defy someone and he didn't know about it, did the act still qualify as rebellion? She placed the business card in her wallet. *Yes.*

She had reexamined her relationship with Trae after her last argument with Jessica. Over the years Trae had invaded every part of her life, and had finally taken over.

Before her argument with Jessica, she would have sworn she was a strong, independent woman, but when she really thought about it— was honest with herself—she even needed Trae's permission to pursue a relationship with Richard. She sighed inwardly, thinking she had allowed Trae to run her life and now was uncomfortable when the decisions were actually hers.

Darryl stood. "There's no rush, Ebony." Everyone in the company was on a first-name basis. He'd asked her to do the same. He swiped his hand on his pants, then held it out. "Nice meeting you."

She shook his hand. "The pleasure was all mine." A new day had dawned. From this day forward, she planned to control her life.

"If you change your mind about Friday, just give me a call. No pressure." A nervous smile tipped his lips. The wrinkles on his forehead deepened. "Not much, anyway." He showed her out.

Darryl took a few minutes to compose himself. He needed Ebony to accept the position. He stared out the window at the office building across the street. He would do anything for his son, but this? He buried his feelings of guilt. Everyone would win, he reassured himself.

The shrill ring of the phone sent a chill along his spine. He chewed what was left of his thumbnail. The phone stopped ringing. He could breathe clearly again. He sat at his desk and scrolled through the caller ID when his cell phone rang. The last call had been blocked.

"Hello." He loosened his collar, wiped the sweat from his brow. Avoidance would make things worse he told himself.

"Why didn't you pick up the damn phone?" came a deep, harsh voice over the line. "Ebony left five minutes ago. Did she accept the job?"

He smoothed his hands over his balding head. The rumors that Trae knew Ebony's every move were obviously true. "I'm sorry, Trae, but she asked for more time. We're a small firm. Candidates of her caliber tend to want to work for large corporations."

"What if you upped the pay another ten grand? No, make that fifteen."

He sorted through his desk drawer for his ulcer medicine. "I don't own the company. My partner will object, and so will the other employees." He propped the phone between his shoulder and ear, then twisted the top off the medication. "I don't know how I would cover that much money up. The most I could allow is another grand or two toward the sign-on bonus." He chugged down the thick white liquid.

Darryl thought about his son's drug addiction. Trae had promised to stop his flow of heroin in exchange for hiring Ebony. When he agreed to the deal, he hadn't realized Ebony was actually a viable candidate. Any corporation in its right mind would snatch her up, leaving him with an angry drug dealer.

"Was her only problem with your firm its size?"

"Yes. I took her on a tour. She loved everything. I even invited her on a business dinner this Friday. We never take associates on business dinners."

"What should she wear?"

"Anything from business to after five will be fine. I want her comfortable."

"I guess you've done all you can."

Relieved, yet confused by Trae's calm reaction, Darryl asked, "Is there anything you'd like me to mention at the dinner?"

"Nah, I got this. You did your part. I'll convince her to take the job with you."

"About my son, he's in rehab now."

"I've got him covered. I put the word out. He can't buy anything around here. Now on the south side, there are a few places I don't have much pull."

"I understand. Thank you, Trae." He couldn't believe he had actually thanked the kind of man responsible for his son's addiction.

Trae fought to rein in his anger. He had to stay in control. He disconnected, tossed the cordless phone over his shoulder, slouched in his recliner, then took in the flat. He had Ebony decorate it years ago in hopes she would change her mind and take him back.

Everything was blinding white or crystal clear, from the carpet to the swirled, painted ceiling. He had so much darkness in his life that his apartment comforted him. It reminded him of the light at the end of the tunnel.

After seeing how she decorated Richard's place, his heart admitted what his head had been saying all along. He had lost Ebony.

He snarled. She decorated his flat for him, and Richard's condo for them. He pushed a magazine out of the way and grabbed his leather photo album. A giant red, black, and green imprint of Africa decorated its cover. Ebony added color to everything.

She had given him the album for Christmas. At the time he wondered what the heck she was thinking, but lately he found consolation in the images. She had compiled pictures from when they were kids all the way through the previous fall.

As he thumbed through the photos, he could tell when she fell out of love with him. In their early photos you could see the love in both of their eyes, then her inner light dimmed and a year of photos was missing.

He kicked the coffee table over, cracking its glass top in the process. That year without Ebony was the worst of his life. He flipped the page to Ebony holding baby Crystal. Sparks flickered in Ebony's eyes, but they were for Crystal, not Trae.

He slammed the album closed. There had to be a way to convince her they belonged together. He wasn't the same stupid kid, and could protect them as he always had. He kicked the table out of his way, then snatched up the *Homes Magazine* it covered.

He had picked out a house for Richard and Ebony. He flipped to the page containing a 3500-square-foot ranch home he knew she would love. *This should be our home.*

He flung the magazine across the room, hopped out of the recliner and flipped it over. "She is mine!" He grabbed the end table and threw it across the room into the stereo.

The Bose system crashed to the floor. He kicked the magazine rack. It flew across the room, causing a huge dent in the wall. Rage consumed him. He wanted to tear the flat up as much as he was torn up inside. The next thing he knew, he was beating what was left of his flat-screen television with a bat.

Skeet burst in with his gun drawn. "What the hell?"

CHAPTER SIXTEEN

Skeet lowered his Colt .45 semiautomatic. "Aw, hell naw!" He stomped into the flat, slamming the door behind him. "Don't even think about asking for your security deposit back." He stepped over broken lamps, glass and furniture.

He pointed at the broken window. "Next time you throw a friggin' trash can out the window, make sure the shit is open first. Damn!" He took off his coat and tossed it and his gun toward the one clear spot on the floor.

Trae stood motionless. The rage in his eyes slowly dissipated. The awkward silence in the room was broken by his uncontrollable laughter.

Skeet stalked up to him, glaring down. "You think this shit is funny? This is my building. Next time you go off, do it on your property." He spun around and uprighted furniture. "From this day forward, I check references."

Still strangely amused, Trae trotted into the kitchen and returned with a broom, dustpan and garbage can. "We need to talk."

"The only thing I want to hear out of your mouth is what the hell set you off." He picked glass out of the carpet.

Trae gathered the torn pages of the magazine he had tossed all over the place. "I can't do this."

"What? Clean? Toss that broom, man. We need to vacuum the carpet."

"I can't give Ebony to Smoke."

Skeet dumped a handful of large glass pieces into the trash, then sat on the edge of the now-lopsided recliner. "The hell you can't."

Trae settled on a clear spot on the floor, shaking his head. "I know I should, but I can't."

"When you first told me you were stepping aside for Smoke, I thought you were crazy. But the more I think about it, you were right. Our lifestyle isn't right for Ebony. I love Ebony and that little girl with all my heart. If something were to happen to them because of us…"

"I can protect them. All I have to do is move them out of the hood."

"You can't move away from our lifestyle. We're drug dealers through and through, Trae."

"I've been thinking about getting out." Still sitting on the floor with his legs drawn up, he lowered his head to his knees. "I love her. I can't lose her."

"But she's in love with Smoke."

"She's just substituting him for me. She went out and found someone like me, except he's legit. I'm what she wants."

He stared into Trae's green eyes a long while. They were becoming more crazed with every second. "Your obsession with Ebony is going to get her killed." He shook his head. "I can't believe I'm saying this, but get some help, Trae."

"I'm not obsessed. She's the one who went out and found a legit version of me."

Skeet laughed so hard he doubled over. "You are out your damn mind. Smoke is not *like you*. Humph. *If* he's like anyone, I'd say he is most like Dan." He leaned forward, driving in his point home. "You know, Ebony's father figure? Dan raised Ebony until Marissa started trippin'."

"You're wrong."

"And you need to step the hell off. The only things you have in common with Smoke are you both play basketball and like to make money. You both being good fathers to Crystal is a given. You know Ebony would never allow a man into her life who wasn't good to her child." He stood and helped clean. "For once in your life, do the honorable thing. We've contributed to the ruin of too many lives. Don't add Ebony to that number. She's in love with Smoke. Back the hell off," he commanded more than suggested.

"Shit." Trae kicked at the couch. "You're right. It's just hard."

Skeet held out his hand. "I got your back, man."

They did a quick brotha shake, hug, pat, release. "I can do this," Trae said half-heartedly.

Richard stood at his hotel window, watching the busy New York streets below. He missed his girls. The prospect of being separated for days affected him more than he had imagined. He seriously considered canceling his plans for Friday to make up for lost time, but pushed the idea out of his head. He didn't want Ebony to think him too needy.

He tried to find everything he could out on Loren, but came up empty handed. Now that he had time for 20/20 hindsight, he should have actually bought the diamond from Skeet so he could have gotten more information. He sighed. He had told Ebony she was wrong for diverting drug money to help drug addicts, yet here he was saying he should have bought a diamond to enable a drug dealer to launder money. He pushed thoughts of the drug trade out of his mind and refocused on the conversation at hand.

He propped the phone between his ear and shoulder, then closed the curtain. After his meeting, he had rushed to his hotel room to call Ebony. "...They offered you the position. I'm so proud of you, angel. I knew you could do it. What's the name of the firm? I'll check them out for you."

"Thanks, but it doesn't matter. I'm not taking the offer. Think of how much a major corporation will offer."

He kicked off his slacks and unbuttoned his shirt. "Don't follow the money. Follow whichever path leads to where you want to go. You want to own a consulting firm someday. If you like everything this company has to offer, stay with them. You don't have to worry about money. I make enough to support us."

He tossed his shirt to the side. He was glad Ebony interviewed at a small minority-owned firm first, thinking they must have been more lenient and understanding about her nails and jewelry. Slowly changing her style would be his next project. He didn't want her fashion sense to keep her from obtaining any job, or cause her to lose her own business customers. She could adorn herself however she wanted when at home, but business was a different story.

"I know how much money you make. But what if you get hurt? I want to be able to support us if need be."

He lay on his hotel bed, dressed in his briefs and a T-shirt. "You want to take care of me?" His heart warmed and libido rose, along with other things. "Have I told you how much I love you lately?"

"Not in the last five minutes."

"I wish you were here. I miss being inside of you."

"You are such a tease."

"Humph. I'm the one lying here with the hard on."

She laughed. "You are a mess."

"Subject change time. How's my baby girl?"

"She's in school right now."

He glanced at his watch. "Oh, yeah, it's only two there."

"Are you still going to the hockey game with Clark on Friday?"

He hated lying to Ebony, but didn't see an alternative. "Yes. If you want, I can cancel our plans and stay home with you. I'd rather make love with you any day."

"Oh, no. Please don't. Go to the game with Clark. I don't want to give him more reason to hate me. You'll do this guys' night out if I have to drive you there myself."

Something in her voice worried him. He shrugged it off, thinking he was probably projecting his own feelings of guilt. "Clark likes you. He just hasn't found someone to spend time with."

"Liar. He's as bad as Jessica. Maybe we should hook the two of them up."

Richard's deep belly laugh filled the hotel room. "Now that would be something!"

She giggled. "Yeah, I thought you'd like that."

"What are you wearing?"

"Oh, lawd, he's slipped into phone sex."

He heard banging over the line. Panic caused his heartbeat to surge. He hopped up. "What's that?"

"Stop, Skeet! I'm gonna tell Mom. Go away!"

He relaxed slightly. Worrying about Ebony and Crystal had become a full-time job. Between the neighborhood, Trae's profession, and her riding the train, he found little peace of mind. This weekend, things would change.

"Sorry about that. Knocking at the door like he had half a brain is too difficult for Skeet to comprehend."

"Did you let him in?"

"He has a key. He bangs because he's an attention hog."

"Why don't you stay at my place?"

"Trying to rush things, huh? Saturday's only a few days away. Hi Skeet, Trae."

"I worry about you. Did you drive to your interview?"

"Yes, I drove that gas guzzling monstrosity. And do you know how much it cost to park downtown? Now those prices should be illegal."

"Promise me you'll drive or have someone take you to school tomorrow. I don't like you on the train so early and late."

"I'll have Skeet drive me." He heard a loud pop sound. "Stop, Skeet. Can't you see I'm on the phone! Dang."

He grinned. Skeet and Ebony had the type of relationship a brother should have with his sisters. "Maybe I'd better let you go. I'll call later. Love you."

"Love you, too."

Richard disconnected. His older sister Gail lived in Chicago. They were only three years apart in age, but a world apart in every other aspect of life. Nonno thought Richard should call her, but Richard refused. He was the new one in town, not her.

He dialed his parents' number.

"Hello, Dubois residence," an unfamiliar female voice answered.

"Hello, this is Smo…Richard. Are my parents in?"

"One second, sir."

Richard leaned against the headboard. He was so proud of Ebony and felt blessed she returned his love. He longed to brag about his fiancée, but knew his family wouldn't give her a chance or appreciate how great she truly was. After all, anyone he picked wouldn't be acceptable.

"Richard, is it really you?" Stephanie asked.

"Yes, Mother. How have you been?"

"It's been months. I've been worried out of my mind. Why didn't you call sooner?"

"You have my number. If you were worried, you could have phoned," he said matter-of-factly. "And you know I speak with Nonno daily."

"So why can't you speak with your mother at least every few weeks?" came her clipped tones over the line.

"I don't know. Maybe because when I do call, instead of asking me how I'm doing, all I get is heartache."

Silence.

"I'm sorry," Richard said. "I didn't mean to be so abrupt. It's been a long day. I'm in New York. I can see the Statue of Liberty from my room."

She sighed. "No, Richard. I'm sorry. You're my baby. My only son. I worry about you." An uncomfortable pause filled the line. "So you're following my advice and moving to New York," she said gleefully.

"I'm afraid not. I'm here on business. I was supposed to leave Friday morning, but I want to finish by tomorrow. I'm ready to go home." Thoughts of waking Ebony up with feather kisses along her inner thigh had him ready to catch the next flight.

"You should reconsider this move to Chicago. You need your father's connections to succeed…"

Ice-cold water thrown on his daydream, he snapped, "Mother, please stop. I can stand on my own two feet."

"Of course you can, darling."

He slumped on the bed, holding his pillow against his chest. He hated the condescending tone her voice took on. He'd rather hear the pissed, clipped tones any day. "I called to tell you I'm in love and getting married. When she has a free weekend, I'm bringing her down to Texas to meet you."

"What! Married? When? Who? What? Did you say married? No!"

He would pay anything to see his mother's face. "Yes, married. We don't have an exact date yet. We're thinking July. That gives you all four months. And not that it matters, but my fiancée is black." He fought the nagging feeling that Ebony's color did matter to his mother, just as his color mattered to her.

"You can't do this, Richard."

"Why not? I'm thirty."

"Wait until I tell your father. He'll be so disappointed. Who are her parents?"

"You wouldn't know them."

"How can you do this to us?"

"I'm not doing anything to you. I've fallen in love, and am getting married. Why can't you be happy for me? Goodbye, Mother."

"No, Richard. We need to discuss this."

"I've changed my mind. We aren't coming to visit. Expect an invitation in a few weeks. Love you." He disconnected and turned off his phone.

He closed his eyes to slow his mind and catch a quick nap before calling Ebony back. This weekend, his prayers would be answered. He would finally have a loving family of his own.

CHAPTER SEVENTEEN

Ebony thumbed through a magazine while four women worked diligently at removing her microbraids. "Mom, if you dye my hair black, will it fall out or break off?"

"It shouldn't. You have that good thick hair. Nice and course." Marissa walked across the salon to the supply cabinet. "We seldom dye anyone's hair black. I hope we have some," she joked.

The bells hanging above the door jingled as Trae and Skeet walked into the salon.

"Hello, ladies." Skeet bowed slightly.

"Hey, Skeet," several young women purred.

Trae marched over to Ebony. The women doing her hair scattered like a school of fish sensing a shark. He kissed her on the cheek. "What did you need?"

He looked angry, but Ebony didn't have time to pamper him today. "For you to watch Crystal tonight."

"You and Smoke goin' out? I thought he was goin' to a game with his boy."

"He is. I have a business dinner."

A grin tipped his lips for about a nanosecond, confusing Ebony. She shook it off as guilt. She was the one hiding something, not Trae. Either way, she wouldn't allow him to talk her out of following through with her plans.

"Business dinner? What kind of business you have I don't know about?"

Ebony motioned for the young ladies to finish her hair. "For your information, I was offered a job with a small consulting firm this past Tuesday. I hadn't planned to take the position. I'm rethinking." She had decided to give Richard and Trae as little information about Banks

Consulting as possible. She knew they would get together, have the place investigated, and then make her decision for her.

"Why didn't you tell me? I would have driven you and made sure they offered what you're worth. You're too trusting."

"Thanks, Trae. I needed to do this on my own." She didn't want to start a fight, so she softened. "I appreciate all you do for me."

"You takin' Smoke with you?"

"No, I haven't told him about the dinner. His flight doesn't even arrive for a few hours, and I don't want him to change his plans with Clark." A set of aw's filled the salon.

"You want me to go with you?"

Skeet stepped between the two. "You'd better not go with him, Ebony. If you're taking anyone, take me." He smiled. "You like me better, anyway." Several women giggled.

They had such good potential. She prayed silently they would leave the drug lifestyle before it was too late. "I don't think I'll take either of you. I still need to figure out what to wear."

By the time evening came, everyone in the neighborhood knew about Ebony's big business dinner. The chilly March weather didn't keep neighbors from gathering on the porch. They reminisced about when she had first moved into the neighborhood as a child, and how she had grown into such a fine young lady.

Dan stopped by to see his baby girl off. He had come close to telling her the truth thousands of times, but couldn't. Ebony's biological mother had died during childbirth. A few weeks later, he signed custody of Ebony over to Marissa, thinking he was saving his child from the drug life. Marissa betrayed him and married that no good drug-addict Bobby not even a year later.

Over the years, he saw Bobby dragging Marissa down. All the women in his family had the same deadly affliction: "heartus softigites." At first, Marissa insisted she could save Bobby. Near the end, she had a drug addiction herself.

Dan felt his rage from Marissa's past betrayal bubbling to the surface. He hadn't given his child away to have her raised by druggies. And then there was Trae.

"Are you all right?" Marissa asked.

"Yeah. I'm fine." He turned away. When Marissa put him out of their lives, he had panicked. At a loss, he used Trae to make sure his child was taken care of. He taught Trae everything he knew, backed him with financing, and cleared the path for him to move up in the organization quickly.

He leaned against one of the porch beams. He wished he had come to his senses earlier. He left the drug life four years after he had begun teaching Trae. Unfortunately, Trae was a fast learner, and loved the life. Dan bowed his head in prayer. *Please help Skeet and Trae leave the life.*

Ebony stepped out to a chorus of ooh's and ah's. She hid her face with her hands. "Why are you all out here?"

Dan hugged his daughter. She had made it, despite her upbringing. "Because we're proud of you."

Trae pulled her into a hug. "You look beautiful."

Skeet stepped up. "Yeah, yeah, yeah, she looks as hot as usual. Can't y'all see you're embarrassing her? That's my job." A round of laughs followed his comment. "Now let the woman get to this dinner." He escorted her to her SUV, with Dan, Marissa and Trae close behind.

She sat behind the steering wheel. "Thanks, Skeet."

"You've finally made it. I always had faith in you. Don't let them sweet talk you into taking the position. You have options. Do what you feel is right." Her family nodded in agreement with Skeet's statement.

"I will." She waved to the people on the porch, then turned back to Skeet. "I love you."

"Yeah, I know." He closed the door.

Richard stared across the table at Clark. He couldn't believe he had allowed Clark to talk him into lying to Ebony. He should have followed his own mind and told her the truth. She was reasonable, and would understand. He stood up, motioning to the others at the table. "I'll be right back." The evening was still young. If he called, she may be able to join them for dinner.

"Something wrong?" Clark mouthed.

Richard nodded his head yes. He scanned the restaurant, and his heart stopped. Ebony stood in the doorway with her trench coat folded over her arm.

His breath caught. She had changed. Not her clothing. She always dressed with class. This was no different. She wore a plum dress that flared slightly at the hips and reached just below the knees, and a matching pair of heels with jeweled straps his sisters would kill for.

Gone were the adornments that detracted from her beauty. There stood his sexy yet classy, statuesque, ebony angel of a fiancée. His heart raced almost as fast as he crossed the room to her. His secretary must have told her about the dinner. He should have known Ebony would understand about a business look, and kicked himself for not speaking up sooner.

Her smile of recognition almost made him lose it. Elation filled him. He wanted to take her home and make love. He drew his hands through her jet-black, shoulder-length hair. "You never cease to amaze me." He kissed her lightly. "I love you."

"I love you, too." She rested her head on his shoulder. "Skeet has a big mouth."

He frowned. He didn't tell Skeet about the business dinner because of his big mouth. Recalling the message Skeet had left for him to call, he was glad he hadn't returned the call. Skeet would have ruined her surprise.

Clearing his throat loudly, Darryl Beacon said, "I take it you know each other."

They broke apart, with Richard answering, "This is my fiancée," and Ebony saying, "Yes, this is my fiancé."

Darryl's eyes darted between the two. "You two are engaged?"

Richard released Ebony's hand. If Darryl was prejudiced, he would take his business elsewhere. "Is that a problem for you?" He glared into Darryl's big brown eyes and saw confusion, not disapproval.

Ebony stepped forward. "Hello, Darryl. It's nice seeing you again. Sorry I'm late."

Richard's head cocked to the side. "You two know each other?" Nausea quickly replaced elation.

Darryl chuckled nervously as he led the way back to the table. "This is the young woman I've been going on and on about. Goes to show what a small world we live in." He nudged his glasses up on his nose.

Richard watched Ebony's reaction to Darryl's words. She looked perplexed—as if the answer to her question was on the tip of her tongue. He kicked himself for ignoring Skeet's call. He must have wanted to tell him about Ebony's first business dinner. He cursed his own stupidity.

Darryl introduced Ebony to everyone at the table, then took his seat.

Richard prayed for the earth to open and swallow him whole. No such luck passed his way. He continued watching Ebony closely. Deep in thought, she stared at Clark.

Richard saw Ebony's inner light literally dying out, and it killed him. He caressed her hand under the table. "I can explain, angel," he whispered into her ear. "I love you. Let's go home and talk. We haven't had stir-fry in a while."

"Did you enjoy the game?" She pushed away from the table. "I apologize, ladies and gentlemen. I'm not feeling well." She grabbed her coat off the back of the chair and ran out of the restaurant.

Oh, God, don't do this to me. Richard stood. "Goodnight." He ran after Ebony.

Darryl walked toward the restroom, dialing Trae's number on his cell phone.

"I told you not to call me," Trae barked. "I'm through messin' in Ebony's business. I'll take care of your son."

"I just wanted to let you know that she ran out of here very upset."

"What the hell happened?" Trae snapped.

He paced the three-stall room. "I don't know. One second she's hugging and kissing her fiancé, the next she's running out in tears."

"Smoke was there? Shit!"

Thoroughly confused, Darryl stopped pacing. "Who's Smoke? I thought you were her fiancé. I was shocked to learn Richard Pacini is."

Skeet, Dan and Marissa had left, but others were still gathered on Ebony's porch.

"Everyone get the hell out!" Trae yelled. "Now, dammit!" He pulled his gun. People scattered.

"I'll kill him." He stalked back and forth, thinking of ways to kill Richard. What seemed like hours passed before Ebony's truck sped down the one-way street. He was glad, though. It gave him time to regain control.

The SUV screeched to a halt close to her parking space. She hopped out and ran for the flat.

Trae had already put away his piece. He stepped in front of her. "What's wrong, baby?" He held her close. She struggled, but couldn't escape. He rocked her gently. "Please, baby, tell me what's wrong."

She stopped struggling, leaned on his shoulder and cried. "He…he's ash-sh-shamed," she buried her head deeper, "of m-m-meee."

As tears soaked his jacket, he became enraged all over again. "I'm sorry, baby." He could feel himself about to lose control, but he couldn't. He would be sent to jail if he acted on his rage. That would leave Ebony without anyone. He chastised himself for thinking anyone could take his place. Only he could care for Ebony. Richard pulled into Marrisa's parking spot.

Ebony swiped at her tears with her hand. "Please, Trae, I can't see him. Not yet."

He dabbed at her tear soaked face. "Go inside." She ran into the flat.

Trae stepped in front of Richard, fully intending to pick a fight without actually picking a fight. It was time for Ebony to see Richard's ugly side.

"Get out of the way," Richard demanded.

He inhaled slowly. Being thrown in jail for murdering Richard wasn't an option. He counted to six by two's. He was in control of the situation. "She doesn't want to speak with you. Go home. You don't belong here." He frowned. If he took Richard to a secluded area, he could make him disappear.

"I have to explain…"

"Explain what? That you're ashamed of your black fiancée? I think you've made that perfectly clear." He reconsidered killing Richard. Ebony would become suspicious if he disappeared. Showing her Richard's dark side would have to do until he came up with something better.

"I don't owe you an explanation." He pushed Trae out of the way.

Trae jerked Richard's arm, spinning him around. "This is the last time I'm telling you to go home, *Richard*. She doesn't want your white ass. Now get to steppin', *Opie*." He shoved Richard.

Richard stumbled slightly, reared his arm back to Texas and brought it around for a connecting flight on Trae's chin.

The lookout ran into the house for Ebony. Trae fell onto the damp ground, fighting the urge to shoot Richard and be done with it. He had to look like the victim; he bit his lip, making it bleed.

Richard stood over Trae with his arms out, hands up. "Come on with it. I won't let your racist ass keep me from Ebony."

Trae rose in one fluid motion. The two men circled each other, shoulder to shoulder. "You wanna take me on, Richie Rich?" Trae growled.

"I'm sick of you, Too Triflin' Trick-Assed Trae."

Trae heard the screen door open. "I should have killed you instead of the Collins boys," he whispered.

Richard froze.

Ebony ran out of the house. "Stop it now!" She hopped down the stairs in her bare feet and pushed Trae away from Richard.

"Don't attack me." Trae made a dramatic swipe of his lip, ensuring that Ebony saw the blood in his mouth. "Your boy sucker-punched me, not the other way around." He pointed at the muddy mark on his pants.

She glared at Richard. "What's wrong with you? Get out. Both of you!"

"Blue and white," a lookout called. "Five-O!"

"Go inside, Ebony," Trae ordered. "I've got this."

She walked into the flat, with Richard close behind.

Ebony dried her feet on the throw rug just inside the door.

"Let me explain." Richard reached forward.

She stepped away from his touch. "No. Let me explain. The only reason I brought you in here was to give you this." She took off her engagement ring and held it out to him. "Jessica was right." She wiped the tears from her face. "You're ashamed of me." Fear gripped her. What if Jessica was also right about him working for Trae? After all, he didn't turn away the hundred grand Trae invested in his firm back in January. And why had he accepted Trae and Skeet as friends so easily?

Instead of accepting the ring, he clasped his hands behind his back. "I love you. It was a mistake."

"Give this back to your boss." She stuffed the ring into his pocket. "I'm not a business deal." His confused stare told her she'd made a mistake. He didn't work for Trae, but she was right about her other fear. "The only mistake was my believing in you." She sat on the couch, hugging herself tightly. "You wouldn't even introduce me to your family."

"Nonno loves you." He knelt in front of her. "You're not a deal. You're my love. I love you."

She rocked back and forth, quietly crying. "You introduced me to the one person of color left in your family. Jessica was right. Your family is lightening up. I throw you back generations. Please just go."

He lowered his head, allowing his own tears to fall freely. "I'll never give you up, Ebony. I love you too much. You are my fiancée, my heart, my ebony angel. I'm sorry I hurt you. I made a mistake. I'm not ashamed of you. I love you."

She lifted her legs onto the couch. "You don't love me."

"Let's go home to our place. I'll make love to you all night." He rested his head on her lap. "Let me show you how I feel. When we're together, you know it's real." He lifted himself, kissing her tears away.

Sex. Jessica always said their relationship was all about sex. Trae had said their relationship was all about sex. They had made love their first night. Now here he was saying he wasn't ashamed of her, yet instead of saying 'let's take the next flight to meet my family,' he was saying 'let's have sex.'

"Go home, Smoke." She pushed him away. "You make me sick."

He took the ring out of his pocket and set it on the coffee table. "You are my heart. I'll never give you up." He kissed her gently, then left.

CHAPTER EIGHTEEN

"Get off my car, Trae," Richard demanded, too enraged to acknowledge any fear.

"We need to talk. Come on, take a ride with me."

"I'm white, not stupid."

Trae laughed. "Damn skippy you ain't stupid. Look, man." He stepped forward, motioning toward the flat. "Ebony's probably in the window watching. We need to talk." He lowered his voice. "In private. I'm not telling the street all of our business."

"I'm not going anywhere alone with you."

Trae held his hands out to his sides, hunched his shoulders. "What, we ain't boys no mo'?"

Richard rounded his car. "You're out of your mind. Please continue sitting on the car. I'm driving off."

Trae opened the door and sat in the passenger seat.

"Get out of my car."

"Get off my car. Get out of my car. Make up your mind. We need to discuss Ebony." He held his hands up. "We can do this at your crib if you want."

Richard wanted to knock the stupid grin off Trae's face.

"I don't know why you're so mad at me, anyway. You started it. Hell, if you weren't my boy, I would have capped your ass for pushing me."

Richard snarled. "I started it?! Were we at the same fight?"

"You pushed me first. You punched me. If you weren't my boy, you'd be dead. No ifs, ands or buts about that shit. Then Ebony came out beating on me. Damn, I'm always the bad guy."

Richard thought back to their altercation as Trae recounted the events.

"First Ebony comes running to me crying, talking about you hurt her. When you came she said to keep you away. I was as polite as a thug could be, but you wouldn't take no for an answer."

"Shoot." Richard dropped his head to the steering wheel. He *had* been the aggressor. "That doesn't change the fact that you killed the Collins boys."

Trae made a sucking, dismissive sound with his teeth. "I lied to scare you into listening. I wouldn't risk jail time on their worthless asses. I wasn't even in town." He paused. "I'm sorry, dawg. I lost my cool when I saw Ebony's tears, but so did you. If you're gonna marry Ebony and adopt Crystal, we have to trust each other."

"I can't lose her, Trae." Unsure of himself, he started the Mercedes and pulled off.

❧

Richard settled in the overstuffed chair at his condo. "I'll give her a few days to cool off. She knows I love her."

Trae stretched his long legs under the coffee table, leaned his head back on the couch and rested. "The first time I saw Ebony she was ten. Our dads did drugs together. Heroin mostly. Dan did Marissa a favor when he killed Bobby."

Richard's mouth dropped open in horror. "He murdered her father?"

"There's no proof. I'd say he did. Dan is very protective of his family. He basically raised me, ya' know."

He shook his head. Ebony had told him about Dan's past, but this was still a light he never imagined Dan in. "Why are you telling me this? What does it have to do with Ebony?"

Ignoring Richard's questions, Trae asked, "Did I ever tell you why we broke up?"

"You were only kids." He didn't have the time or energy to travel down memory lane.

"What is the first thing you noticed when you saw Ebony and Crystal together?"

"Are you serious? I'm not in the mood to play twenty questions."

"Humor me. You'll see where I'm headed shortly."

He slowly exhaled. "The first thing I noticed was the difference in their complexions. I've never seen anything like it."

"Did you wonder why?"

"At first I did." He nodded at Trae. "But you have green eyes and, as Skeet would say, 'You is one high yella brotha.' "

They both chuckled at his terrible impersonation.

"Crystal's complexion is a touch darker than her biological mother's."

Richard choked. First Dan, now this.

Trae went into the kitchen, pulled two beers out of the refrigerator, returned to the living room and handed Richard one. "I've always loved Ebony."

"You cheated on her with a white girl!" He guzzled down the beer, processing this new information. "How could you say you loved her?"

"I was only seventeen. Hell, I never thought Ebony would find out."

"Why would you cheat on her, anyway?"

"It was all about sex. Ebony wasn't giving it up at the time. I'd go across town to have my needs met. That ho' got pregnant and confronted Ebony." He leaned forward. "She lied to me, dawg. She said she was on the pill."

"How did Ebony end up with this other woman's child?"

"Ebony kicked my dumb ass to the curb. I put Shelly up in an apartment and kept her off the drugs until the baby was born. The day Crystal was born I had a DNA test done. She's my baby."

"This is freakin' unbelievable."

"Shelly didn't mean shit to me. I loved my baby from day one. Even before the DNA test, I knew she was mine."

"What happened to Shelly?"

"I was on the birth certificate and had the DNA test to prove I was the father. I took my baby home with me to raise properly."

"Shelly didn't want her?"

"I literally had to lock that ho' up to keep her from gettin' high when she was pregnant. She'd had at least seven months clean when Crystal was born. I offered to set her up nice someplace else."

Richard shook his head. "So she took the money and ran."

"Nope. A few weeks after having Crystal, she was gettin' high again. I gave her all the money I had in the world, twenty thousand, to sign her rights over to me. Shelly died of an overdose by the end of the week."

"You gave a drug addict twenty thousand dollars?" He'd never seen anyone as conniving as Trae. The man had manipulation down to a mathematic equation.

"Yeah. Single fatherhood and my movement in the organization didn't mix. Dan gave me two totally legit businesses. He said I couldn't raise a child and be in the business. I knew he was right, so I asked Ebony to help me. She was still angry with me, but you know her kind heart. There was no way she would leave Crystal for me to raise. Everything would have worked out perfectly if Dan hadn't stuck his nose into my business. He had a stipulation."

"You had to sign custody of Crystal over."

"Exactly. Some say I'm controlling, but I don't have squat on Dan. Ebony should have been Crystal's mother, anyway. I'm not stupid. Dan planned on pushing me out of the picture, but time worked on my side. Ebony was still a minor and broke. I knew the judge wouldn't give her custody.

"To make Ebony feel more secure, I legally changed Crystal's last name to Washington and told Ebony I'd give her joint guardianship when she turned eighteen. She didn't want to do it. She wanted outright custody and for me to trust her to do the right thing by Crystal. Hell yeah, she'd have done the right thing and ran off with Crystal. I turned the shit and told her she'd have to trust me. I know how her mind works. In order to save Crystal, she'd do things my way."

Extortion, thought Richard. *Ebony didn't have a choice.*

"When Ebony turned eighteen, I didn't hold up my part of the deal. She fought me on it, but I wouldn't budge. I had a guaranteed way of always being a part of Ebony's life. I just knew she'd forgive me and take me back. Damn. I was half right. She forgave my infidelity eventually, but she never gave us a chance."

"Why didn't Ebony tell me?"

"Hell, Dan would have had my hide. I made her promise to pretend we did the adoption route and never tell anyone, or I'd take Crystal from her. I did a few payoffs and had forged documentation in case Dan's nosey ass checked things out. That was the only time I ever threatened to take Crystal from her. She is Crystal's mother. I'm sure Ebony doesn't even think about the arrangement anymore."

Everything finally made sense to Richard. If Ebony had taken Crystal, it would have been kidnapping, and Trae would have gone after her. Trae had literally held Ebony captive in the life. Yet he had more pressing issues to deal with. He hadn't seen Trae's bag of tricks in weeks, but felt he'd be pulling a doozie out pretty soon. "You're a drug dealer, Trae."

"I counted on you, Smoke. You let me down."

Richard saw Trae's evil alter ego emerging, heard it in his voice. "It's time for you to leave."

"Not so quickly. I like you, but I love Ebony. I've decided to marry her myself."

"Hell no!" Richard jumped out of his seat. "She would never marry a drug dealer."

"Sit your punk-ass down. Damn." He unzipped his jacket. "It's hot in here."

"She's in love with me. Yes, she's angry with me right now. In a few days she'll be ready to talk." He crossed his arms over his chest. Trae wouldn't be manipulating him into giving up Ebony.

"I'm getting out of the business. I choose Ebony."

"You can't have her."

"Of course I can. I just need for you to stay out of the picture and give us a chance." He walked about as he spoke. "I need for her to see I've changed, that we belong together."

"You've lost your mind." He stepped before Trae. "I'm not giving her up."

"Here."

Out of reflex, Richard grabbed what Trae held out. He quickly realized the cards were blood-covered driving licenses. His stomach churned angrily. Hands shaking, he turned them over.

Trae pulled out his piece, then pointed it between Richard's eyes. "Yes, I killed the Collins boys. With this very gun, as a matter of fact."

The scent of gunpowder burned Richard's nose. His breathing became ragged. Fear invaded every fiber of his body. He dropped John and Morris Collins' licenses to the floor, bent over and vomited.

Trae returned to the couch. "Someone had to pay for your indiscretion with my woman," he said with an air of nonchalance one would use to tell the day of the week. "You weren't around, so I had to settle. If they hadn't stolen your car, you and Ebony would have never met again."

Visions of Ebony and Crystal flooded Richard's mind. He felt lightheaded. He reached back for the overstuffed chair. "I love Ebony."

"That's the only reason you aren't dead. They would be devastated." He lifted his brow. "You'll stay alive unless you interfere with me and Ebony's relationship. You had your chance. Now it's my turn."

Trae's cold expression had murderer written all over it. "I'll back off," Richard reluctantly said.

"That's what I'm talkin' about." He raised his beer in toast. "I love Ebony. I won't hurt her."

"Get the hell out of my house!"

Trae's eerie laugh filled the condo. "See. I told ya, you my boy. I would have killed anyone else who yelled at me like that. We cool. Just stay away from Ebony, and we'll stay that way." He headed toward the door. "I can't believe you're making me walk home from this neighborhood." He closed the door on his way out.

Richard threw the lamp on the end table across the room. It crashed against the wall, shattering into pieces.

CHAPTER NINETEEN

Nonno opened his door and stepped to the side. He had moved from the ranch-style home where he raised Richard to a retirement community when Richard went away to college.

"Papà, whose Mercedes is that out front?" Stephanie hugged her father, then sat on the couch.

He put his finger to his lips. "Keep your voice down. It's Richard's. He drove in yesterday and hasn't left his room since." He closed the door. The two-bedroom, bi-level town home was more than large enough for him.

"Richard's here? Why didn't you call me?"

"Something's terribly wrong, Steph. I wanted to give him time." He drew his hands through his thinning, gray hair. "I'm worried. I've never seen him like this."

She patted her father's hand. "Don't worry, Papà. I'm here now. I'll take care of my baby."

His smoky gray eyes locked onto her warm sepia ones. "I know you want to help, but I think he needs to be left alone." She sniffed. "Don't do that, baby." He pulled her into his arms, rubbing her back as if she were still a child. "I'm making shrimp gumbo. Let Papà fix you a bowl."

"Can I take some home?"

He smiled sadly. "Of course, darling." He never understood Stephanie's distance from her youngest child. One second she'd want to take the world on for daring to look at him crossways; the next, she'd act as if he didn't exist. He harped on her for years about her treatment of Richard, but to no avail. At his wit's end, he finally took Richard to raise as his own.

"Why doesn't my son love me?"

"Stop this. He loves you, but now he needs to do things his way." He released her. He loved his daughter, but she had always been self-centered. And Phillip…Well, he had no respect for people who stood by and watched a child be mistreated, especially their own child. "Put Richard's needs first."

"It's that woman."

Oh great, now you want to be protective. He continued patting her back. The phone rang. Nonno answered, "Hello…Oh yes, Richard told me all about you, Skeet…Yes he's here…" He tilted his head to the side. "Well, I was born and raised in Italy. I should have an Italian accent."

He glanced at Stephanie. They didn't move to the United States until she was fifteen, but she had lost her Italian accent. He frowned. She hadn't lost it; she had worked to erase it. She wanted to sound like a real American. "Hold on a second." He lowered the phone. "Do not go to his room, Steph. You hear me?"

"Yes, Papà."

"I'll be right back." He walked into the kitchen to stir the gumbo and find out what the heck happened to his grandson.

Richard ran his hand along the fine oak arm of the rocking chair, thinking how much Ebony would love the chair. When Stephanie's limo parked in front of Nonno's house, he locked the bedroom door. The last thing he needed was a confrontation with his mother.

He saw an older couple step out of the ranch-style townhouse across the street. The older man took his wife's hand and kissed it gently, then guided her along the walk. In forty years, that could be he and Ebony taking their evening stroll.

Trae threatened to take his life, but didn't understand that by taking Ebony and Crystal away, he had already taken his life. He watched the couple as they ambled down the boulevard. No way would he allow a madman to take his family.

The smell of shrimp gumbo wafted through the vents, causing Richard's mouth to water. He hadn't eaten in two days, but wouldn't leave the room until he was sure Stephanie was long gone.

He rubbed his belly. Gumbo was Richard's favorite. He watched the limo, thinking it was too bad his mother had come along.

"Richard." Stephanie tapped on the door.

"I don't feel like talking, Mother. I'll call you tomorrow."

The doorknob creaked. "Unlock the door, darling."

Richard lowered his head into his hands. "Mother, please…"

"Stephanie, get down here this instant!"

"Papà, I'm sorry. I was only…"

"Don't make me repeat myself, young lady!"

A short time later, Richard saw Nonno escort Stephanie out of the house and nudge her toward the limo. His grandfather's protective streak was the main reason he didn't tell him what happened with Trae or what he had been up to the past few months.

He chuckled. He could imagine his eighty-year-old grandfather chartering a flight for Chicago to go after Trae.

As usual, Nonno's face softened when he saw his daughter's tears. As usual, he didn't give in. Instead, he hugged Stephanie and handed her a large Tupperware bowl. Richard was amazed at how loving his mother was toward her father. Nonno could do no wrong, while Richard could do no right.

He crossed the room and unlocked the door. He already had more than enough on his mind. Figuring out his mother would have to wait for another day. He flopped onto the bed to calculate a move that wouldn't end in his funeral.

Nonno tip-toed into the bedroom and set the serving tray on the nightstand. He sat on the edge of the bed and watched his grandson sleep.

"Something smells delicious," Richard said, as he stretched awake.

"Something? Have I lost my touch?"

"What, are you kidding me? You're still the best cook this side of the moon."

Nonno handed Richard the tray, then watched him eat.

"Have some with me."

"You know I can't eat spices like I used to. What good is gumbo without spices? You enjoy."

Richard tasted a spoonful. "Ummm." He devoured the bowl of gumbo in record time.

"Want more?"

He rubbed his stomach. "I'm stuffed." He set the tray on the nightstand, then drank his cola.

Nonno pulled the rocking chair around from the window to the bed. "We need to have a man-to-man talk." He held up his hand to stop Richard from interrupting him. "I'm disappointed in you, but like Ebony, I'll get over it. It's time for you to go home and face the music."

"You don't understand."

"I understand you humiliated the woman you love. I have a good mind to take a switch to you." He shook his head. "I taught you better than that."

"I'm sorry, Nonno. I just…" He shrugged. "I don't know what came over me. I knew I had made a wrong turn, but kept down the road, anyway."

"I'm not the one you should be apologizing to. Get on the next flight home. Show Ebony how you really feel. I'll have your car sent to you."

"I wish it were that simple."

Nonno stared at Richard, knowing there was more to the story. Some part Skeet didn't say. "What did you do?"

After a long hesitation, Richard told Nonno about Trae and Skeet's drug ties, then reached into his jeans back pocket and pulled the driver's licenses out. Richard had been withholding vital information from him, and Nonno didn't appreciate it one bit. This man was obviously still a boy, and needed to be cared for.

"Oh, my God." Nonno's gray eyes slowly rose from the images of the young men to Richard. He felt sick to his stomach. "Why do you have these?" Richard had told him about the Collins boys stealing his car and their subsequent murders when it first happened.

"Trae killed them for my indiscretion with *his woman*. He's decided he wants Ebony back. If I don't stay out of the picture, I'll meet the same fate with the same gun. I don't know how to save Ebony."

Overwhelmed by the new information, Nonno could barely manage, "He wouldn't hurt Ebony or Crystal, would he? From everything you've told me, he'd die first." But there had been so much Richard hadn't told him, it scared him.

"Trae has lost his mind. She's mad, but Ebony's in love with me. What happens when she tells him? He's a psycho. He may kill them all so they can be together forever."

"Tell Ebony and Skeet." Richard had always said Ebony and Skeet were close. Hopefully, Skeet would protect Ebony instead of siding with Trae.

"They haven't seen his crazy side. Hell, I didn't see it until Friday." He stepped out of bed. "They'll think I'm making things up as a distraction to turn the heat off me to him." He hit at the dresser as he passed between the bed and the window.

"What about the police?"

"And tell them what?" Richard's face took on a look of déjà vu.

Nonno held out the two licenses. "Last I checked, murder was illegal."

"I don't have any proof. If anything, the cops will think I killed them. I had a motive, not Trae. I'm the one without an alibi, not Trae. I'm the one with their licenses, not Trae. He's a master of manipulation."

Nonno rocked slowly in the chair. "Same fate, same gun. How do you know it'll be the same gun?"

"That asshole pointed it at me."

Nonno lifted his head. "What?"

Richard explained how he had been conducting his own investigation. Nonno wanted to strangle him for being so arrogant, and thinking he could ride in to save the day. This was no game. These were dangerous people. Richard also explained how Trae manipulated him into taking him to his condo.

"I feel like such an idiot. He played me."

"Where does he keep the gun?"

"I've never seen him carrying, so I'm thinking his car."

"We have to involve the police."

Richard shook his head. "I know he has cops on the take. Going to the police would be suicide."

"Listen, he has you scared, and rightly so, but not all police are crooked. I know some people. I'll arrange things." He tapped the licenses. "These will be found by 'honest police' in Trae's car. If he's moved the gun, they'll still find evidence he can't explain away."

"You plan to have someone plant evidence?" Richard laughed. "You are too much. I can't let you do this. I'll think of another way."

"We don't have time to find another way. The authorities need to be brought in now." Nonno was so disappointed in Richard he didn't know what to do. Hanging out with these thugs had corrupted his grandson and had him thinking the police were the enemy. "Maybe I should visit my granddaughters. Both of your sisters live in Chicago now."

"No!" He covered his mouth, apologizing for raising his voice. "I can't risk you getting hurt. Make the arrangements, but that's it. I'm heading back to get Ebony. As soon as Trae is taken in for questioning and, hopefully, arrested, I'm getting her and Crystal out of there. Promise me you'll stay down here."

"I'm not promising a damn thing."

"Nonno!"

His face tightened and voice hardened. "What? You honestly expect me to stand by while this hoodlum tries to kill you?" He crossed his arms over his chest. "Not in this lifetime."

"You're giving me an ulcer." He knelt at his grandfather's feet. "You've always protected me, but I need to fight this battle on my own. This is my family."

CHAPTER TWENTY

Trae ran through the rain to the lookout standing across the street from Ebony's flat. "Did she leave yet?" He drew his hood tighter.

"No movement." The wind caught in Meechie's umbrella, turning it inside out. He threw the umbrella to the side. "I'm worried about her. If that white mutha comes around here, I'll kick his ass ma damn self."

"You'll get your skinny ass kicked, you mean. Everyone is to leave Smoke alone unless I say otherwise." He checked his watch. "It's almost seven. What time is her first class?"

"Nine, I think."

He handed Meechie a hundred bucks. "Run along and get yourself a new umbrella." He pulled out his key as he skipped up the steps to Ebony's flat.

Dan had taken Crystal and Marissa to his place to give Ebony space. Trae did a quick scan of the dark flat. All the curtains were drawn and lights were off. He went into her bedroom. The nightlight provided the only light.

"Ebony." He touched her side. "Time to get ready for school."

"Go away." She rolled onto her belly and hugged her pillow.

He turned on the light in the closet. "What do you want to wear today?"

"Go away!"

"Something simple, she says." He selected her favorite Tigger T-shirt and a pair of jeans. "Now for the good part." He searched through her drawers for a clean pair of underclothes. "I'd kill to see you in these." He held up a pair of red thongs.

She looked up briefly. "You can have them if you leave."

"Nice try. Now are we doing this the hard or easy way?"

"Go away!" She threw her pillow at him.

"The hard way. Okay." He left, then returned a few seconds later. "Shower time." He pulled her out of bed. She fought him, grabbing onto the spread, the doorway, dragging the kitchen table, grasping at anything within her reach. He pushed her into the bathroom and slammed the door closed. "Why must you make everything so damn difficult?"

She folded her arms over her chest. "I hate you."

Wide-eyed, he made spooky fingers. "Oooooo, da big bad Ebony said she hates me. I'm wounded. Now get your ass in the shower." He blocked the door.

She looked over her shoulder at the running water. "You can't make me shower if I don't want to. Go away and let me die in peace."

His eyes roamed from her wild hair to her angry yet enchanting face; down her cotton nightshirt to her bare legs and her perfectly pedicured toes. He could use a cold shower himself. Allowing his hormones to rule was the reason they weren't a couple now. This time, he planned to be patient. "Wanna bet?" He took his jacket off and tossed to the side.

"What are you doing?"

He pulled off his jersey but left on his T-shirt. "Undressing." He unsnapped his pants.

"Not in here."

"This is the bathroom. Where else should I undress?"

"Your bathroom. Get out, or I'm telling Mom."

Now in his underclothes, he moved so quickly Ebony didn't stand a chance. He pushed her into the shower, turning his body so he'd receive the majority of the impact. His back hurt like hell. *No more of this movie shit.*

"Trae! You make me sick! This water's freezing."

He stared at the outline of her hard nipples poking through the shirt. "So I see." He held onto her wrist and helped her stand. He needed to escape before she saw what part of him had hardened.

"You have lost your mind. Let me go."

"Since you're all wet, put a little soap on your body." He handed her the soap, stepped out of the tub and grabbed a towel. "You have thirty minutes before we leave." He walked out with his clothes and a towel.

❧

"What the hell have you been doing that you need more drawers?!" Skeet tossed new packages of briefs and T-shirts at Trae. "Stay away from Ebony."

Trae picked the packages up off the floor, then closed the blanket wrapping him. "Get your mind out of the gutter."

Skeet followed him into Ebony's room. "So what's up?"

"She smelled like crap, so I threw her ass in the shower. Let's just say she wouldn't go peaceably."

Skeet laughed. "So that's why the house's a mess. You better clean before Marissa comes home."

He changed his briefs and T-shirt, then put on his jeans and Cubs jersey. "Do you know what her class schedule is? I can tell she's not gonna cooperate."

"Ebony has never missed class a day in her life. You know she exercises in the morning. She probably doesn't have any morning classes."

"You didn't see her. She's miserable." He wrung his hands. "I could break Smoke's neck for hurting her."

"Chill out, Trae. They had a lover's quarrel. You need to step back, and let them do their do."

"I'm staying out of it," he paused, "for now."

"Don't start trouble."

"I didn't start shit. He did, when he disrespected Ebony. You can't expect me to let this shit slide."

"Don't get me wrong. I want to kick his ass for hurting Ebony, but we can't jump in every time they have a fight."

"This is more than a fight. He disrespected her. No one disrespects my girls."

"I'm with you. I just think it's best to let her handle things her way. Give her time to cool off."

"I can't stand seeing her like this, Skeet."

"Come on. Let's get out of here before she comes out." Trae had acted unpredictably lately. When Skeet heard Richard had actually punched Trae, he was shocked Richard was still alive. Allowing Trae to spend the day with Ebony had *bad idea* written all over it.

"Nah, you go ahead."

Skeet folded his arms over his chest. "What are you up to?"

"Nothing. I just want to make sure she goes to school."

"I'm tellin' ya, she won't miss class. Not Ebony. You're trying to get some rebound action."

Trae stalked out of the room with Skeet close behind. "I wouldn't do that to Ebony. I told you I was steppin' out, and I meant it." He moved the kitchen table back to the center of the room. "I gotta clean up this mess. You can stay and help if you want. That way you can keep your eye on me."

Skeet shook off the uncertainty. Trae loved Ebony. He wouldn't do anything to harm her. "I don't need to keep no eye on you. I'm out." Skeet beat on the bathroom door as he passed.

"Go away, Skeet!"

"Ah, the sound of love. See ya, dawg." He nodded on his way out.

Ebony rubbed sweet pea lotion into her legs. The soft fragrance calmed her. *Smoke.* She pinched the bridge of her nose, massaging lightly.

The humiliation and embarrassment that had clouded her judgment had dissipated. She set the lotion bottle on the sink, then wiped the foggy mirror with a face towel. She could think clearly again. She combed her fingers through her thick, black hair. Richard seemed to like it much better than the blonde.

She turned away from her reflection, then dressed in the Tigger T-shirt and jeans Trae had laid out for her. She had preached to Jessica about the appropriate corporate America appearance. If the shoe were on the other foot, she wouldn't have invited herself to a business meeting the way she had looked. And she hadn't. She had changed before the interview, then again before the dinner.

Richard said he wanted to take her business shopping, but she had blown him off. She quickly cleaned the bathroom, then rushed out.

"I hope you're running for your book bag," Trae said from the couch. He flicked off the television.

"Nope." She grabbed the phone.

He quickly crossed the room and snatched the phone before she could finish dialing.

"Hey, what are you doing?" She stretched across his body, reaching for the phone. He moved his arm further away. "Stop fooling around, Trae."

He unplugged the cord from the wall. "Who you tryin' to call? It's time for school, not socializing. You've come too far to blow it now."

"Not that it's any of your business—Mr. Freezing Shower—but I'm calling Smoke to apologize." She turned to find her cell phone.

"What, are you crazy?" He stepped in front of her. "I can't let you do this."

"Get out of the way."

"Why are you calling him? He's the one who was wrong."

"Because I overreacted. He isn't ashamed of me. I need to let him know."

Trae dragged her into the living room. "Listen to me, then you can call."

She sat on the couch. "I can't believe I doubted him. I have to apologize. He needed me to listen, but I shut him out." She blinked her tears away. "I'm no better than his family."

He sat on the coffee table, facing her. "I'm not saying you can't apologize to Smoke. I think you should." She cocked her head to the side. "I know. I sound crazy, don't I? All I'm saying is he should apologize first. He was the one who was out of pocket."

"You didn't hear the horrible things I said to him, Trae. I accused him of working for you."

"You were angry."

"Well, I'm not angry anymore."

"What kind of precedent are you setting for your relationship? He makes an ass of himself, lies, humiliates you, punches me, disappears for days, then you call him and apologize. Wrong freakin' answer, baby girl."

"But I told him it was over." She wiped her misty eyes. "I love him." She reached for her engagement ring, which was still on the end of the coffee table.

He grimaced. "He knows you were angry. He'll call and apologize, or he doesn't deserve your love. Don't you have faith in him, Ebony?"

"Of course I do." She studied the exquisite diamond ring, priding herself in learning from her mistakes. Her lack of faith in him was what led her wrong in the first place. She slipped the ring onto her finger. "I fully believe in Smoke."

"Oh really? Can you explain why you were about to apologize to him first? If he's so in love with you, he'll give you time to cool off, then call and apologize." He gently nudged her hair behind her ear. "I know this is hard for you, but this fight was minor. You still have to deal with his snobbish parents. If he can't bring himself to apologize for this stupid shit, how will he stand up to them?"

Disheartened, with the fight knocked out of her, she leaned on the arm of the couch. "I'll wait for him to call."

"Don't worry, baby. He'll call."

She caught the anxiety in Trae's voice. He sounded as if he had as much riding on Richard calling as her. She sighed. In a way, he did. Trae seldom allowed anyone close enough to let him down. She prayed Richard called for both of their sakes.

"Where are your school books?"

"I'm skipping class today. He may come by."

"He knows you have class. He won't come by." His cell beeped with a text message.

"Missing one day of class won't hurt anything. I'm staying and you're leaving." She needed time alone to sort out her feelings.

"Promise you won't call or visit him."

"I promise, Big Daddy Trae."

He looked at the number displayed on the cell, then grumbled.

"Is something wrong?"

"Nah. I'm just tired of all the shit." He paused. "I'm tired."

His cell beeped again with another text. Without checking the message, he tossed the phone toward the table. It skidded across and dropped onto the carpeted floor.

"I'm really proud of the way you handled yourself the other night." She examined his face for bruises and found none. "I'm sorry I thought you hit Smoke. He picked a fight in front of the whole neighborhood, and you acted like a real man." She patted his cheek. "You made me proud."

With all the signs of change he had been displaying, she prayed he would allow her to adopt Crystal, soon. When Richard said that Trae had asked him to adopt her, her immediate reaction had been fury. She had been *begging* Trae for years to relinquish his parental rights, but he had refused; yet he hadn't even known Richard two good months and was *asking* him to adopt her.

She buried the resentment and anger she felt. This was no time to allow it to surface.

He chuckled lightly. "You're proud of me for being knocked on my butt? What has the world come to?" He wrapped an arm around her.

"I haven't issued a beat down in at least five years," he lied. "That's why I wasn't ready."

Emotionally drained, she leaned her head on his shoulder. "You're lying."

"Think what you want, baby girl."

"You're serious, aren't you?"

"Don't tell anyone. Not even Skeet. I'd never live it down."

"I won't tell." He was so close to giving up the life. She could feel it. Spending so much time with a legit man close to his own age had paid off. She still couldn't figure out why he had asked Richard to adopt Crystal instead of allowing her to. Maybe it was to show her he was in control.

His cell phone rang. "Damn." He leaned over the table, snatched the phone off the floor, then checked the caller ID. "What?" he answered.

She watched him pace the room as he listened. For a second she thought she saw panic in his eyes.

"Son of a bitch!" he spewed. He sat on the floor by the shoe rack, disconnected, put on his Nikes.

"Trae."

Without a word, he drew his legs up and lowered his head to his knees. "I can't live like this," he finally mumbled. He looked over his shoulder at her. "I'm tired, Ebony."

She quickly crossed the room and wrapped her arms around him from behind. "It's time for a change," she whispered. The urge to preach the same old lines about giving up the drug life, reiterating how unhappy it made him and how unfulfilled he'd become, were all shelved. He knew. Now she prayed for him to take action. She hummed softly.

"Soon we'll both have what we've always wanted. I promise." He pulled away. "I planned to spend the day with you, but I have something to take care of."

She watched him ready himself to leave. "I'll be fine."

CHAPTER TWENTY-ONE

Skeet needed time to cool off before talking sense into Richard. He pulled his BMW over to the curb a few blocks from Richard's condo. The quiet residential neighborhood was only a mile and a half from Ebony's flat, but was a totally different world. Her world was a war zone, while his was utopia.

The streetlights were out. He smiled. There was one thing the two neighborhoods had in common. The power had gone out in Ebony's neighborhood several times over the winter. The outages never lasted long, but were a real pain.

He rested his head on the steering wheel, inhaled deeply, then exhaled. Maybe Ebony was right, maybe he was no better than any other drug-dealing thug. He viewed himself as a businessman. No worse than an owner of a liquor store, tobacco company or gun dealer. If he didn't supply the need, someone else would. Why shouldn't he make the profit? Yet, there he sat a few blocks from her fiancé's home, ready to beat the man. He wiped his hands over his face. *I'm not a thug. I'm a businessman. I'll talk sense into him.*

He took out his cell phone and dialed Ebony's number.

"Hello, Smoke?" Ebony's fretful voice came on the line.

"I'm afraid not." He heard her sniffle. "Please don't. I can't stand to hear you cry." He felt his rage increasing.

"I'm sorry." She hiccupped. "I'm not crying."

He checked the clock on the dashboard. "It's after midnight. I shouldn't have called so late. Go to bed." He'd called to see if the trip to Richard's was necessary.

"I'm too upset to sleep. Instead of believing in him, I shut him out."

"Don't start. This ain't your fault. He's the one…"

"I've already had this conversation with Trae. I can't go through it again."

"It'll work out, Ebony. I promise."

Breathing labored, eyes swollen almost completely shut, Richard lay on his dining room floor rolled in a ball with his arms guarding his head. He knew he wouldn't survive many more kicks. "Pees, Tae," he breathlessly eked out.

Trae stood over him. "Why don't yo' trick ass go to the cops now?" He kicked him in the back. Richard cried out in pain; every inch of his body hurt. "Did you think they wouldn't warn me, you stupid-mindless ass? I have people everywhere! I should kill you for being stuck on stupid."

The blood he tasted in his mouth and smelled in his nose couldn't be real. Trae beating him to death couldn't be real. Him lying dying couldn't be real. This was all a bad dream. Ebony would wake him any minute and save him.

"Let me tell you how this is gonna work." Trae crouched down, leaned forward. "You listenin' to me? This is important." He pried Richard's hands from his face. "Damn, man. I let my anger control my ass on this one. I didn't mean to beat you this bad. You'd better not die on me. I have big plans."

Lightheaded, Richard knew he'd faint any second. This was real. He couldn't die and leave Ebony unprotected. His lungs burned as if he had been stabbed with a flaming knife. Inhaling was harder than inflating a balloon with a hole in it. He silently prayed for divine intervention.

"This is how we're gonna work this. You won't tell anyone about our little altercation here. I've already arranged for the police to find evidence that your attacker is one of my rivals. All you remember about your assailant is he's black and wears braids. Not nice ones like mine."

He smoothed his hands over his hair. "Frizzy, short shit, straight back, no imagination."

The lights had come back on, but Richard's world remained dark, and one of his ears rung. He strained to see. He hadn't realized eyelids could hurt so much and were so heavy.

"That's a good boy. Look at me. First you'll tell Ebony the engagement is off. She keeps the ring. You stay out of her and Crystal's lives."

Richard couldn't focus or open his eyes fully. He saw a blurry Trae and gray blotches. Staggered breath after staggered breath, he fought for life. "I…" his head barely moved side to side, but it felt like someone used it as a tennis ball at Wimbledon, "wond…oo," he drew in a breath, "et."

"The hell you won't."

Fear of death disappeared; he had to save his family. "N-no…" He used all of his strength to grab Trae's arm, scratching him in the process.

"Y-yes," mocked Trae as he brushed Richard's hand away. "You see, I'd kill you, but Ebony would eventually think I had something to do with it. This way you break up with her, and she has to move on to me."

The police could check his nails for trace evidence. He'd seen it done a million times on "Forensic Files." He relaxed and awaited death.

"I'm about to call the ambulance for you, but I need to make sure you understand this before they arrive. I know you wish you were dead, but you're not. You stay away from Ebony and don't tell anyone any of this, or I'll kill your precious grandfather."

"N-no," he forced out as he hacked up blood and wrapped his arms tighter around his body.

"Oh, yes, yes." Trae chuckled. "Tell Ebony that you needed her to believe in you. To prove I mean business, I think I'll kill those bitches you call your sisters. They both live in Chicago now."

"Pees…Tae…don…"

Trae stood. "Damn, you're lucky you're my boy. I won't kill them for now, but slip up with Ebony, and they're dead. Don't even think about contacting anyone about this. For one thing, I have everything tapped, and trust me, if you contact someone, it will get back to me, and your family will die." He reared his foot back for one last kick.

Richard could barely see Trae's foot coming toward his face. He winced and drew his arms up, but the foot never connected.

Skeet stood in the doorway. "What the hell is going on?" he snapped as he closed the door and went to Richard's aid. "Step off." He pushed Trae away. "What the hell have you done? He's our boy." He knelt beside Richard. "Don't worry, dawg." He snatched his cell phone off his belt clip.

His initial shock on seeing Skeet worn off, Trae said, "You didn't see her crying. I couldn't let him disrespect her like this." He crouched beside them. "Shit, man. I didn't mean to beat him so badly. I came to talk sense into him. He said he didn't want anything to do with Ebony. I—I snapped."

"Take your ass in the kitchen and get ice, water, towels." Richard relaxed in Skeet's arms. "Hold on, man." Skeet dialed 911 and gave them the pertinent information.

Trae walked into the kitchen, saying, "I'm going to jail for this shit. You have to take care of Ebony for me."

"Shut the hell up, and hurry with the ice." He felt Richard's lumpy face. "Damn, what the hell you hit him with? If he swells any further, I think his face will burst."

Richard could hear Skeet, but didn't have the strength to acknowledge him. He forced himself to focus. The anguish in Skeet's expression touched him. They had truly become friends.

"You'll be fine, Smoke." He rocked him. "The ambulance will be here soon."

Trae knelt beside them with a bowl of ice, a glass of water and a face towel. "I can't believe I did this, not to my boy." He dabbed the towel in water and cleaned Richard's wounds. "Shit, Skeet." He lowered his head. "I swear I didn't intend on…" He shrugged. "In a way I wanted to live through him and Ebony. He was my way of getting out, then he…We're the monsters Ebony said we'd become.

This is the second time I've done something I'll never forgive myself for."

Skeet exhaled an exasperated breath. "I understand. We have to stop this madness. Don't say anything to the police. You might get lucky, and Smoke will let this go. I wouldn't hold my breath on that one, though."

A few seconds later, Richard lost consciousness, thinking Trae, master manipulator, had won again.

Richard slowly opened his eyes and saw Skeet sitting beside his hospital bed. Fortunately, the drugs pumped into his system dulled the pain drastically. Unfortunately, they also dulled his thinking.

"Damn, Smoke. You look like shit." Skeet's face usually lit up when he smiled, not this time.

Richard chuckled, coughed, moaned.

"I know you won't believe me, but Trae's really sorry. He didn't mean to…" he trailed off. "Well, he meant to beat your ass, just not so severely. I know you don't understand our world. I'm asking you as a friend not to tell the cops. They think it was those south side punks."

Trae's threats to kill his family ran through his mind. He had to figure out a way to save Ebony without endangering the rest of his family.

"I don't blame you for being angry." Skeet scooted his chair forward, then rested his elbows on his knees. "How can I explain?" He lowered his head. "A few years ago Trae did something really jacked up to Ebony. I lost it." He ran his large hands over his braids. "I beat him so bad he was in the hospital for a week. He didn't tell the police I had done it."

"Woo swaved me," he slurred through fat, busted lips. "I wontell."

"Thanks, man." He straightened his shoulders.

Richard's vision was still blurred, but it looked as if Skeet would tear up.

"About Ebony…" Skeet cleared his throat, composed himself. "If you take her back," he walked to the window, "I promise to stay out of you all's life, and keep Trae out also." He stared out the window into the night. "I know you love her. It's her baggage you don't want." He wiped his eyes. "Damn allergies are bad this time of year."

Richard watched his big friend fighting an "allergy attack." His own eyes were watery from tears, so the allergens must have been high. He'd have to play along with Trae until he healed and calculated how to save Ebony.

Skeet returned to the chair. "When Crystal asks for us, we can meet wherever you decide. That way she won't feel like we abandoned her. Ebony never got over Dan leaving."

"No, Keet. Ahm da wan who should wheave. She es to cose to woo an Tae. I can…can…t…tahmatize her," he said slowly.

"But you love them. I see it in everything you do and say."

"Ebney will neva beweave in me like she," he drew in a few staggered breaths, "does woo an Tae." He turned his head to the side. "I don—t won her." All he could think about was the message she had left on his answering machine saying she loved him and apologizing for overreacting. How he wished he had retrieved the message sooner. Now it was too late. Trae had to be dealt with.

"You're scared and lying to yourself. You love Ebony."

"Pees, Keet. Ahm tired." He gazed into Skeet's big brown eyes, pleading for him to drop the subject.

"Get some rest. I called your family. Don't worry, I used my business voice. Your father's secretary said your parents were on some cruise, but they're on their way." He chuckled. "You should have heard me convincing Nonno to stay his old ass in Texas. He has a lot of fight in him. I know you don't want him seeing you like this." Richard's face was still swollen, black and blue, a lumpy mess.

"You have three broken ribs, all kinds of bruises and contusions, and that cast there isn't for decoration."

Richard focused on the cast around his left forearm and hand. His injuries would take weeks to heal. That would give him time to create a game plan. Skeet would protect Ebony, just as he had years ago. "Wha tom es et?"

Skeet glanced at his watch. "Almost nine."

"How wong ave I been out?"

"Since last night. Ebony still doesn't know. I'll bet she's left about a thousand messages on your service."

Ebony didn't know, but his sisters did, so why hadn't they come? Fear gripped him as echoes of Trae threatening to kill them resounded loudly in his mind. "Where's Tae?"

"With Ebony. We need to tell her soon. I just wanted to prepare you first."

"Ah don wan to see her."

A broad smile flashed across Skeet's face. "Like anyone can stop her. She will find out. Shit, you think your ass was beat. Hell naw. I'm not taking the heat for keeping news like this from her. You two love each other. Everything will work out. I think you need at least one more day. These drugs have you sounding crazy. This will give more time for some of the swelling to go down."

CHAPTER TWENTY-TWO

Trae maneuvered the truck into the hospital parking lot. "Speak to me, Ebony." Silence. "This is stupid. Why are you mad at me? Hell, if I hadn't come along, he'd probably be dead."

She tilted her head to the side. "Why didn't you tell me immediately? He needed me here!" She stuffed her fists under her armpits and stared out the window. "Just drop me at the emergency room door."

He backed her SUV into a space. "It's after visiting hours. Let me go in and make sure they'll let you see him."

"You'd better believe they'll let me see him," she snapped.

His lips thinned. "You have a lovely disposition, but I think you should calm yourself before you go into his room."

"Fine."

Richard flinched at the sight of Trae standing over him.

"Don't worry, Smoke. I just wanted to make sure you remembered our conversation before I bring Ebony in."

Richard remained silent.

"Blink once for yes, twice for no. Do you remember our conversation about your family?"

"Yes, I remember, you bastard," Richard slowly replied.

"Still talkin' shit, huh. No problem. Ebony always liked men with balls. You sound way better. Watch what you say." Trae walked out the room.

Richard pretended to be asleep when Ebony entered the hospital room. She argued in an undertone with Trae for a while. Trae wanted her to leave, but she wouldn't. Instead, she insisted he leave. She finally fell asleep leaning on Richard's bed, holding his good hand.

The room was dark except for the moonlight from the window and the hallway light seeping under the door. He caressed her hand, whispering, "I'll always love you."

She stirred, woke. "Hey, stranger. I love you." The sight of all the swelling and bruises had Ebony wanting to cry. She wondered what type of animal could do this. She found the one clear spot on his face and kissed him lightly. "I'm so sorry, Smoke. I was wrong. Please forgive me."

"I'm Richard, not Smoke."

Slapping herself inwardly, she tilted her head forward in apology. "Of course, Richard. I'll never call you Smoke again." His speech had slowed drastically, but at least he didn't sound drunk, as Skeet had informed her.

He sighed. "Thanks for the visit. I think you should leave."

Hurt, afraid of rejection, she forced a smile. "I don't mind. I want to stay with you. The man I love." Adjusting to the limited light, she strained to see past the bruises and swelling into his eyes, searching for the truth.

He closed his eyes. "I mind. It was nice while it lasted, but I want out. We made a serious mistake."

Her ears were deceiving her; this couldn't be happening. "I know I overreacted. I was embarrassed."

"I needed," he turned his head away from her. "My mother never believed in me."

"I believe in you. I'm here for you."

He caressed her hand, squeezed it gently.

As usual, his touch calmed her. The medications must have had him talking out of his mind. She patted his hand. "I'll take care of you, Richard."

"I know this is hard for you, but I…"

"Look at me, Richard. Look at me, and tell me you don't love me."

"Listen to me carefully. I need someone who, no matter how things appear, loves me enough to know my heart. I..." he trailed off. "It isn't your fault. That first day you, a stranger, showed me true kindness and acceptance. Something I'd missed in my family. I wanted it so bad. I wanted someone besides Nonno on my side."

"I am on your side."

"You're on everyone's side. Your heart is like none other, but..."

"But what?"

"We made a mistake. I wish you well in your life." He closed his eyes. "I'm too tired to argue. There's no need for you to stay."

Tears streamed down her face. "After your family arrives, I'll leave your life."

The pain on Ebony's face had hurt Richard worse than all the wounds Trae inflicted combined. He'd never forget her look of agony and confusion, or that he'd caused it. He stroked her hair. She'd fallen asleep leaning on the edge of the bed. Someday he'd make it up to her, but for now he had to play along with Trae's game. The room door creaked open. He pretended to be asleep.

"Well, what do we have here?" Bianca asked as she strode across the room, high heels clicking on the floor all the way. "Come on, Gail."

Ebony stretched. "Pardon me." She stood, straightening her jeans and blouse. "Hello, I'm Ebony Washington." She held her hand out to shake. "You must be Bianca and Gail, Richard's sisters."

Bianca placed her hands on her imaginary hips, turning her narrow nose up at Ebony. "You *are* dark, aren't you?"

Ebony frowned. "Excuse you."

"You may leave now, Elbowknee."

Gail laughed. "I know he had no intentions on marrying this one. What a cruel joke."

Richard peeked at his sisters. They were still both anorexically thin, tall for women but shorter than Ebony, had long, bleached blonde hair, and were bitches. Ebony looked as if she was praying for patience.

"How was your flight, ladies? Will your parents be arriving soon?"

"We live in Chicago," Bianca said.

"What?"

"Yes, we live in Chicago. You didn't actually believe he wanted to marry you, did you?" Gail asked. "Oh please, he'd take you to bed, but that's about it." She giggled. "And these *hoodrats* are supposed to be so street smart."

Pimp-slapping his sisters into purgatory seemed like a good idea to Richard. Remaining silent while they belittled Ebony killed him slowly, but it would work in his favor.

Ebony gritted her teeth, softly counted to a hundred by tens, then glared into Bianca's cold black eyes. "When were you notified Richard was in the hospital?"

Bianca seemed tongue tied, so Gail answered, "Some jerk had the audacity to wake me at two in the morning talking about it was an emergency. Last I checked, we're not doctors. What could we do?"

"Wait a second. You were informed two days ago and you're just coming in today? Aw, hell naw!"

Richard had to watch. He'd never heard Ebony curse. She stood with her back to him, hands on her hips, neck twisting, railing at his sisters. He loved every second of it.

"...You want audacity. Let me tell you about audacity. A few nights ago, at two o'clock, Richard almost died, and his *loving family* was nowhere in sight. Not because they didn't know, or they were too far away to see him. That would be too much like right. Nope, nope, no. His loving family didn't come because they don't exist, and the family he does have never gave a damn.

"You are two cruel, heartless, mean-spirited, unhappy, evil wastes of human flesh. You tormented Richard so badly as a child he still has nightmares to this day. Why are you here now? Not for his well-being."

"You can't speak to us like this," Bianca interrupted. "Who do you think you are?"

"No need to think about it. I'll tell you exactly who I am. I'm the dark-skinned hoodrat that will put her foot up your ass if she hears you upset Richard in any way, shape or form!"

"What's all the noise?"

Everyone jumped at Trae's sudden entrance. The sisters backed away. Richard pretended to be asleep.

"I'm ready to leave now." Ebony gently brushed her lips over Richard's. "Goodbye," she whispered.

Comfort and the hospital lounge chair were mortal enemies. Skeet twisted and turned his large body, finally giving up. Ebony was still with Richard, Trae had disappeared and Skeet wanted sleep.

He took the cheap leatherlike cushions off the chairs and love seats, then scooted one of the love seats and end tables away from the wall. *Damn, they need to dust back here.* He placed his temporary bed behind the love seat frame, stretched his long body out and drifted into sleep. The sound of a woman's heels clicking against the hospital floor woke him a short time later.

"Stop pulling on me, Steph," Nonno demanded as they entered the lounge. She'd been acting strange—stranger than usual—ever since he insisted on accompanying them to Chicago.

Stephanie released her father's arm. "I'm sorry, Papà. I just wanted to…" She covered her mouth with her hands. "I'm sorry."

He hugged his daughter. "Don't worry, baby. Richard will be fine."

"I need to ask you something, but I don't want to hurt you."

"Stephanie, my patience has worn thin."

"Papà. I love you. You've always been my hero."

Sorry he had spoken so harshly, he softened. "You're my baby." He caressed her face. "Don't be afraid. Tell Papà what's bothering you." He glanced at Phillip, who looked as confused as Nonno felt.

She lowered her head. "I'm Richard's mother, and have to do what's best for my son. Would you please not tell people…" She lifted her head. Tears streamed down her face. "Don't tell them you're his grandfather."

"What?" he snapped.

"Stephanie!" Phillip spun her around to face him. "What are you saying?"

She turned back to her father. "I'm sorry, Papà, but I can't allow the same thing that happened to me to happen to Richard. He could die. If the doctors find out about you, they won't give Richard the best treatment. Please, Papà." She hugged him tightly. "I love you so much. Please understand. I'm not ashamed of you. I love you. You're my papà. You're my hero."

Nonno gently rocked his daughter, trying to alleviate her fear. The way she paraded him around, there was no way she could be ashamed of him. "Who hurt you, Steph?" Her treatment of Richard finally made sense.

He stepped out of denial. She wouldn't allow the child to play outside. He had convinced himself she wanted pretty little girls that sat around the house, but in his heart he knew she didn't want Richard to appear any darker. Unlike his sisters, Richard had been born with an olive complexion, and darkened quickly in the sunlight.

When Richard went through the finding-his-black-self stage in college, Nonno thought it was hilarious. Especially since Richard was an Italian-American, not African-American. Stephanie almost had a heart attack, literally. Richard only hung out with black students. He minored in African-American studies. He felt comfortable in the culture.

"I love you, Papà."

"I'll always love you, Steph. I just want to understand. I need for you to tell me what happened." He held her hand and led her to the lounge chairs. He frowned. Some idiot had taken most of the cushions. He guided her to a seat, then pulled around an upright chair for himself. Phillip stood by silently.

He took her hands into his, warming them. "You're trembling."

"Don't hate me, Papà."

"I love you." He fingered her graying shoulder-length hair behind her ear. "Tell me what happened." After high school she had decided her accent wasn't cute any longer so worked to lose it. She had told him others wouldn't accept her unless she sounded and acted American. It hurt him that she chose this strange culture over his, but he eventually accepted her choices. She had never said a word to him about his color being an issue. He worried she had been protecting him all of these years.

"We can't remain silent any longer, Steph. The family is a mess: my granddaughters barely acknowledge me or their brother, my grandson is in the hospital fighting for his life and has never felt he fit in, my daughter's afraid people will find out she's…"

"No," she cut in. "I'm not afraid people will know you're my father. I'm proud of you. Always have been."

"I know. What I don't know is what happened."

Phillip knelt beside the pair. "Stephanie has always been proud of her papà. During college, she bragged about you all the time and showed your letters to her friends. The girls were jealous of Stephanie. She was beautiful, smart. Her being Italian made her more exotic. They used to tease her about her accent."

"That's why you worked at losing your accent," Nonno said.

She slowly nodded yes.

Phillip continued, "Lucy wanted to knock Stephanie down a few pegs. One time Lucy said Stephanie was lying, and that you didn't own restaurants all over the world. She said Stephanie had just capitalized off a common Italian name and written the letters herself. Of course, Stephanie had to prove Lucy wrong. A week or so later we all dressed in evening attire and drove from Boston to your restaurant in New York.

"Lucy knew Stephanie was about to make a big fool of herself. You see, Stephanie had insisted we not make reservations." He shrugged. "I have to admit, I thought we would be turned away. Pacini's was a five-star restaurant before they had five stars. None of us could afford Pacini's. You had to make reservations at least a week in advance. I knew Stephanie was a relation, but thought she was embellishing about her father being the owner."

"Phillip, how could you?" Stephanie snapped.

He patted her hand. "Darling, everyone in our circle stretched the truth concerning their father's wealth. We all wanted to be Rockefellers or Vanderbilts." He faced Nonno. "When we walked into the restaurant, the staff knew Stephanie. They fawned all over *Miss Pacini*, tripping over themselves to serve her. They asked how her father liked California, and made our whole group feel welcome."

Nonno chuckled. "My baby the show-off."

"Well, I had to teach them a lesson, Papà." Her smile faded. "I didn't understand. I mean, I knew how blacks were treated, but that wasn't my life. We're Italian."

"I asked Stephanie to marry me. She said she wouldn't without your blessing. She called and asked for you to come over for Easter break. In true Stephanie style, she paraded you all over the place."

Her smile lit her whole face up. "You were so handsome, Papà. I felt like royalty having you at my side." She lowered her head. "After you left, things changed. My friends, except Phillip, started acting funny. When I finally confronted them, they said I should have told them I was a nigger. I was so confused."

Phillip continued on her behalf. "At the time she didn't understand that to our snobbish friends, black was black. They treated her miserably."

"I'd always been Italian, and even when I was working to sound American, I knew I'd always be Italian. The people I thought were my friends called me names and treated me like a criminal."

"Oh, baby." Nonno embraced his daughter. "That was forty years ago, Steph. Times have changed."

"The type of people I went to school with are now the heads of companies Richard has to work for. The doctors that should be saving him."

"Why didn't you tell me?"

Her grin drew his mind back to her mischievous teen years. "Because you would have come ready to fight for your daughter's honor. I was getting married, and never had to see them again." She had married over the summer and didn't finish school.

"You're going to therapy."

"What? I don't need therapy."

He raised a brow. Her expression made her look closer to six than sixty years old. "Are you talking back to me?"

"No, sir."

He rubbed her back. "After you've had a few sessions, I'll go also if it will help. Right now you need to go see your son."

"Aren't you coming?"

"Of course. I just need a few minutes alone." Nonno didn't know what to do about Stephanie or Richard. He had condemned Phillip for ignoring Richard's suffering, yet he'd done the same thing with his child. And Richard...*I almost got my grandson killed.*

At a loss, the only thing he was clear on was he would never forgive himself.

CHAPTER TWENTY-THREE

Trae stood in the doorway of Ebony's room, watching her work diligently at the computer. In the month since Richard's unfortunate mishap, she had continued with business as usual. Well, almost. Her fire was gone, and she was always on the defensive. Helping her get over Richard was more difficult than he thought it would be.

"Where's Crystal?" Ebony had asked him if she could adopt Crystal. He explained that he had made a mistake asking Richard to adopt her. He was her father, and couldn't give up custody. She didn't take his explanation well, and while she had started speaking to him again, the hostility remained.

"Skeet took her with him to visit Richard."

He cursed under his breath for his miscalculation. Richard cooperated, but Skeet kept the door open. "I'm worried about you." She ignored him and continued working.

"Look at me, Ebony."

"I'm busy, Trae."

"Ever since you broke up with Smoke, all you do is work, work, work. You're burning yourself out."

"I took Crystal to see a movie yesterday."

He held his hands up slightly. "I stand corrected. You work, work, work, take care of Crystal, work, work, work. You're a mess. When's the last time you went to the gym, ate a good meal; hell, fixed your hair?"

"I cook for Crystal daily. My aerobics class was a twelve-week course, not sixteen, and a ponytail has always been my preferred style."

"I know you. You're hiding from your feelings. When's the last time you walked the neighborhood? Hell, it's spring. Your favorite time of year. There are flowers all over the damned place, the trees are blooming, but this place looks like a morgue. This isn't like you. Why are you shutting me out? I'm here for you."

"Men." She continued editing her report.

How could he be the shoulder she'd lean on if she wouldn't open up to him? He buried his frustration in exchange for love, care, patience and a bit of cunning. He knelt beside her. "You're hiding your pain behind your responsibilities. No matter what happens, we've always been friends. I can't stand by and allow you to close yourself off from the world."

She sighed, stopped typing and slowly turned to him. "I truly appreciate what you're trying to do. I'm fine. Honestly."

"How can you be fine when the man you love walked out of your life? You can't tell me you aren't affected."

"What do you suggest I do? Beg him to take me back? Stop living my life? Yes, I love Richard, and I'm hurt. But you know what? I'll survive, just as I did when you broke my heart. I've learned from my mistakes. It's time to move on."

Stunned by her response, as well as the harsh tone, he was at a loss for words. He quickly searched his mind for a new angle.

"Are you finished?" she asked. "I have work to do."

"You've been done with your thesis since December. You're hiding behind the computer screen, making excuses to avoid people. This snappy, bitchy woman that's been here these past few weeks isn't you."

"Yes, I handed in my thesis to the committee, but I still have an important presentation in a few days." She saved her work, then shut down the computer. "Okay. Let's get this over with." She turned, giving him her undivided attention. "I'll give you one night to play Mr. Psychology. After tonight, the subject of my love life is closed. Deal?"

"Deal." They moved to the living room couch.

"So how do you want to do this?" she asked.

"I want for you to stop being so damn hostile."

"I'm sorry." She drew her legs up, then leaned her body against the armrest of the couch. "I shouldn't take my bad mood out on you."

"You're always in a bad mood. Closing yourself off from everyone isn't working. It's time to try something different. We'll always be friends. Let me be here for you." As of late, she always looked worn out. He moved to her end of the couch, drawing her into his arms so she'd rest on his chest. As she relaxed her weight on him and softly cried, he knew she'd be his again.

"It's all right. Let it all out." He rocked her slowly, allowing her to finish her cry.

After she quieted, he asked, "What did you learn from our relationship?"

At first he thought she wouldn't answer, then she finally said, "That being in love isn't enough. I thought because we loved each other, we could conquer the world. It didn't matter that your life wasn't headed in the direction I wanted to go. Nothing mattered but the love we had for each other."

"I screwed up, and you changed your mind."

"I'm not stupid, Trae. I knew about the other women. Yes, I was embarrassed when I was confronted, but I had always known."

"Why did you change your mind?"

"I loved you, but I discovered I love myself more. Women accusing me of taking food out of the mouths of their children was not what I wanted out of life, but a wake up call. I never wanted to run in the drug world. We wanted to move in different directions, so why was I following you?"

He listened closely. He had changed directions, and would prove it to her. He stroked her back, encouraging her to continue.

"When you gave me Crystal, I had to grow up. I decided what I wanted, how I would get there and worked toward my goals. Don't take my Independent Woman card away, but it's been a lonely journey. I want to share my life with someone."

"What kind of man do you want?"

"Ooh, goin' in for the kill tonight. I didn't think he existed until I bumped into him on the train."

Trae regrouped. Listening to her sing Richard's praises was the last thing he wanted to hear. He hoped she'd give him some useful insight to use. "What was your mistake with Smoke?"

"I've been thinking about this since I visited him at the hospital. At the time I didn't see it, but now it's crystal clear. Rome wasn't built in a day."

"What?"

"You heard right. I thought I had met the man of my dreams. Instead of taking time to develop our relationship, I skipped steps so I could have the life I always wanted. I tried to build Rome in a day."

"You did your part. It's Smoke who messed things up."

"We both rushed into the relationship, needing something we thought the other could provide, telling ourselves it was love at first sight. We both rushed to make the family we always wanted. When our relationship was tried, we found out we didn't really know each other. Richard needed someone who believed in him. It took me days to realize something that if I had known him, I would have realized in seconds."

He didn't agree with her assessment of the situation at all. He knew she spoke out of pain. He needed to make his move before she began thinking clearly again. "Every couple fights. He ran out without trying to work it through. He gave up before he gave it a chance."

"He needed time to cool off and regroup, just as I did when I found out you were about to become a baby daddy and was selling drugs. I'm sure he reevaluated our relationship. Did he want a woman who didn't believe in him, in hopes that she would have faith in him someday? Is that what he wanted out of life? He was at the crossroad I was at years ago with you. Then the realities of my world were literally beat into him. I know I said we could talk about this all night, but I'm tired."

"Some day you'll love again."

"Love's highly overrated. My next relationship will be a business deal. Where are marriages arranged these days, India?"

"Can I pick him out?"

"I think I might be onto something here."

Confident he would win her back, he wrapped his arm around her.

Trae thumbed through the pages of the photo album Ebony had given him for Christmas. If everything went according to plan, he'd have his happy family, but he needed to work quickly. The doorbell rang. He set the album on his new glass coffee table, then answered the door.

"Come on in, Skeet." He stepped to the side. "Why are you wearing a suit? Did someone die?" He closed the door, then returned to his seat.

"I always wear a suit to the hospital."

"Why?"

"I didn't want to scare Richard's family to death. I told them I'm a professional football player."

Trae laughed. "You are out of your mind. How is he?"

"His grandfather's taking him back to Texas for a sabbatical of sorts."

Turning cartwheels inwardly, looking saddened and concerned outwardly, Trae said, "Follow him to Texas and convince him to take Ebony back. She's miserable without him."

"Why the hell you think I've been taking Crystal to see him? Damn!" He kicked at the table, then leaned back in the recliner. "If he believed his lame-assed excuse for their break-up, I'd have a chance."

"What do you mean?"

"He loves Ebony. He knows she believes in him."

"So why doesn't his trick ass tell her? This is jacked the hell up. If he loved her, he'd tell her."

"He's scared. I see it in his eyes. His fear keeps him away." He smoothed his hands over his braids. "This is some stupid assed shit. They love each other."

Trae rubbed a kink out of his neck. Soon Ebony would love him. All he needed was time to show her he was what she really wanted. But first he needed to finish his snow job on Skeet. "Why the hell did I go over there?"

"It's too late now."

"I feel like shit."

"Good. This is all your fault. I should tell her you're the one who beat Smoke."

"No!" His mind ran faster than the speed of light. "She'll never let me see Crystal again. Hell, Ebony still has scars from when Marissa kicked Dan out of their lives. Don't do this to Crystal."

"Calm the hell down. I already thought of that. Smoke and Ebony will survive. I'm staying quiet for Crystal."

An awkward silence filled the room.

"There's been something I've been meaning to talk to you about, but you've been busy with Smoke," Trae mumbled.

"What?"

"I'm getting out."

"Out of what?"

"The drug life. Damn! You ain't smoking that shit, are you?"

"Ebony won't fall out of love with Smoke for you because you leave the drug life."

"For a second I considered staying in, because I knew you'd think I'm doing this to win Ebony back. I realized that's some stupid elementary school shit. Hell, I'm a grown-assed man. I shouldn't have to lead a life I no longer want because *you* think I have ulterior motives. I've been wanting out for over a year now. After the way I acted with Smoke, I know I need out before it's too late."

"You're serious, aren't you?"

"Dead serious."

Skeet's deep, hearty laugh filled the room. "What the hell is this world coming to? I've been wanting out also. I can't believe I'm saying this, but I want kids of my own. Kids I don't have to give back. I want a family."

Trae held his hand out to his friend. "I guess we've both finally grown up." They did a quick brotha shake, then settled in their seats.

"We can't both cut out now, though," Skeet said.

"I know."

"You've had this on your mind longer than me. I'll finish up our business."

"You don't have to do this."

"One of us has to minimize the war we're about to start. In a few months, we'll both be free."

"I don't want you telling Ebony. She'll think I'm getting out to chase after her. I love Ebony, but I'm doing this for me." He knew Skeet couldn't keep his mouth shut. By the end of the day, Ebony would begin realizing that he was the new and improved man of her dreams.

"I ain't sayin' shit."

"Remember that row of condos I showed you over by Chinatown? I bought them. I had planned on giving them to Ebony as a wedding gift. I figured if they ever divorced, she'd have property of her own. Now that I'm getting out, I want her out of the neighborhood. I can't keep her safe. Do you think she'll take an early graduation gift?"

"She's so funny. You'd better make sure she knows they come from legit channels. Give me a few minutes. I'll think of something. How are you gonna clean up your businesses?"

"Dan's been helping me for the past year."

"Your ass really was serious. Damn, dawg, I'm sorry I doubted you." He fidgeted in his seat. "Dan's been helping me tie up loose ends for the past few months," he lied. "At least we were smart enough to clean the money as we received it. Think of the mess we'd be in now if we didn't." He picked up the album and flipped through the pages. "If you tell Ebony Crystal's in danger, she'll move. The only problem is money. She doesn't have any."

Trae smiled. Having Skeet think he came up with the idea to move Ebony away from her family and friends was brilliant. "She decided to take the job with Banks Consulting. They offer a sign-on bonus. I'm sure I can convince her new boss to slide her a few extra thousand."

"Sounds like a good plan." He stretched his long legs out. "I'm not stupid, you know."

Trae choked on the lump of anxiety caught in his throat. "What are you talking about?"

"You've been after Ebony since y'all were shorties. Here you are changing your life around. You're becoming the man she's always wanted. You expect me to believe you won't go after her?"

Trae smoothed the imaginary wrinkles out of his jersey. "I've never hidden my feelings for Ebony. I've also always done my own thing in spite of those feelings." He was relieved to see Skeet nod in agreement. "Do I want Ebony? Hell yeah! But I'm still gonna do my do. She has to accept me as I am, just as I've accepted her."

"Damn. That's some deep shit there." He stood to leave.

"Don't tell Ebony my plans. She doesn't need anything else put on her plate. I'll tell her after I've arranged for her to receive a nice-sized sign-on bonus."

"I know when to shut my mouth."

CHAPTER TWENTY-FOUR

The aroma of rosemary and other herbs wafted from the kitchen as Ebony stirred the simmering chicken quarters.

"Would you cut the onions for me, Skeet?" He washed his hands and took a chopping board and knife to the table. He had been visibly upset all afternoon. "You've barely said a word today. What's wrong?" She diced tomatoes.

After a long silence, he said, "I have a lot on my mind."

"Such as?"

"I can't tell."

"Oh, I see. It's work." Disheartened, she scooped up the tomato pieces and placed them into a bowl. At least Meechie had agreed to speak with one of the counselors from the rehabilitation center. Now all she had to do was beg Dan for the money to pay for the program she prayed Meechie would agree to attend.

"Cut the onion into wide strips, please." She started dicing another tomato. "I want to apologize for how I've been acting lately. I know I haven't been the most pleasant person to be around."

"No problem."

"I'm worried about you, Skeet. I've never seen you so withdrawn."

He chopped the onion in half, quarters, eighths…The pieces got smaller and smaller as he kept whacking away.

"Pretty soon I'll have onion juice instead of slices." She waited for him to crack a smile, but it never came. She took his chopping board over to the stove and scraped the chopped onion into the stew-pot.

He took the potato peeler, pulled the trashcan between his legs, and began peeling carrots. "I'm angry at Trae."

"Why?"

"I thought we told each other everything. I found out he's been keeping a big secret from me. Now I'm pissed. He doesn't trust me."

"Of course he trusts you. You just seem to think everyone else's business is yours."

"But this directly affects me."

She diced tomatoes. "Well, how did you find out about this secret?"

"He told me."

"Skeet!" She threw a half tomato at him. He ducked. The tomato whizzed past his head and splattered against the edge of the counter, ending up on the floor. "How is he keeping secrets from you if he told you? Stop being a baby. People talk in their own time, not yours."

He finally flashed a smile. "You'd better clean that up before Marissa gets home. He should have told me sooner."

"Why don't you ask him why he didn't tell you sooner, instead of coming here pouting?" She tossed the tomato into the trash, and then sponge-cleaned the mess on the counter and floor.

"Because I already know why. I just don't agree with it. I'm his best friend and business partner. He's been preparing to leave our business for over a year, and only told me because he had to. What kind of crap is that?" He bit off a piece of carrot. "How can he hold out on me?" He was too busy rambling to notice Ebony was bending over the sink, shocked. He continued gnawing on the carrot.

It took Ebony a few moments to process his words. She shouldn't have been shocked. She had noticed the gradual changes in Trae herself, yet was afraid to believe. But Trae actually taking steps to leave the drug life was big news. She bowed, silently thanking God for the miracle, and prayed Skeet would be next. This must have been the reason he said he wouldn't allow her to adopt Crystal. He was actually going to be legit. She and Crystal would be free.

"Well he didn't tell me, either. He only hinted around."

"Ebony." He blew out a long, labored breath. "Could you stop thinking about yourself for five damn minutes? Shit, woman, this is about me!"

She sat at the table, fighting to keep from laughing. Skeet needed her to be serious, but she couldn't hold it in. She leaned back in the chair and laughed so hard her stomach hurt. She could barely catch her breath.

"This shit ain't funny."

"I know." She giggled. "I'm sorry." She rounded the table and hugged him. "I love you, Skeet. If you weren't my cousin, I would marry you."

He chuckled. "Well, I wouldn't marry you. I can't stand self-centered people." He tapped her nose with his knuckle. "I'm overreacting, ain't I?"

"And being melodramatic. Why didn't Trae want to tell you what he's been up to?"

He smiled peevishly. "Because he thinks I talk too much. He doesn't understand that it's not what ya say, but who ya say it to. I know who I can say what to. I don't just go blabbing all over the place. If I did, we'd of been dead years ago."

"Why doesn't he want me to know?"

"I don't know. I think he doesn't want to get your hopes up. He could always change his mind. Then there's your safety. We've made a lot of enemies, and some in the organization won't want him to leave. The only way to control Trae is through you and Crystal."

A chill ran down her spine. "I've always feared someone would come after us. I'm so tired of all of this, tired of being scared."

"I've got your back. I won't let anyone harm my family."

"I know you keep us safe. But the reason the protection is needed…I shouldn't have to live like this." She diced another tomato. Trae held all the cards, and made the rules to the game. She didn't want to celebrate Trae's conversion to a legit life too soon, just to be disappointed. "I'll be glad when this is all over. When are you getting out?"

"I'm not. If Trae says I am, he's wrong. I lied and told him I was leaving to make him think I'd kept secrets also." He paused. "At least I was sort of lying. I've been thinking about getting out, but I haven't acted on it."

"Don't worry. Your secret's safe with me. Unlike you, I don't have a big mouth." She winked, transferring the diced tomatoes to a bowl. She took the bowl over to the stove and dumped the tomatoes into the pot. "You talk entirely too much."

"I do not. I know you won't tell anyone what I say. You should feel honored I trust you so much."

She bowed slightly. "I'm honored. Now finish with the carrots."

He peeled more carrots. "I know things that…oh, never mind." He kept glancing over his shoulder at her, as if he wanted her to ask him something. "Is this enough?"

"Yep. Chop them into wedges and dump them into the pot. Nah, make them thin slices. They'll have to cook fast. I should have put them in the pot earlier." She took a bag of fresh spinach leaves out of the refrigerator and dumped them into the sink for cleaning.

"Don't you want to know one of the things I haven't told?"

"Not if I have to pry it out of you." She turned on the faucet and ran cold water over the spinach.

A few minutes later, he put the carrots into the pot. "Where's the ladle?"

She pointed at the far drawer. "Could you also take out the tongs and remove the meat from the bones?"

"I overheard something I shouldn't have. They didn't know I was in the room."

"How can anyone miss seeing you?"

"I'd fallen asleep on the floor behind the sofa."

She opened a jar of macaroni shells.

"No one knows I overheard." Skeet stirred the soup as she poured in the shells. He proceeded to give her a word-by-word replay of Nonno and Stephanie's conversation.

"Oh, my goodness. Poor Richard." She didn't know what to do. She wanted to help him, but he would refuse her help. She added the spinach to the pot, then sat at the table trying to think clearly. "Does he know?"

"Pay attention to the conversation, Ebony. I haven't told anyone. He has no idea why his mother's so batty. At least he won't admit it. I've watched them for the past few weeks. He knows. They all know." He shrugged. "It's the strangest thing. The Stephanie I heard crying to her father is not the cold bitch I heard nagging at Richard. Phillip stays out of the line of fire. And Nonno. Well, all I can say is that man's a trip. And don't get me started on those bitches he calls sisters."

Ebony remembered Richard saying his family life was like a Broadway production. She had tried to get him to open up about them several times, but he had always changed the subject or started cooking. "I wish there was something I could do to help him."

"Call him." He took out his cell phone. "It's number three on speed dial."

"He doesn't want me to."

"That never stopped me."

"I'm not you." She turned away from Skeet to hide her tears. "Crystal will be home soon."

"Changing the subject doesn't change anything. You two are in love with each other."

She wiped away her tears. "Well, love isn't enough." She walked out of the room.

Richard sat in the rocking chair, absently watching the couple who lived in the ranch-style town house across the street from Nonno. The separation from Ebony was killing him. He couldn't stand her thinking he didn't want her. Skeet had continued bringing Crystal around. This had to tell Ebony he still wanted to be in the picture.

A few days ago, when he arrived in Texas, he hired a private investigator to find indisputable evidence that Trae killed the Collins boys. Once he had the evidence, he would tell his family the truth so they could leave the country until Trae was arrested.

He prayed the investigator found evidence before Trae had time to manipulate Ebony into taking him back. If Ebony felt even half as discombobulated as Richard, she would be easy pickings for Trae.

The older couple across the street slowly rocked on the porch swing. "That will be us someday, Ebony."

"Who are you talking to?" Nonno walked across the bedroom with two large bowls and a paper grocery bag.

"No one."

"You need to contact Ebony and tell her the truth." He sat on the edge of the bed. "Get on over here and help me with these string beans. My hands have been hurting me."

He chose to ignore Nonno's remark. The man had been itching for a fight ever since he found out Richard would fully recover. "You don't even like green beans. I think they're the one food you hate."

"Well, you and Stephanie love them."

Richard took the bowls and bag from his grandfather. He set the empty bowl on the floor to his right, the paper bag to the left, and the bowl of green beans in his lap. "You spoil us. I'll do the cooking while I'm down here."

"You trying to force me into retirement?" He moved from the bed to the straight-back chair from the desk. "That's much better. I'm too old for this."

"You're not old." He snapped the ends off a bean, broke the bean in half, tossed it into the empty bowl at his side and the ends into the paper bag. Cast removed, it felt good to use his left hand again.

"You're making me old. Apologize to Ebony, leave the country, get married, and make me some great-grandbabies."

"It isn't that simple." He hadn't told his grandfather about Trae's threats against the family, or that Ebony didn't have legal custody of Crystal.

"The hell it isn't. What are you scared of, Richard?"

"Nothin'." Unable to stand Nonno's penetrating gray stare, he snapped the beans faster. "I'm not ready for a commitment right now."

"Don't hand me that bull. Your mother isn't around. It's just us. I'm sorry I told you to bring the cops into this. I'll never forgive my…You're miserable. Hiding from problems never works out in the end. We have to face this head on. Be straight with me. What's going on? You love Ebony. I've seen you with Crystal. How can you walk away? What aren't you telling me?"

"You don't understand."

"Explain it to me." The snap, snap, snap of the beans was the only sound in the room. "I know you, Richard. That cock-and-bull story you gave us about Ebony not having faith in you didn't pass the smell test. Trae's the one who beat you, isn't he? He somehow found out about the police."

"No. That's not it."

"Get your head out of that bowl, look me in the eyes and tell me Trae didn't beat you. Tell me he isn't keeping you from Ebony. Tell me you're not in love with her."

The lie sat on the tip of his tongue, but he couldn't force it out. "Nonno, please just drop it."

"You could've been killed. I will not drop this."

"Yes you will!" He stood, knocking the bowl of green beans to the floor. He dragged his hands down his face. "I'm sorry I yelled at you, but you will not interfere." He knelt at his grandfather's feet. "I know what I'm doing. This is my fight."

Nonno's face softened. He patted Richard on the shoulder. "I'm proud of you."

"For what, disrespecting you?" He picked a few beans off the floor and tossed them into the bowl. "Making a mess of my life?"

"For finally standing up to me. My fighting your battles almost got you killed. I'll never forgive myself. You're a man. I should have let you be a man. Trae isn't the only thing keeping you from Ebony. You need to stop bickering with your mother about this superficial stuff and get at the real issue. Stand up to her, and let the pieces fall where they will. You can't build a future with Ebony when you're stuck in the past."

Richard sat with his legs crossed on the floor. "How'd you get so wise?"

"A wise man would have acknowledged his daughter's pain years ago."

"What are you talking about?"

"Take the blinders off. Don't be afraid to face the truth. Speak with your mother. She'll always love you." He walked out.

Richard leaned back against the bed, searching within himself for the feelings he had buried: The ones that were emerging in the dreams; the ones that hurt too badly to acknowledge; the ones he needed to confront in order to have a real future with Ebony.

He picked the remaining string beans off the floor, wandering what Ebony was doing. *I miss my angel.*

CHAPTER TWENTY-FIVE

A few weeks later.

Instead of moping around, wallowing in self-pity, Ebony focused on the positives in her life: She only had one day of class left; she had accepted the position at Banks Consulting, and she received a larger bonus than expected; Crystal was happy; Meechie agreed to enter rehabilitation; Trae was making major strides toward turning his life around, and Skeet was on the brink of turning over a new leaf.

Trae looked up from the chess game he was playing with Crystal. "Well, look who's actually smiling. Welcome back."

"I'll have you know I've been smiling quite a bit all afternoon. Skeet kept me entertained while I prepared roast."

"Don't tell me you let him touch my food. What were you thinking?"

Crystal moved her bishop across the game board, capturing Trae's king. "I win!"

His jaw dropped. "Why, you little cheat." He picked up the offending bishop. "A few moves ago this thing went straight. Now you have it going diagonal. She's cheating, Ebony."

She leaned over the board, quickly assessing the situation. "Crystal, how did you end up with both of your bishops on black?"

"If you ain't cheatin', you ain't tryin'," Crystal boasted.

"What a crock of crap. Who told you that?" Trae asked.

"John at school." She set the board up for another game.

"He's an idiot. Don't listen to him." He tapped his Rolex. "It's almost eight. You need to start your bath."

"Oh, no. I forgot to call Smoke! I promised Skeet I would call him every night. Mama, can I call now? I'm sure he's not in bed yet."

Ebony suddenly had a tremendous headache. She would deal with Skeet, but first she needed to placate Crystal.

"That's a long-distance call," Trae said. "Those are extremely expensive. I'm sure Smoke will understand if you wait until he returns."

"I'll be right back." Crystal ran off to her bedroom.

"Thanks, Trae. I thought with Richard out of town she would have more time to…"

Crystal ran into the room and stood in front of Ebony. "Skeet gave me this." She held out a small cell phone.

Anger built within Ebony, but she tried to remain calm. "You're too young for a cell phone, darling. Skeet should have asked me first."

"But this isn't a real cell phone. It only calls you, Trae, Skeet, Granny, Uncle Dan, and Smoke. It's a phone for kids, and the calls are free." She pointed to the seven. "All I do is hold down the seven and Smoke's phone rings. I call him every day. You're number two, Mama."

Strangling Skeet was not an option. *Maybe a slow poison.* "Trae, would you start her bath? I have a call of my own to make. Only ten minutes, Crystal." She went into her bedroom, dialing Skeet's number on her cell phone.

"How could you?" she snapped at Skeet over the line, closing the door behind her.

He calmly replied, "Hello. This is Ebony. May I speak to Skeet? Or, since this is my private line, hello, Skeet. Now hang up and try again." He hung up on her.

She mumbled a few expletives under her breath and prayed for strength. She redialed. "Hello, Skeet, this is Ebony," she said calmly.

"Oh yes, I like this sweet, polite woman much better."

"Why, thank you." Maintaining her cool veneer, she continued, "If you pull any of that manipulative phone crap you did with Crystal again, I'll cut you out of our lives completely." She disconnected, tossed the phone on the computer desk, grabbed her pillow and sprawled out on the bed.

A few moments later the phone's ringer played Beethoven's "Fifth Symphony." Unable to deal with Skeet, she ignored it.

Trae came into the room, picked up the phone and answered it. "What?"

"You're not Ebony," Skeet said.

He frowned. "I know I'm not Ebony. What the hell you want?"

"I called Ebony's phone because I want to speak to *Ebony*."

"Well if she wanted to speak with you, she would have answered the damn phone herself. Now what the hell possessed you to give Crystal a cell phone? She's only seven. And how the hell you gonna tell her to call Smoke?"

"I'm taking care of business."

"You need to take care of your own business and step out of ours. Don't make me put my foot up your ass."

"What the…You threatening me? Aw, hell naw! I have something for your ass." He hung up.

Trae pinched the bridge of his nose with his thumb and index finger. "Shit." Disconnected. "Skeet's on his way over."

"Oh, great. Just what I need. Clash of the titans. Hand me the phone." He handed over the phone. She dialed for reinforcements. "Hello, Auntie Genevieve, it's Ebony. I have a favor to ask. Would you please call your son? He's on his way over here to cause trouble with Trae. I'm not in the mood for him tonight. Thanks." She disconnected and tossed the phone to the side.

Trae sat on the edge of the bed. "Don't be too angry at him. His heart's in the right place."

"Weren't you just threatening to put your foot somewhere not too pleasant?"

He chuckled. "I'm just protecting my girls."

She smiled, then sobered. "I don't know what to do. Richard's leaving was the perfect opportunity for him to back out of Crystal's life. By the time he returned, she wouldn't ask for him as much. But Skeet's been interfering this whole time."

"I can't believe she was asking for him. That has Skeet written all over it. I'll talk to him. He's making this harder on Crystal, not easier."

"I agree. I can't just cut Richard out of her life, but I don't want to encourage their relationship."

"It'll all work out. I hate to rush off, but I'm heading to Genevieve's."

"She can handle Skeet. Give him more time to cool off."

"He won't be cooling off anytime soon."

She watched him fidget with the crease in his jeans. He looked as though he had just been caught drinking milk out of the carton. The more she thought about it, the more shocked she was he hadn't confided in Skeet. Skeet wouldn't have told if Trae had been upfront.

"I did something really screwed up to Skeet. I mean really jacked the hell up."

"Skeet's been moping for weeks. Don't let this get out of hand. Go apologize."

"He knows I'm sorry."

"I know Crystal loves me, but it always feels good to hear her say it. What did you do?" She opened the door for him to tell her he was going legit and waited for him to walk through. She would never be truly free of the drug world until he went legit, went to jail, or died.

"You've been through enough these past few weeks. I won't put more on you. Let's just say I was trying to do the right thing, but ended up doing wrong in the process. Something I definitely had no call to do. I'm off to apologize. What are you doing after class tomorrow?"

"I'll be here cooking dinner."

"Call me when class let's out. I'll pick you up. I need to talk to you about something. I'm off to straighten things out with Skeet. I'll ask Marissa to watch Crystal." He kissed her on the cheek and left.

She found her cell phone and dialed Skeet's number. "Hello, Skeet."

"How you gonna sic my mom on me?"

She sat in the computer chair, laughing. "You made me do it. I won't tolerate you and Trae fighting."

"I was totally out of line for giving Crystal the cell phone. I'll discontinue the service tomorrow. Ever since Smoke was hurt, I've been trippin'. I'm just trying to set things right."

"I know you were only trying to help, but I have this under control." She prayed she sounded more confident than she felt. The more she thought about Richard, the more she wanted to confront him. He said he needed someone who would believe in him no matter what, and she did.

"He loves you, Ebony."

"Maybe he does, but love isn't enough. He's made his decision, and we have to live with it. Love isn't enough…"

"So what are you going to do?"

"Provide a safe and loving environment to raise my child in."

"What about falling in love?"

"Love hurts too much. I've been down that road twice now. I'm a slow learner, but not that slow."

His low rumble laugh came over the phone line, warming her heart. "Yeah, right. You're slow, and I don't talk too much. But you're wrong about something."

"Well, no one's perfect." She heard Crystal splashing in the tub.

"I'm being serious. You've only been in love once. You were never in love with Trae."

"Of course I was. I know my feelings."

"You loved Trae. You still do. But you were never in love with him. You two played house so many years, it was a given you'd be married someday. You were comfortable with him. Not in love."

"We were so young."

"I remember when you broke up with Trae. You were angry with him and yourself, not hurt like you are now. I gotta go. Trae's here. Call Smoke. True love only comes once." He disconnected.

Ebony lay across the bed, thinking about Skeet's words. *For a knucklehead, he sure is insightful.* In the larger scheme of things, her past feelings for Trae didn't matter. All that mattered was providing a safe and happy home for Crystal.

CHAPTER TWENTY-SIX

Stuck in a traffic jam on the Dan Ryan expressway, Ebony opened the bag of jumbo fried shrimp Trae had brought with him. "Want one?" She took a bite, savoring the flavor as it rolled over her tongue. Goose Island Restaurant made the best shrimp in town.

Trae glanced at her. "I was saving those for when we stop."

"It's almost two, and I haven't eaten all day." She rubbed his bottom lip with a shrimp. "Come on. You know you want it."

The passion that flared in his eyes suffocated Ebony. The two had always teased like this, but he hadn't looked at her like this in years. When they were teens, his passion scared her, as it did now. Unlike Richard's warm, loving passion that was somehow liberating, Trae's was an all–consuming, confining passion that made her feel trapped. She still didn't understand this reaction to him.

"You're playing with fire," he said huskily. He took a bite and brushed his lips over her fingers. An awkward silence filled the car. She watched the traffic, her mind darting here and there. For early May, it was awfully warm—in the eighties. She wished her mind were half as clear as the beautiful spring day, but it was as jumbled as the traffic jam they were weaving through. Trae merged his black Jaguar into the lanes headed toward Chinatown.

His look scared her for another reason; it told her he had decided to pursue her. She buried the thought. He had to know by now that she wouldn't have a relationship with a drug dealer. Then again, Skeet had said Trae was leaving the life.

He waited at the Chinatown entrance stoplight, turned right, away from Chinatown, and went under the viaduct to the next set of lights. "You all right?" He turned the corner and headed toward downtown Chicago.

"Yeah." She prayed for something to talk about besides how *not all right* she was. She focused on the buildings they passed, and was surprised. "They've really built this area up, haven't they? These town houses are nice. I'll bet they cost an arm and a leg."

"Nah, they aren't that much. Just a leg and a finger."

She laughed.

"Do you like them?"

"I love them, but I wouldn't want to live on a busy street. In a few years, I'll be able to afford something like this."

"Check this out." He turned the corner into the town-house complex, drove to the center of the community where the park was located, and pulled into a parking space.

"Hidden Oasis. I love the name," Ebony said. "And this park is too cute." The small park, about the size of two neighborhood blocks, was surrounded by town houses. "This is really nice. The folks who live across the street are lucky." She stepped out of the Jaguar and ran to the swing set. Trae followed with the shrimp.

He handed her the bag of shrimp, and then stood behind her, pushing her gently in the swing while she ate. "This is a nice neighborhood," Trae commented.

"It sure is." She handed him a shrimp. She didn't make the mistake of facing him. "This is what a neighborhood is supposed to be like. It's so quiet. People are actually at work instead of roaming the street getting into trouble." She watched a woman pushing a stroller around the walking path, a few kids in the middle of their terrible twos climbing all over the slide and a small team of four-year-olds playing at wiffle ball.

He continued pushing the swing. "I can imagine Crystal running around this park. She would take over in no time. The trees would become her second home."

In her mind's eye she saw Crystal climbing trees, hopping from limb to limb, worrying Ebony to death. "Yeah, it would be nice for her to have somewhere to run besides in the house. I'm moving Crystal to a place like this someday."

"Oh, really?"

"Yep." She handed him the last shrimp.

He held her hand and led her toward one of the sets of five town houses. He took the empty shrimp bag from her, and tossed it into the trashcan as they passed. Each set was similar. The end homes were ranch styles, perfect for a small family, and the middle three were bi-levels. The center home was the largest.

He stopped at the bottom of the steps. "Let's go inside."

"We can't walk into people's homes, Trae."

He pulled her along. "Don't be ridiculous. This one's a model." He led her up the steps and opened the door of the center home. "Ladies first." He moved to the side, allowing her to enter.

"This is fantastic!" The sunken living room was spacious. A wide, curved-metal stairwell led out of the living room up to what she assumed were the sleeping quarters.

She took the two steps down, slipped off her shoes and placed them on the plush burgundy carpet. "This is amazing." She walked across the room to the open area behind the living room. It had a maple Woodstock floor. The pattern of the wood flowed nicely with the feel of the town house. She bent, brushing her hand over the wood. Its rich deep coloring took her breath away. She sat on the floor, imagining how she would decorate. She saw her computer desk sitting along the wall.

"Come on. There's more."

"I think I'll stay here forever."

He chuckled. "Let's check out the kitchen. You know how you love to eat."

She pointed to a room off to the left. "What's that?" She went to investigate. "Oh, cool. This would make a perfect office. Everything in this place is huge. I need to be rich." She wandered through the down-stairs bathrooms and the kitchen, then ventured upstairs.

The upper level contained three medium-sized bedrooms, a full bath and a small loft area lined with built-in bookshelves. And then there was a finished basement. "This is simply amazing."

He escorted her into the living room, where they sat in the middle of the burgundy carpet and looked through the floor plans and brochures about Hidden Oasis.

"You really like this place, don't you?"

"Stop talking crazy, Trae. I love it. Now I know where I want to live."

"We never got to have our talk."

She forced her mind away from the fabulous home she had just walked through. "Oh, I'm sorry. I totally forgot. How did it go with you and Skeet?"

"I ate a little crow, so we're cool again." He fidgeted with the tongue of his Nikes. "I don't know why this is so hard. It was easier apologizing to Skeet."

"Why not just say it? I won't break, you know." She couldn't fathom why it was so hard for him to tell her he was leaving the drug life.

"I scared you in the car, didn't I?"

She looked away. "I don't know what's wrong with me."

"I'd die before I hurt you." He took her hand into his.

She knew he didn't understand. By refusing to give her freedom from the drug world, he hurt her. By keeping her from raising her child as she saw fit, he hurt her.

"The anxiety in your eyes took my mind back to when we were teens," he continued. "I'm not the same person anymore. I can't continue living as I have. I'm leaving the drug life behind."

Skeet telling her Trae was leaving the lifestyle registered in her brain; hearing Trae confirm his life change registered in her heart, became real. She felt overjoyed and teared up. "I'm so proud of you." She hugged him. "Sorry I'm acting so crazy. I've been through a lot lately." She rested her head on his shoulder. "Everything's finally coming together. We're all gonna make it out alive."

"I have a favor to ask. You see, my getting out will place you and Crystal in more danger. I have a plan to keep you safe."

"What?"

He lifted himself slightly, taking a set of keys out of his pocket. "I'm giving you your graduation gift now, instead of after the ceremony next month." He held the keys out. "This whole set of homes is yours."

Her mouth opened wide. "No way! What are you talking about?"

"I bought them with legit money as a wedding gift. Since your plans changed, now they're a graduation gift."

"I can't believe this. You're actually giving me this town house?"

"All five. You can collect rent on the other four. You can't go wrong owning property. I already have a prospective renter for one of the units."

"You're serious, aren't you?"

"Yes, this is all yours."

Overwhelmed with everything that had gone on since the new year, she took a few seconds to gather herself. "I love the house, but I can't accept this."

"The hell you can't."

She closed her eyes and lowered her head. "I'm so tired of this. Trae, please…" She sat up straight. "I was wrong. I should have never accepted a dime from you. This," she motioned around, "was bought with drug money. How many addicts did you create to pay for it?"

"I'm leaving the life."

"And I'm grateful to God for sparing you, but don't expect me to live under a roof paid for in dollars of sin."

"Listen, you can't stay on the west side. I've already started a rumor that I'm the one who beat Smoke. By the time I drop you off, everyone will know."

His words took a while to process because she knew he couldn't have said what she thought he said. But just in case, she asked, "Why would you do something like that?"

"To keep you safe. People have to think you've given me walking papers. We need to have a fight over Smoke, and you move to get away from me while I'm out of town."

"You put this cockamamie scheme into action without even consulting me? This is ridiculous. I'm not into playing games."

"I'm trying to protect you."

"From danger you put me in. This isn't the life I want, Trae."

"You don't have a choice. You have to move away. Take the damn house."

She held up a finger. "That's where you're wrong. If you had come to me *before* you set this crazy ball to rolling, you'd know that I deposited my sign-on bonus in the bank. I planned to take Crystal out this weekend to go condo shopping."

Trae just stared.

She tapped the prices listed on the brochure. "I can't afford a whole set, but I could swing a middle and an end unit. I may have to ask Mom to cosign a loan, but so be it."

"Fine! Do it your way, but this is a bunch of bull! I want you to move this weekend. Don't tell anyone where you're moving. Tell the boys you're afraid I'll find you. I'll bet they'll try to keep you hidden from me." He snarled more than smiled.

"Does Skeet know the plan?"

"Whose idea do you think it was?"

"Figures."

"I also told Dan and Marissa."

"So everyone knew except me. I need to get control of my life."

CHAPTER TWENTY-SEVEN

Trae watched Ebony as she paced her flat, arguing with her mother on the phone. He had known separating Ebony from Marissa would be easy. Marissa was the type of person who refused to move out of the neighborhood. He didn't understand the mentality, but thanked God she felt that way. He also knew that she would give Ebony a hard time, but would cosign the loan. With the way Marissa's shops pulled in the dough, he would bet she could have bought the entire Hidden Oasis.

"I'm not deserting you, Mom. I asked you to move in with us." She massaged her temples. "I know I grew up here and came out fine…Are you going to cosign or not?"

Trae rested on the recliner. Separating Skeet from Ebony would be impossible, so he would have to keep Skeet close. Dan was the real danger. If his plan for coming between Dan and Ebony backfired, Trae would never recover. He also feared he would create more than a temporary rift between the two.

"…this weekend, Mom. Trae will be out of town, so I have to move fast." She sat on the couch, then covered the receiver with her hand. "This woman is driving me crazy," she whispered through clinched teeth. "I'm not trying to keep your grandchild away from me. Please, Mom. I need for you to back me on this."

Why he was shocked that Ebony wouldn't accept the complex from him was beyond him. He should have known not to even try. Over the years, she had even been wasting the money he gave her for Crystal on a bunch of junkies. He would have stopped the flow of cash to her long ago, but chasing crackheads seemed to make her happy.

"Yes, Crystal can stay with you at Dan's for a few days…if that's the way you want it." She held the phone in front of her face, stared at it a few seconds, then tossed it to the side. "She hung up on me."

"She'll cool off."

"She says not to speak to her unless it directly relates to Crystal, but she'll cosign the loan. Talk about mixed messages."

"She's been worrying about your moving for years. Give her time. She's always been melodramatic. All of you Washingtons are."

"Why can't she just be happy for me? Why all the drama? I need a drink. Do you want something?"

"Nah." He could see her retreating to some place deep inside as she headed for the kitchen.

Orange juice, milk, Kool-aid, tea. Ebony closed the refrigerator door, took a glass out of the cabinet and ran cold tap water in the sink. She wasn't thirsty; she was hurt. Why she continually put her faith in people just to be let down time and time again never ceased to amaze her. She should have been prepared for Marissa's reaction. Yes, she had said she would cosign the loan, but only because she knew Ebony would get the money from Dan if she didn't, and she didn't want anyone saying she didn't provide for her child.

"You get lost in there?" Trae called from the living room.

"I'm fine. I just need a few minutes—alone." She cut the water off and sat at the table. Marissa would never change. She could remember when she had rushed home from school with her letter of acceptance from the University of Chicago.

"Mom, I made it! I made it!" Ebony kicked off her shoes and ran into the kitchen.

Marissa smiled. "Made what, child?" She stopped breading the fish momentarily, placing her finger close to her lips. "Keep your voice down. Crystal's finally asleep."

"I'm sorry. I'm just so excited." She held up the letter so Marissa could read it. "I made it! I made it! I made it!"

One glance at the letter and Marissa's smile faded. "Girl, you don't have no time for no college." She pointed toward the bedroom, cornmeal and seasoning dropping from her fingers. "You have a child to raise."

"But, Mom, read all the way to the bottom." She pointed out the lines. "They're giving me a full scholarship. I don't even have to pay for books."

"That baby in there will be five by the time you finish school, and then find a job. How will you support her until then, Ebony? Rent, diapers, food, clothes, health insurance and childcare all cost money."

Ebony had thought she'd live with her mother and continue working at the convenience store to earn extra money.

"Does their scholarship pay for that? I've supported you long enough. After you graduate, you're going to beauty school. That's one job you'll always have financial security in."

"But I don't want to be a..."

"No buts. I finally have enough money to buy us our own salon. I have eight beauticians lined up to rent space at six hundred a month each. You're a smart girl, do the math. I have a large clientele. If you would waste less time at the library and spend more time braiding hair, you'd never have to worry about money."

"I work. I make money."

Marissa returned to breading fish. "Sorry, but that measly hundred a week won't cover it. You'll stay here with me and work at the salon."

"I could work full-time. People work and go to school."

"When would you spend time with your child, Ebony? She needs you."

"Who are you to tell me about spending time with my child? I spend more time with Crystal in a week than you did with me my whole childhood."

Marissa caught Ebony by surprise with a slap across the face. The letter flew out of Ebony's hands. Refusing to cry, she stared at her mother.

When Ebony was accepted to Whitney Young, one of the top high schools in the city, Marissa threw a fit, saying she should go to the neighborhood school, which happened to be one of the worst schools in the city. *School is whatever you take out of it,* Marissa used to say. Ebony hadn't allowed Marissa to talk her out of going to Whitney Young, and she had no intention of being talked out of attending the University of Chicago.

"Who do you think you're talking to? I did the best I could for you. After your father died, I didn't have a choice but to work two jobs to keep a roof over your head and food in your belly. What did you want from me? To take Dan's drug money? Is that your plan? I hear Trae's dabbling in the drug trade."

Rubbing her cheek, Ebony continued staring at her mother. She had remained silent for years, but no longer. She had her own child to raise, and wouldn't be stopped. "You did have a choice. We could have moved in with Auntie Genevieve. Instead, *you* chose to leave me alone."

"You weren't a baby."

"No, I wasn't a baby, but I was far too young to be left alone. Everyone knew I was home alone. I lived in fear of being raped, mugged or murdered. Do you know how many perverts are out there? Do you think their remarks were only for other kids? Give me a break." She bent, picking up the letter. "I'll get a second job if I have to. My counselor said something about grants. I'm going to the University of Chicago with or without your support—and I'll do it without Trae's drug money. I don't need anyone's help."

"What about the shop? It isn't good enough for you, I guess. You've always thought you were better than others. Hell, how many kids you know around here call their mother Mom?"

Ebony set the letter on the table. She had a smart-aleck remark but held off. She didn't want to be slapped again. "This is ridiculous. When I was fourteen, I tired of people teasing me for calling you Mommy, so I shortened it to Mom. If you had a problem with it, you could have said something. And of course the shop is good enough for me, but it isn't my dream. That's your dream."

"It's our dream. I've been saving for us. You don't belong out at that highfallutin' school. They'll treat you like crap because your pedigree isn't up to snuff." She softened. "I'm sorry I hit you, baby." She caressed Ebony's face. "You belong here with me. I'm sorry I wasn't there for you. Let me be here for you now. You can't raise Crystal on your own."

"But I want to go to college. I want to own my own business someday, not take over yours."

Marissa wet a towel in the sink, then cleaned the cornmeal off Ebony's face. "Let's compromise. When I open the shop, quit your job at the convenience store and work for me as a shampoo girl and braider. I found a place with a room we can turn into a nursery for Crystal."

Ebony smiled, glad Marissa was finally cooperating. Her mother always gave her a hard time, but in the end she usually came through.

"Malcolm X Junior College is right down the street from the salon. You can take a few classes there. I'll even pay for it."

Ebony looked at her mother crosswise. "I have a full scholarship to one of the top universities in the country. People would kill to have this opportunity, and you want me to throw it away! Why are you trying to hold me back?"

"I love you, baby, but you're young, idealistic and dumb. I'm not holding you back; I'm giving you a head start. You have a baby and don't have time for four years of college before you start your career. You can have your beauty license in a few months, then earn a degree in two years from a junior college if you decide to continue school. I'm telling you the fastest way to become independent."

"You don't understand."

Marissa crossed her arms over her chest and narrowed her gaze. "And who does, Dan? I know you've been sneaking to see him again."

Ebony folded her arms over her chest.

"I didn't graduate number one in my class, but I'm not stupid. Trae giving you Crystal has Dan written all over it."

"At least Dan supports me."

"Ebony," Trae called from the living room, ending her trip back in time. "It's getting late."

"Here I come." She thought about Richard. They had both grown to be disappointments to their mothers.

Trae moved from the recliner to the couch. "I have something for you." He took a typed letter out of his pocket and handed it to her.

She read the letter. "This says you beat Richard and threatened to kill his family if he didn't stay away."

"I know. I wrote it."

"That's horrible, Trae. What is wrong with you? Why would you write something like this?"

"The words been spread around the street that I beat Smoke, but no one would dare to tell you for fear of crossing me. In comes the anonymous letter." He flicked the letter.

She pushed the letter toward him. "I don't know about this."

"It'll work."

"It sounds stupid, but I guess we don't have a choice." She set the letter on the coffee table, then leaned on the arm of the couch. "I'll be glad when this is all over."

He toyed with the manila folder he had brought with him. "There's something else I need to discuss with you." He paused. "I'm truly sorry I didn't give you legal custody of Crystal. Now that I'm going legit, I pray you can forgive me."

"I need time to think. Maybe we should have our showdown tomorrow. Mom's drained the fight out of me."

He fingered the folder. "You didn't legally adopt Crystal, so I had to do some research."

"Trae," she paused, "I'm tired, upset and trying to figure out how to pull off this deception."

"It's just, I found something. Have you ever seen your birth certificate?"

"Of course. I trust you're coming to a point." She curled her legs under herself and used the armrest as a pillow.

"I know you're tired, but I don't know when I'll see you again. I've been putting this off for weeks."

She straightened up. It wasn't like Trae to hem and haw. "What's wrong?"

He found a certificate in the folder and handed it to her. "Dan was married."

"No way!" She examined the duplicate of Dan's marriage license. "Oh my goodness." She laughed. "I can't believe this. Wait 'til I tell Skeet." She reached for the phone.

"There's more." He took the phone and set it to the side. "She died two years after their marriage."

"Poor Dan. No wonder he never talks about her." She read the vital statistics on the marriage license. "She died the year I was born. I guess when she died his dreams of family died with her."

"He has family. He's your father."

"You don't know how many times I wished Dan was my father. I love Mom, but she never understood my needs, and emotional support was out of the question. Our dads were too busy getting high to care about us. He didn't even give me his name after they married."

"They had a baby, Ebony." He handed her Savannah's obituary. He had stolen the original from Genevieve's years prior, made a copy, and replaced the original in case he ever needed to blackmail Dan.

She looked up from the obituary. "She died on August sixteenth." She felt queasy.

"Your birthday."

"Yes, my birthday." She silently read, "…Savannah leaves behind her husband of two years, Dan Washington, and her newborn baby, Ebony Washington." Hands shaking, she dropped the obituary.

He drew her into his arms, rubbing her back as she sobbed.

"Why didn't they tell me? I don't understand. Why would they do this? They knew how much I wanted a real father. He's been here all the time." She thought about the nights she'd spent hiding in a corner of the room, worried someone would break in. She had called Dan many times, begging him to come get her, but he told her he didn't have any rights and Marissa would have him arrested. He did have the right. How could he allow a drug addict to raise his child? How could he leave her alone? How could he?

"I know this is a shock."

"Please, Trae, leave me alone."

"Why are you angry at me? I thought you had a right to know."

"I'm not angry at you. I'm upset, period: My fiancé dumped me, my mom's not speaking to me; my father never claimed me. He knew I needed him and said nothing. Nothing, Trae! Well I don't need any of them. I'll raise my baby on my own."

He stared at her.

"What?" she snapped.

"Nothin'." He raised his hands slightly. "I thought I'd stay away for a while, but I've changed my mind. I can sneak by and…"

"I'm sorry. I didn't mean to yell at you. I don't need you to babysit me, Trae. I'll be alone, not lonely." She sorted through the documentation of Dan's marriage, her birth, her adoption and Savannah's death.

"Melodramatic and arrogant," he said. "I don't want Crystal to think I'm abandoning her. Talking on the phone isn't the same."

She slapped her forehead. She had been so busy wallowing in self-pity she hadn't taken into consideration how Crystal would react. "You're right. Don't pay any attention to me. So how are we doing this fight?"

He rose, calmly picked up the lamp and hurled it across the room, smashing the front window.

She jumped up. "Trae! Are you out of your mind?"

"I didn't do it! They're lying."

"Get out!"

He tried to kiss her cheek. She hit at him. "Get away from me. How could you?"

"I love you," he whispered.

She snarled. Yes, she was supposed to be playing along, but she was actually angry. How could he break the window?

"I'll send someone to fix that."

"Go away now."

CHAPTER TWENTY-EIGHT

"Come on up, Skeet." Richard unlocked his front door and continued packing. He didn't know what his mother was up to, but she said she needed him to get down there immediately. Nonno wasn't sick, so he had no idea what could be so urgent.

Skeet walked into the bedroom. "Why didn't you tell me you're selling your condo? How many times have I said I want to buy this place?"

"I didn't know you were serious." He tossed two pairs of jeans on the bed. Trae had violated his home, and Richard no longer felt comfortable in it.

"Hell, yeah, I'm serious. I put your for-sale sign in the trunk of my car. I get first dibs on this joint." They both laughed. Skeet plopped down on the chaise lounge. "You find a new place yet?"

"I haven't even tried."

"I found the perfect place, but it's a rental. The only problem is the location. I love the west side. Oak Park is as close to leaving the west side I'll ever get."

"Where is it?"

"About a mile from Chinatown." He scratched his head. "Now that I think about it, it's in a perfect location for you. Let's go."

Richard took a few pairs of socks out of his drawer. "Can't you see I'm packing? I'm leaving town in the morning." He continued his work.

"Damn, man. It's only seven. You have all night. This place won't be free for long. If you like, we can start the paperwork for me to buy this condo before you leave."

"You are entirely too impatient."

"I just know what I want, and don't see why I should wait to get it. You want to sell this place. I want to buy this place. I don't see the problem. Now let's go."

Richard stood in the foyer of the two-bedroom town house. "Hidden Oasis is right. I would have never found this place." Royal blue carpeting covered most of the floors. The kitchen, living room and dining room were part of a large hexagon. "I love this layout." The bedrooms were off the 10 o'clock and 2 o'clock sides of the room.

"These are sweet, ain't they? I'm tellin' you, if someone had moved them to the west side, I'd of bought one."

"It's perfect for me." Richard inspected the kitchen. The cabinets had plenty of storage space, and the appliances were new. He pointed at the dark-gray ceramic tile. "Nice. Who do I contact?" He didn't want to buy another place until he and Ebony were together again.

"So it's a done deal. Cool. What's your realtor's number?"

"I'm not contacting anyone tonight. I'll call whomever from Texas—tomorrow."

Skeet walked out. Richard ignored Skeet and stepped out onto the patio through the sliding door in the kitchen. The patio stretched from one bedroom around the back of the town house to the other bedroom. He wondered who tended the patches of lawn surrounding each home.

Skeet stepped onto the patio, handing the phone to Richard. "I have your realtor on the line. I've already explained everything to him. All you need to do is confirm."

"You're not serious, are you?"

"Just tell the man you've found a buyer for your place, and you want to sign a lease for this place before you leave tomorrow."

Richard was anxious to move out of Oak Park, so he took the phone and made arrangements with the realtor, then went into the kitchen. "Don't ever pull anything like that again. How did you get his number?"

"Off the sign you had in your yard."

Richard laughed. "You really did take my sign. I didn't even notice. You're out of your mind." He sat on one of the stools at the breakfast bar. The park across the street would be perfect for Crystal. "Do you know if any of the units out here are for sale?"

"I'm sure some are." Skeet's cell phone played "Bohemian Rhapsody." He looked at the caller ID, then went into the living area answering, "What's up?...No way!"

"Skeet, I wouldn't joke about something like this. Dan is my father. I saw the birth certificate, his marriage license and everything. I'm so angry I could spit. How could they keep this from me?" Ebony switched the phone to her other ear, rolled over on the bed and hugged her pillow.

"That's jacked up. What did he say?"

"I can't speak to him right now. I feel so betrayed. First Mom, now this. I need time to sort out my feelings."

"Forget that feelings crap. I'll three-way his ass right now. I want answers."

"No, Skeet."

"And what the hell did Marissa do this time?"

Ebony smiled. Skeet was the only person who had always supported her decisions. He could be meddlesome at times, but she realized he was the only one who truly had her back. "It doesn't matter. Do you want to go to the movies? I'm home alone and bored."

"I'm still trippin' off Dan bein' your father."

"Wild, huh?"

"I'm not tryin' to rush you off or nothin', but I got company. I'll come by tonight. We can catch a late show."

"Oh, no, don't rush things on my account. Love ya."

"I'll be there."

"I'm heading home to finish packing," Richard said.

Skeet walked into the kitchen. "Things are getting crazy around here. First Trae leaves the business, and now Dan's actually Ebony's father."

"Trae doesn't deal drugs anymore?" He told himself not to panic. He had known Trae would make this move sooner or later, but had hoped it would be later. Much, much later.

"This is his last trip to St. Louis. He's legit. I'm sticking around a few more months to watch his back."

"Did you say something about Dan being Ebony's father?" For some reason, this news didn't shock Richard, but he knew it would knock Ebony off-kilter. He needed to settle his business with his mother and speed up his plan to take Trae out of the picture.

"Now ain't that some crazy shit? Ebony's a mess. She won't even talk to him. And don't get me started on Marissa."

"What's wrong with Marissa?"

"You got me. Something happened between her and Ebony."

Richard nodded knowingly. He would bet Trae was at the root of all the turmoil in Ebony's life. When Trae finished with her, she wouldn't know left from right. "We need to get up out of here." He headed for the door.

CHAPTER TWENTY-NINE

Richard stretched his legs out in the backseat of the limo Stephanie sent to the airport for him. It had been a long flight, made to seem longer by his private investigator not answering his phone. Now that he finally had him on the line, he wanted some answers. "Hello, Mr. Graves."

"Sorry I couldn't call you sooner. I just arrived in town about an hour ago."

The limo was stuck in traffic. *Good*, thought Richard. That would give him more time to speak with the private investigator before he arrived at his parents' home. "It's been over a month. What's taking so long?"

"I know you're worried about your fiancée, Mr. Pacini. But you have to remember that it often takes the police department years to solve cases."

"I don't have years." He tried to rein in his frustration but couldn't. There had to be a way to stop Trae.

"I'm severely handicapped here. You didn't know his real name or the name of his parents. I can't work with the police. I don't have any connections in Chicago."

"That's why I hired you. He has people in the police department. Hell, he has people all over the Midwest." Richard rubbed his left temple, frustration mounting. "Please tell me you at least know his name."

"His real name is Trinity Miles. He did have enough time to murder the Collins boys before his flight. I'm searching for any and everything. Murder has no statute of limitations, and he hasn't always been so careful."

The private investigator idea wasn't panning out. He would have to gather his family and tell them the truth. Once they left the country, he would approach Skeet and Ebony.

"Give me another month. I'm close. I can feel it."

"I don't have a month. He could convince her to marry him by then."

"I know you don't want to hear this, Mr. Pacini, but you've lost your objectivity. Your number one priority should be keeping your family safe, not keeping him from marrying Ebony."

"I can't stand by and allow this to happen. I'll tell my family to leave the country."

"For how long, until he murders you? Someone's already hired a private investigator from Chicago to investigate you."

Richard gripped the phone so tight his fingers hurt. "What the…Who?"

"I don't know. I wouldn't be surprised if Trae hired someone to keep an eye on you."

He cursed under his breath. "Does this investigator know about you?"

"I'm covering my tracks; he isn't even trying. That's another reason I believe he's one of Trae's men."

"Great," he drawled. "I want to be posted daily, even if you don't find anything."

"Yes, sir."

Richard walked into the grand hall of his parents' home. "Have you seen my mother?" he asked a passing maid.

"Your parents are in the study, Mr. Pacini."

He thanked the maid, then went to the study. The layout of the study hadn't changed much since he was a child. The sofa was still far enough from the wall for a child to hide behind. The end tables had ceramic lamps instead of antique vases. The built-in bookshelf was still full of books most normal people wanted nothing to do with. He looked at the floor. Stephanie had the marble replaced the day after he'd scratched it.

"Hello, Mother." He nodded a greeting to his father and the man sitting at the round reading table. His parents seemed nervous, especially his mother. They joined the man at the table.

"Richard, this is Dr. Joyner. He's here to help," Stephanie said. "Have a seat with us."

"Is someone sick?" He sat at the only remaining chair, which was across from the doctor.

"We're concerned about you, son," Phillip said. "You've changed so much these past few months."

Richard's eyes slowly traveled from his father to Dr. Joyner to his mother. "Why are you all staring at me? What's going on here?"

"Dr. Joyner is my psychologist," Stephanie answered. "I asked him to be here."

Richard released a breath he hadn't realized he had been holding. Nonno had told him Stephanie had started seeing a therapist.

Stephanie tapped her perfectly manicured nails on the oak table. "We know who you are. We want to help you."

"What? Help me with what?"

"We know everything," Phillip said. "Your street name is Smoke. You've been laundering money for drug dealers. You're under surveillance by both drug and gang task forces in Chicago. You are part of a double-murder investigation. Your best friend Skeet isn't a football player but a major drug dealer. Your fiancée is the lover of the man who we believe beat you."

"So *you're* the ones who hired the private investigator. This is freakin' unbelievable."

Stephanie cleared her throat, calling his attention. "We'll hire the best lawyers to keep your record clean. Dr. Joyner has given us a list of excellent rehabilitation clinics."

"So now I'm a druggie, too. What am I on, Mother?" He couldn't help but laugh at how easily his parents thought the worst of him. He stood to leave. "I can't believe you called me down here for this." He tipped his imaginary hat at the doctor. "Sorry they wasted your time. Charge them double." He stalked toward the door.

"Richard. Wait. Don't leave." Stephanie followed him.

He spun around, practically knocking her over. "Why not? I'm a drug-dealing, money-laundering druggie who doesn't have enough sense to find his own woman, but instead goes after the woman of the top drug dealer in the Midwest. And, oh, I forgot—I also belong to a gang. I'm a busy man. I don't have time for this."

She wrapped her arms around him. "Allow us to help you."

Phillip stood beside Stephanie and studied his son. Richard was so hurt and angry he almost turned away. He wouldn't hide from the pain this time. He would confront his fears, and let the chips fall where they may.

"I don't want or need your help." He pried her arms from around him, then returned to the table. "I refuse to live like this any longer."

Stephanie and Phillip retook their seats.

"We've misjudged you, haven't we?" Phillip asked.

"I'm saying my piece, then leaving and never returning," he stated with a confidence he didn't feel.

"No, Richard," Stephanie cried.

"I won't go if you explain one thing to me." He rubbed his hands over his face. "How is it you can accept your son being a drug dealer, a money launderer, a junkie, and a gang-banger, but you're ashamed of him being black."

"You're not black."

"You are correct. I'm not black. I learned a long time ago that it takes a lot more than a tan and a black great-grandmother to make a person black."

"Stop trying to change the subject. We're only trying to help you."

"Stephanie, stop," Phillip interrupted. "We were wrong."

"But, Phillip." She turned to Dr. Joyner. "You're supposed to be helping."

"Listen to your son, Stephanie," the doctor answered.

"You're all turning this on me," she snapped. "I'm not the one in the gang."

Richard had reached the point of no return. He wanted a family with Ebony. Until he hashed out his problems with his mother, that wasn't possible. He also wanted peace for himself. Bottling up his feelings and fears was eating him from the inside out. "Let me get this straight. You don't mind people, such as the good doctor here, thinking I'm a criminal as long as he doesn't think I'm black. What kind of sick logic is that? You do realize Nonno is black, don't you?"

"He's Italian. You're ashamed of who you are."

"You have your work cut out for you, Dr. Joyner. I'm proud of my French, Italian, and Moor blood. Can you say the same? Nonno's still hurt that you worked to lose your accent and everything associated with your Italian heritage. Being Italian wasn't good enough for you. Being a black Italian was unspeakable." He nodded at the doctor. "Good day."

Phillip followed Richard out while Dr. Joyner stayed behind and consoled Stephanie.

"I'm sorry. I should have known."

"Yes, you should have." Richard crossed the grand hall. "I lost Ebony because I was ashamed of my family." He stopped and considered his father. Phillip was a big man: dark hair with graying edges, blue eyes, stern features. He always wore power suits, and didn't look like the type of man to be pushed around by his wife. "I don't even know what to call you." His eerie laugh echoed off the walls. "I'm thirty and don't have a comfortable way of addressing my father."

"I love you, Richard. I've made mistakes. I regret my inaction. There is no excuse, but you were always such a strong-willed boy, while your mother was weak. She always has been. But I love her. You had Papà. Instead of protecting her, I should have protected you. I should have insisted she go to therapy years ago." He held his arms out and hands up in surrender. "I'm asking for your forgiveness."

Richard stepped into his father's embrace. He relaxed in Phillip's arms, releasing the anger and disappointment festering in his heart. Tired of fighting, he wanted to work toward healing his family. "I need your help."

"Anything, son." They went into Phillip's office, where Richard brought him up to date on everything that happened with Trae.

"This private investigator hasn't found anything you can use?" Phillip asked.

"Not yet."

"Tell Skeet the truth."

He shook his head. "If he believed me, he'd go after Trae. He saved my life, Papà." Richard smiled. It felt awkward saying Papà, but it also felt right. He saw the joy on his father's face. It was odd, but he felt at home.

Phillip nodded. "You don't want to risk your friend's life. I understand." He moved his hand over his face. "I've been thinking about retiring."

"What are you saying?"

"Papà misses Italy. Stephanie and I want to travel the world. I can hire protection for you and your sisters."

"You would quit your job for me? But you've worked so hard."

"It's time for me to take care of my family."

"I appreciate your efforts, but he could hire a sharpshooter. I don't want to live under siege, and I don't want that for you." He leaned back in the chair. "I think I should tell Dan. He'll be able to find evidence against Trae."

"Didn't you say he killed the man Ebony thought was her father?"

"I've finally figured Trae out. He likes to separate his victims from their support. He knew I'd go to Dan, so he said something to make me fear Dan."

"Are you sure you can trust Dan?"

"I should have gone to him from the start. Trae has all of the phones bugged. He probably has me being watched."

Phillip poured himself and Richard a rum and coke. "Can you bug a cell phone?"

"I have no idea. I don't want to take any chances." He took the drink offered. "Thanks. I'll have my P.I. contact Dan and set up a time and place for us to meet."

"Sounds like you have a plan." Phillip held his glass up in toast.

Richard tipped his glass. "Let's pray it works. By the way, I'm moving." He chuckled. "I wouldn't be surprised if Skeet hasn't moved my furnishings over to my new place already. He's been after my condo for months."

"Do you think it's wise to have friends like Skeet?"

"Wise? No." He tasted his rum and coke. "I don't know how it happened. The Skeet I know isn't a drug dealer. I'm told he is, but I haven't seen it. In my head I know it's real, but in my heart…" He stopped mid-sentence, unable to find the words to explain this odd friendship. Ebony had said similar words to him. "I'm his friend and can't turn my back on him. He needs someone to show him a different way of life."

"I'm proud of you. You've grown to be a fine young man. I only wish I had more of a part in it."

CHAPTER THIRTY

Ebony rested on the living room couch of her new house. She was exhausted. She had spent the weekend, and what was left of her bonus, purchasing second-hand furniture and having the utilities turned on. She'd even unpacked everything.

The guys from the block were great. They had scrounged enough money together to buy her a few sets of towels, dishes, glasses, and eating utensils as a going-away gift. They had told her Trae was out of line, and she should find Richard.

Of course, Skeet had to harass them about paying full price for the items instead of buying them from him. "D-damn, Skeet," Stam said. "W-we ain't givin' our Miss Ebony n-no hot gifts. We g-gots more class then that." Skeet acted wounded, but everyone laughed.

But the highlight of the weekend was Meechie. They had gone to the rehabilitation clinic together, and he was admitted.

She called Crystal and told her about their new home, and that she loved her and would be picking her up from school the next day.

Everything had finally fallen into place. Almost, anyway. She got a second wind and went into the kitchen to prepare stir-fry. Her mind went back to the first time Richard had prepared it for her. He would be pleased that she could now prepare the dish to perfection.

Listen to me carefully. I need someone who, no matter how things appear, loves me enough to know my heart. His words haunted her. She closed her eyes and ears to the noise of her problems with her parents, her resentment toward Trae, her breaking up with Richard, her having to move, her finishing school, her starting a new job, and listened to her own heart.

Ebony and Richard loved each other and wanted the same things out of life. What was the real obstacle between them? She opened two packages of linguine and poured the noodles into a gallon glass jar on the counter. It couldn't be her ties to the drug world, because he didn't break off his friendship with Skeet. She smiled. *Like Skeet gave him a choice in the matter.*

She knew he wasn't ashamed of her, but he still didn't want her to meet his family. The entire time his sisters were in the hospital room, he had pretended he was asleep. She'd seen him peeking, and had noticed his jumpy reaction when Trae entered the room.

She snapped her fingers. "That's it," she said aloud. "He's ashamed of his family." She sat at the kitchen table, waiting for the water she had put on for the pasta. He'd introduced her to Nonno, the one member he wasn't ashamed of.

Skeet walked into the house as though he owned it. She met him in the living room with her hand held out. "Give me my key, Skeet."

"What if you lock yourself out?"

"I'll give a spare to Mom."

"Like I don't have copies. You're cute."

"You make me sick. Wash your hands. Dinner will be done shortly."

He turned the water on in the kitchen sink. "Has Dan called?"

"What did you do?"

"I cussed his ass out and told him to stay the hell away from you." He grabbed the dish detergent and washed his hands.

She smacked him on the back with a dishtowel. "How could you? That wasn't your place. Call him up now and apologize."

"Hell, naw. He's the one who's been lying all these years." He chuckled. "I asked him if he's my daddy, too."

She dropped noodles into the boiling water. "I wanted to approach him my way, and in my time."

"Your way and your time takes too damn long. By the way, you have a new tenant."

Arguing with Skeet was like arguing with the television. Sound came out, but it ran on its own programming. "When are you moving in?"

"It isn't me, smarty pants. I found a spot in Oak Park I like. Bought the whole building yesterday." He reached in the back pocket of his jeans and took out the lease. "Here's your copy."

"Thanks. Just put it somewhere. The realty company takes care of everything, right?"

"I set it up exactly like you wanted. Read the lease."

She glanced over her shoulder at him. "What are you up to?"

"Why I always gotta be up to somethin'? I think you should know who you're letting rent your property. Especially since you live on the premises."

"Yeah, right." She skimmed through the lease. "Richard's my renter? I'm gonna kill you!" She chased him into the living room.

He hopped over the couch and headed for the front door. "What'd I do?" He laughed and ran outside with her close behind.

The beauty of the sun saying its final farewell for the evening over the rooftops of the western houses stopped her in her tracks. Children were playing in the park. People were walking their dogs, talking and laughing. Others were working in their flower gardens or washing their cars. Skeet stood on the sidewalk, showing all of his teeth.

She smiled, shook her head and walked into the house. All of her dreams were literally within her grasp. All she had to do was reach for them.

"What are you doing?"

She fingered through the index of her cookbook. "I want to bake a cake. Do me a favor and steal Auntie Genevieve's caramel cake recipe."

"You tryin' to get me killed?"

"Do you plan on eating a home cooked-meal tonight? And what about that hair? It's awfully frizzy."

"You blackmailin' me? What has this world come to? Don't fix mine until I get back. Cold stir-fry is straight up nasty."

"When is Richard moving in?"

"He'll be back from Texas tonight."

"That's nice, but I asked when he's moving in."

"Pay attention to the conversation, Ebony. He'll be back tonight. I bought his condo complex, so I doubt he'll want to stay there."

"You bought his place?"

"How else did you think I tricked him into renting here?"

"You are the devil."

He bowed like the perfect gentleman. "Thank you. I'll be right back."

Ebony smiled at her reflection in the full-length mirror. Richard would love the contrast between her bright yellow sundress and her dark-chocolate skin. She combed her hair back and put on a wide yellow headband with black shadow imprints of animals spread around. According to Skeet, Richard planned to spend Monday unpacking and organizing his new place. She baked a caramel cake and cooked breakfast.

She organized the bacon, eggs and grits on a serving tray, along with orange slices, coffee and toast, lowered the tray cover and walked over to Richard's unit. She used her elbow to ring the doorbell.

Richard opened the door wearing his Bulls T-shirt and shorts. Flashbacks of their first night filled her mind. "Welcome to Hidden Oasis," she said.

His crooked smile lit up his face. He poked his head out, looked up and down the street, across the park, took the tray and rushed her in. "Come in, come in."

Confused, she followed him into the kitchen. At first he appeared happy to see her, then he started acting paranoid and nervous. After the beating he had received, she couldn't blame him for being extra careful. "I was worried you'd already eaten breakfast."

He opened the tray. The aroma of bacon, eggs and grits filled the room. "This smells delicious. Thanks." He took out a second plate.

"Come and eat with me." He dumped half of his food onto the second plate. They sat at the kitchen table together and said their blessing.

"I see you unpacked the kitchen first."

"Kitchen and bedroom. How did you find out I moved?"

She second-guessed herself. "Skeet," she replied softly. "I didn't mean to intrude." His genuine grin removed all doubt.

"Of course it was Skeet," he said. "I'm glad you came. Really."

"He's been busy lately. He helped me move in this weekend. I'm your neighbor."

He stopped eating. She saw the passion in his eyes and warmed instantly. But this time she intended to take it slow.

"What a coincidence. Skeet *has* been busy."

"I'm done unpacking. How about I help you out today?"

"I'd like that. I have an appointment later this afternoon, but until then I can tell you what's been going on in my family while we work."

"I'm picking Crystal up later anyway. Wait until I tell you about my family dynamics. What a mess."

Trae searched through the town house and garage for Ebony. The truck was there, but Ebony wasn't. He walked around the park. Still no sign of Ebony. He called her cell phone from the house. "Where the hell are you?"

"Hello, Ebony. How was your weekend? Now hang up and try again." She disconnected.

He grumbled a few expletives, calmed himself and redialed. "I'm sorry. I just don't have much time. I wanted to see you."

"No problem. How was your trip?"

"Mission accomplished. I'm a free man."

"I'm so proud of you, Trae. Skeet said he's getting out in a few months. I can hardly wait."

He pushed the curtain back to the large picture window facing the park. "Where are you? Your truck's still here."

"I'm glad it's there. I'd hate to move out here just for my truck to be stolen. I'm helping my new tenant move in."

"Put Skeet on the phone." He went to the kitchen for a cola.

"It's not Skeet. The point in me moving was to get away from you guys, remember?"

"I didn't say anyone could move in." He saw the lease setting on the counter next to the jar of linguine. He picked up the lease and skimmed through it.

"I didn't ask. This is my place. I have a realty company managing the property for me. I intend for them to earn their pay."

He saw Richard's name and ripped the lease into small pieces. "I have a few minutes. I'll come over and help out."

"No, Trae. Stop treating me like a baby. I know what I'm doing."

He checked his watch. If he hurried, he'd have time to curse Skeet out in person before he tied up a few loose ends.

"How the hell you gonna rent Smoke one of Ebony's units?" Trae stalked into what used to be Richard's condo, flinging the lease pieces into the air.

"It was really quite simple," Skeet replied in his most formal voice. "They didn't know what hit them until it was too late. Damn, I'm good."

"You know I'm interested in Ebony. Smoke walked out on his chance."

"He didn't walk out. You beat his ass." Skeet set a gallon of primer and two gallons of forest green paint in the purple bedroom. "You my boy, but Ebony's my heart. I'm not stupid. I know what you're up to. I'm leveling the playing field."

"So you want Ebony with Smoke?"

"To tell you the truth, I don't care. You're legit, and Crystal loves you both. Either of you would be a good choice for Ebony. But it's her choice to make. You gonna help me with this, or what?"

Trae cursed under his breath. He was furious with Skeet, but knew there was no way to stop him. Killing him was not an option; Ebony would never recover. Counteracting Skeet's meddling would become his full-time job. "I can't help today. I have a lot to do." He paced the room. Now there would be no way to keep Ebony away from Richard. "Why don't we have a painting party next weekend? We can all chip in and have this done in no time."

"Sounds good to me." He dropped the paintbrush. "We haven't had a party in a while." He pulled out his phone. "I'm inviting Smoke. Don't cause any trouble if he comes."

"I'm done playing games. We'll do this heads up. Let the best man win." Trae needed to arrange for Richard to have an accident he wouldn't survive. An accident no one would suspect was foul play. "I'll catch you later." Finding someone Skeet didn't know to organize the accident would take more time than he wanted, but he needed to do this properly.

Richard arrived a little late for his appointment with Dan at a pancake house in a small town northwest of Chicago. He'd never been to Rockford before, and took several unnecessary turns to ensure he wasn't being followed. It was 3 o'clock in the afternoon, so the place was virtually empty, which suited Richard just fine. He didn't want anyone overhearing their conversation. Dan had listened to everything Richard said as he retold the tale from beginning to end.

"…The only way to stop Trae is having him arrested for murder, but I need solid evidence," Richard said. "I know he killed the Collins boys. When I went to the police, someone tipped him off. I'm not sure who to trust in the department, maybe a state prosecutor or something.

My father's researching for me." Richard could feel himself rambling. "I'd appreciate any information you could give me."

Dan sipped his coffee. "I'll take care of everything."

"Thank you, Dan. I should have come to you sooner."

"I've had my suspicions ever since you were beaten. When he told Ebony I'm her father, I knew what he was up to. I hear you've moved next door to Ebony."

"Skeet is a mess."

Dan chuckled. "That he is."

"He's throwing a painting party this weekend. He bought both of the condos at my old place. Says he's renting out the bottom unit."

"Ebony invited me—after she apologized for Skeet showing his ass. I'm not mad at him. He's protecting his family. Always has. He's a good boy. She baked me a cake."

"I'm glad Trae's plan to come between you and Ebony didn't work. That would have been tragic."

"Be extra careful. Trae will be desperate now that he can't keep you and Ebony apart. It would be the perfect time for you to have an accident. You hear what I'm saying? Stay close to Ebony and you'll be safe."

A chill went down Richard's spine. "I'm not hiding behind Ebony."

"Don't go stupid on me now, Smoke. Put that ego of yours in check."

"Okay. Fine. I'll do it." Trae had called him when he was driving to Rockford, cursing Skeet for butting in. Trae told him that he didn't have a choice but to allow Ebony to pursue a relationship with Richard, and that he wouldn't harm his family unless he told Ebony of his threats. Before he hung up, he said that the best man had won.

Trae's phone call was surreal. Richard's path to Ebony had been cleared, yet not cleared. He took a sip of coffee. Now it all made sense. Trae would arrange an accident.

CHAPTER THIRTY-ONE

Richard handed Skeet a bottle of beer, then took more books out of the box. He and Ebony had unpacked the boxes for the rest of the house. All that was left was the living room bookshelf.

He wasn't sure he should confide in Skeet about Trae's misdeeds. He trusted Skeet, but after hearing how he had put Trae in the hospital for cheating on Ebony, he didn't know how Skeet would react. He didn't want to be responsible for sending Skeet into a rage that might lead to murder. "Thanks."

Skeet read through the titles on the bookshelf. "For what?" He alphabetized the titles by author.

"Me and Ebony living here is one amazing coincidence."

"I'm only settin' things straight." He ordered the Asimov novels by series. "I'm gonna ask you something that doesn't leave this room." He stopped organizing the bookshelf and gave Richard his full attention.

"Go for it."

"Tell me what actually happened between you and Trae. I don't want to continue assumin' shit."

Richard averted his eyes. "Nothing." He took a swig of beer, then set the bottle on the bookshelf.

"Don't give me that shit. How about I tell you what I think happened? Trae threatened to kill your family if you went near Ebony."

Richard choked.

"I'll take that as a yes. I knew his obsessed ass was up to no good."

"How long have you known?"

"Trae totally trashed his crib back when Ebony had that interview with Banks Consulting. He said he had changed his mind about giving her up to you. I told him to back the hell off. After he kicked your ass, I knew Trae needed to be dealt with."

Richard's mouth dropped open. "You had a hit put out on Trae!"

"Hell naw! Damn, man, what kind of person you think I am? Trae's my dawg. Yeah, he's crazy as hell, but he's still my boy. I just kept interfering in his plans. There's no way he can keep Ebony from pursuing you now. He'll have to deal with it."

"Not if he arranges for me to have *an accident.*" Richard made quote signs in the air.

"He won't be able to find anyone that doesn't have a connection to me in one way or another. He won't want word to get back to me."

Richard dragged a second box of books over to the bookshelf. His ribs still hurt from the beating, but he didn't want to let on. "What if he had you killed?"

"You worry too damn much. He's my dawg. He won't kill me. And Ebony would never believe our deaths weren't connected. He's crazy, not stupid. Now what you gonna do about Ebony?"

"Trae said he'd stay out of my way, but I'm not sure what to do. I don't trust him. I can't push Ebony away or she'll never take me back."

"It's time for me to have a man-to-man with him. I'll make sure he knows I'm onto him and you'd better not have any accidents. I have one favor to ask of you, though."

"Anything," he grinned, "legal."

"Got jokes, huh." Skeet chuckled. "Seriously, though, don't ever tell Ebony what Trae's been up to. I'll have him under control in a bit. I'll make him face facts and get help."

"Why don't you want Ebony to know?"

"Short answer: to save her and Crystal heartache. What they don't know won't hurt them. Now what you gonna do about Ebony?"

"I love her. I can't continue lying to her."

"Did you settle things with your parents? That was a real issue between you two. You need to tell Ebony what's going on. Have faith in her to understand and support you."

"You're right. She tried to get me to open up, but I kept putting it off. I should have told her a long time ago." He selected a few books out of the box. "I think I'll ask Ebony to take a trip to Texas with me.

I need to introduce her to my parents. I might as well get it over with."
He smiled. "And I haven't been with my angel in a long time. I can't tell
you how hard it was for me to stay away from her this morning. She
was wearing this yellow sundress that…"

"Shut the hell up! Damn. I don't wanna hear that shit."

"She just…well…never mind."

"You need to keep your horny butt in check. That's another reason
you're in this situation. Hell, you don't even know how to court properly."

"Court." He laughed. "You said court. What year do you think this
is, anyway? Need I remind you she came to me this morning?"

"Okay, yuck it up. But until you show her you aren't ashamed of
her and that you think of her as more than a sex object, you'll get
nowhere with Ebony. I know my cousin."

Richard stared at Skeet. "Ebony's your cousin?"

"Hell, yeah. I can't believe you didn't know. Where the hell you
been, man? Have you looked at us lately? Hell, Dan could be both of
our fathers."

"I guess I do have a lot to learn. Trae is gonna flip if Ebony agrees
to go to Texas with me."

"I'll handle Trae. You just handle those hormones."

"We'll stay with Nonno. If he isn't getting any, no one gets any."

"You telling me that old fart's still knockin' boots? He'd better
watch out using that Viagra shit. He gonna have a heart attack."

Trae paced Ebony's bedroom. "How the hell you gonna leave town
with Smoke? Crystal needs you here!"

"Lower your volume or get out." Ebony continued folding towels
and stacking them on the bed. "You leave Crystal at least once a month.
She doesn't seem any worse for the wear. I'm sure she'll live without me
for a few days. I'd take her, but she doesn't want to miss her last week

of school." She snatched a towel off the bed, snapped it out, then folded it.

He wanted to kill Richard, but his hands were tied. "And what am I supposed to do? Maybe I had plans." Skeet had snapped on him about interfering in Ebony's love life, and warned him that Richard had better not have an unfortunate accident.

"If Crystal is too much for you, Mom can keep her. I thought you would enjoy this extra time with her."

He hit at the curtain. "Of course I want to keep her. Damn, stop twisting my words. When you comin' back?"

"By Friday. Don't forget we promised to help Skeet paint on Saturday."

"Why the hell does Smoke need for you to go to Texas with him?"

"I'm tired of this line of questioning, Trae. Smoke is ready to confront his parents. He wants me there as moral support." She shook her head. "What's wrong with you?"

"Are you serious? Damn, woman, I thought we were getting back together."

She dropped the towel she was folding. "I truly apologize for whatever I did to mislead you."

Afraid of letting go, he pulled her into his embrace. "You didn't do anything. It was all in my head. I'll back off." He had to find someone to arrange for Richard and Skeet to be in the same accident. Unfortunately, everyone he could think of had a link to Skeet. He'd have to search out of the Midwest.

"You'll find the one meant for you."

I already have.

Richard lay across the couch in Nonno's living room, staring at the staircase. Exhausted from the flight, Ebony had taken a shower and was in the spare room, dressing for bed. They had discussed everything from their first memories, to how his smile went from perfect to crooked—though Ebony insisted his crooked grin was perfect—to how she felt about Dan being her father.

It was only 9 o'clock, but Nonno had already retired for the evening. Richard contemplated helping Ebony apply her sweet pea lotion. Nonno would never know. He crept up the stairs.

"Where do you think you're going?"

Richard spun around. "Nonno, you scared the hell out of me. I was about to check on Ebony. Make sure she didn't need anything."

Nonno raised a brow. "Get down here."

"I thought you went to bed." Richard returned to the couch.

"Leave that girl alone. What have you told her?"

"Everything." He paused. "Skeet overheard your conversation with Mother when you first came to the hospital to see me."

Nonno swiped his large hands over his toffee colored face, then took a seat in his favorite ladder-back chair. "I'm sorry I didn't insist on Stephanie seeking help sooner. I allowed the family to live in denial."

"You haven't done anything wrong. I'm glad Ebony told me. It helps me understand Mother better."

"How did Skeet overhear?"

Richard explained what happened, then continued, "I'm worried about tomorrow, Nonno. I don't know how Mother will react to Ebony. You should have seen the way Gail and Bianca acted. The way they spoke. I was so angry and embarrassed." He lowered his head into his hands. "I honestly didn't realize how racist they are. At least I couldn't admit it until I heard it for myself. If Mother is even half as bad as they…" he trailed off. "I won't allow her to treat Ebony like that." He shook his head. "I should have stopped Gail and Bianca."

"I have faith in Stephanie."

"Nonno…"

"What's wrong?"

"Do you consider yourself black? I mean, you've always stressed that we're Italian."

"Of course I'm a black man. But I'm not African-American. Everyone can see I'm a black man. I love my homeland and sing its praises every chance I get. When I came to this country, I barely spoke the language. I gravitated to the Italian immigrants with whom I shared more common bonds."

"Why did you move from Italy?"

"Your granny was dying. There were experimental treatments here that I prayed would save her life. After she died, I couldn't go home." The chair creaked as he leaned back. "I want to go home now."

"You're moving back to Italy?"

"After you marry Ebony, you'll have to bring my great-grandbabies to see me."

"Hello, gentlemen." Ebony descended the stairs wearing a royal blue silk nightshirt that reached her knees and a matching robe.

"Did you find everything?"

"Yes, Nonno." She sat beside Richard. "So what's on the agenda for tonight, a DVD?"

"I'm tired," Nonno said. "I'll see you two in the morning." He waved on his way out. "I'm a light sleeper, Richard."

Richard laughed. "Okay, okay."

"What was that about?"

He ran his hand along her leg. "He knows how much I want you." He traced her soft lips with his finger. "I don't want to, but I need to stop now." He flopped back on the couch. They'd agreed to stay away from each other sexually until after he dealt with his parents.

She snuggled next to him. "I love you."

"Not half as much as I love you." He wrapped his arm around her, still dreading his mother's reaction. "About tomorrow. If Mother says anything out of line, don't feel that you have to hold your tongue."

"Don't worry, she won't scare me away. I can take anything she can dish out."

"I'm just not sure if you should come along. This battle is between me and her. It started before I knew you, and she'll try to use you as its reason."

"I know you aren't ashamed of me. If you don't want me to go, I'll understand. You have nothing to prove."

"I'm not sure what to do."

"If you think I'll increase the rift between you two, maybe I should stay behind."

"Rift? We passed rift years ago. We're at least a universe apart." He was glad she would be behind him, whatever he decided. He held her hand close to his heart. "I heard you in the hospital when you went after Bianca and Gail. I'm sorry I didn't speak up. I appreciate how you've always been willing to fight for me, but…" he stopped, not sure how to proceed.

"No apology is necessary. You were in no condition to take them on." She grinned. "Don't worry. I won't go after your mother. I know this is your fight."

Glad she understood, he hugged her closely. "I have to save myself this time, angel."

CHAPTER THIRTY-TWO

"I should have put a stop to your treating Richard as a second-class citizen years ago, Stephanie," Phillip chastised. He stalked across the study from the bookshelf to the couch. "I'm so disgusted with myself. I can't believe I stood by and allowed this to happen."

"I've made his life easier. He's only one-eighth black. Why should he advertise it? Instead of claiming that tiny eighth, he needs to keep it hidden. I want our son to be a success. I expect you to discourage his relationship with this black woman."

Phillip glared down at his wife. "Listen carefully. I don't give a damn what color he associates with, as long as he's happy."

"That's easy for you to say, you're not black."

"Am I interrupting?" Richard asked.

Phillip stiffened, praying Richard hadn't heard Stephanie's words. He smoothed his suit, stalling. "I'm just talking sense into your mother. Come and sit with us." He walked toward the reading table.

"I'd rather stand if you don't mind. Mother, I'm in love with and marrying Ebony. Your grandchildren will be black. I won't tolerate your treating them as you've treated me."

"You can't be serious," came her clipped reply.

"I'm dead serious." He paced the room. "How could you disrespect Nonno like this? I don't understand. Do you even care how much you're hurting him? Or is pretending he isn't black easier for you?"

"Papà isn't black, he's Italian."

"I heard everything, Mother."

"Oh, no," Phillip gasped under his breath. Mortified, he clenched his hands into fists.

"Could you please explain how you want to hide my being black if there is nothing to hide? Nonno is half-black. How do you think it makes him feel that you deny half of who he is?"

"You don't know what you're talking about. You're diverting the focus from Ebony. She's corrupted you. I know her type. She wants you for status. She's no better than any other gold digger. You're doing this to get back at us. Just like when you went to that black college."

"I didn't bring her here to be insulted. You know…" He ran his hands over his face and burst out laughing. "Whoa."

Stephanie frowned. "I'll call Dr. Joyner."

"I'm not crazy, Mother. I've reached the point where I really don't give a damn how you feel. I almost lost the woman I love because I was holding on to something I've never had. As a child, I tried to convince myself I didn't need you. As an adult, I honestly don't need you. Now I'm laughing at myself for taking so long to figure that out."

Stephanie crossed her arms over her chest. "Don't be ridiculous, Richard. Of course you need me."

"There's no reasoning with you. You stay out of my way, and I'll stay out of yours." He turned to his father. "Papà, would you like to meet my fiancée? She's in the library waiting."

"She's here?" Stephanie asked as she stalked out.

"Mother, wait." Richard followed behind her.

"How can you bring that woman into my home and expect me not to meet her?"

"Slow down, both of you," Phillip said. "She'll think we're attacking her. You had best behave, Stephanie."

"I know what I'm doing."

Ebony stood as the three entered the library. Richard went to her side. "Ebony, these are my parents, Phillip and Stephanie Dubois."

She nodded. "Pleased to meet you."

"The pleasure is all ours," Phillip said, tugging on Stephanie's sleeve in warning. Richard had not exaggerated. Ebony was truly a beautiful woman. Her eyes were stunning. Before Ebony, he had never seen sepia eyes that could rival Stephanie's. Ebony wore a white linen kulak outfit, and her hair was held back with a large white banana clip. The straps of her sandals wrapped around her shins.

Stephanie scrutinized Ebony from head to toe. "I'll pay you two million dollars to stay away from Richard."

"Stephanie!"

"Mother, that's it! You've gone too damn far this time…"

Ebony's anxiety-laden laugh stopped Richard's tirade. "She's joking, right? This is a whole new spin on *Guess Who's Coming to Dinner*." She kissed Richard on the cheek. "I love you." She turned to his father. "It was nice meeting you, Mr. Dubois."

"I'm sorry about my wife's behavior."

"Don't apologize for me, Phillip!"

"No need to apologize, Mr. Dubois." She peered into Stephanie's dark eyes. "No wonder your son is ashamed of you. Peace." She walked out.

Richard paced along the wall of built-in bookshelves, wringing his hands. "I can't believe this."

Stephanie folded her arms over her chest, tapping her heels on the marble floor. "She'll take the money. She couldn't say yes in front of you."

"Poison. You are poison, Mother. I'm out of here, before I say something you'll regret."

Stephanie moved in front of Richard to keep him from leaving. "You can't be serious, darling. I'm your mother. I know what's best."

He looked at his father. "She really doesn't get it, does she?" He gazed into her eyes. "I am in love with Ebony and marrying her. She is the mother of my children."

"Oh, God no." Stephanie drew the back of her hand across her forehead with a dramatic swipe. "She's pregnant?"

"No, Mother, I misspoke. She's not. She completes me. She's made me a better man, but all you see is she's black." He hunched his shoulders. "You know, like your beloved father. Ebony and I are one. You reject Ebony, you reject me." His eerie laugh sent chills down Phillip's spine. "Well you've always rejected me, so I guess that's no big deal."

"What are you saying, Richard?" she asked shakily.

Phillip stood beside Stephanie, feeling as if he was about to witness a train wreck, and there was nothing he could do to prevent it. He didn't want to lose his son.

"I'm saying, consider me dead."

Phillip felt the impact of the train hit him full force. He'd been a party to Richard's mistreatment by his inaction. Now his son had disowned them. He couldn't breathe.

Oblivious to his father, Richard continued, "I'm changing my phone numbers, and I've moved. I'll instruct Nonno not to give you my new information. If you call my office, I swear to God, I'll quit. I want nothing further to do with you."

"Richard, no!"

"Yes, Mrs. Dubois."

Phillip felt too weak to stand. He staggered over to the window seat. He'd always thought someday he'd make things up to Richard, but someday never came. Now it was too late.

Richard saw his father's broken state. "I'm sorry, Papà." He knelt beside him. "I can't live like this. I don't want what she has to offer."

He looked at the fine young man his son had grown into. "I'm proud of you. Do what you feel is right. You have my support."

"What are you saying?" She stepped in front of them.

Phillip ignored her. "I don't want to lose our relationship. It's too valuable to me. I'd like your new information. I promise not to tell Stephanie."

"What are you doing?" she snapped.

Without raising his voice, he answered, "What I should have done years ago—placing my children before their mother." He looked into Richard's eyes. "I love you, son." He grinned. "I saw Ebony walking toward the boathouse. I don't think you should keep her waiting. I'll deal with your mother, and tell Nonno you'll be staying here tonight."

Richard hugged his father. "I love you."

Unsure how to proceed, Richard stood in the doorway of the cabin and watched Ebony sleep. He'd taken the scenic route to the boathouse for more time to cool off and think. In his heart, he had always known the day would come when he had to admit his mother would never accept him and he would have to move on, but the pain was still stifling.

Ebony had fallen asleep on the bed while reading a magazine. He stooped beside her, wanting her to save him again, but there was no saving. Not this time. He placed his loafers next to her sandals, lay in the bed and cupped her into his body.

She woke and turned in his arms. "How did it go?"

"I lost my mother today."

"I'm sorry, baby."

"I've always feared this day." He closed his eyes. "I've been running from it for years. I can't do it anymore. I don't want to." He rested his hand on her waist. "I'm exhausted, but relieved it's over."

"I want to do something, but I don't know how to help."

"Love me. Marry me."

"I do." She kissed the tip of his crooked grin. "And I will."

"You've saved me again."

CHAPTER THIRTY-THREE

Dan checked his watch, then did a head count and position check of everyone in the condo. He loved Trae, but he had to be stopped before he could harm anyone else. Ebony, Richard, and Crystal were painting the master bedroom. Dan pulled on Ebony's bandana. "You have more paint on you than the wall, little girl." She was covered with multiple-colored splotches of paint.

She set the roller in the pan, wiped her hands on her jeans and straightened her long-sleeved T-shirt. "I'll have you know this is the latest fashion."

Crystal stood beside Ebony, copying. "Yes, this is the latest fashion."

"Get back to work, my painted queens." He went into the spare bedroom. Marissa, Genevieve and Oscar were painting it forest green.

"When you gonna start helpin', Dan?" Genevieve asked.

"Wait a second." He stepped into the living area. Trae was taping baseboards, and Skeet was painting. "Trae, I left my phone on the charger in my car. Would you get it for me?" He held up his keys.

"Sure."

Dan tossed the keys to him, then went to help his sisters. Soon it would all be over. "Okay, women, let's do this. Where's my roller?"

"Get the ceiling edges for me," Marissa said.

He moved the ladder to the corner, set the paint and edger on the top rung, then climbed.

"Do you all have more tape in here?" Trae asked.

Dan whipped his head around. "I thought you were getting my phone."

"Here you go." Marissa handed Trae a roll of tape.

"Ebony was going outside anyway…"

"No!" Dan tried to hop off the ladder and slipped, toppling the ladder and spilling the paint. He reached for Trae. "Save her," he pleaded.

Trae ran as fast as he could out of the condo. Everyone else ran into the spare bedroom to see what the commotion was about.

Ebony saw Trae tear out of the condo. His panicked green eyes were more than enough to tell her to run. She quickly surveyed her surroundings. There weren't any trees, cars or anywhere close enough to hide. She ran for the condo.

"Lie down!" Trae yelled.

Ebony could hear the car's engine revving as it quickly approached. A few more feet and they would both be safe. She reached out for Trae. As Trae grabbed her hand, the shots rang out. The first shot tore into her shoulder; the second her arm. She cried out in pain.

Trae turned their bodies, holding her close. She could feel the impact against her chest as the bullets riddled his back. His weight and the force of the shots sent them both crashing to the ground.

Skeet ran out of the condo, gun drawn, running down the street shooting. He hit the rear window of the car. The car crashed into a large oak tree.

Richard handed a crying Crystal to Marissa. "Keep her safe." He ran out of the condo to Ebony and Trae. "Oh, God, please, please help me." He didn't know where to touch. They were both covered with blood and unconscious.

Dan lifted Trae's lifeless body off Ebony. "What have I done?" he whispered.

Oblivious to Dan, Richard held Ebony in his arms. He saw where her shoulder was shot, but wasn't sure if there were more wounds. He ran his shaking hand along her back, checking for wounds. "It's gonna be all right, angel." He saw the wound on her arm. "I'm here, angel." He rocked her.

Skeet ran up and knelt beside Trae. "I got 'em, dawg. I got 'em."

"You have to leave, Skeet," Dan said. "Take my car. The police will be here soon." He picked his keys off the ground and dropped them into Skeet's outstretched hand.

"Is Ebony…" Skeet cut his question short.

"She's alive," Richard said. "She's alive."

"I'll meet you at the hospital." He took off toward Dan's car.

Richard held Ebony close, his heart breaking. "You are my heart, my life, my ebony angel."

EPILOGUE

Fifteen months later.

Ebony swore her back ached worse than the wounds she had sustained from the drive-by. She set the clock on the nightstand. "Honey." Though she felt like punching him, she gently shook Richard until he woke. "My water broke." The contractions were a little over three minutes apart.

"No thanks. I'm not thirsty," he said groggily.

She dropped her feet over the edge of the bed as she massaged her lower back with her hands. Her nightgown was soaked. "I said water broke." The pain gripped her again, refusing to let go. "Richard!"

He hopped out of bed. "What? Is the baby coming?" He ran around to her. "Is Savannah Pacini ready to make her debut?" He grabbed her overnight bag, then helped her stand. "Crystal, it's time!"

Contraction over, she could speak normally again. "I can't go like this. I need a new nightgown. And you're only wearing briefs."

He helped her clean and change to her gown, then he dressed in jeans and a T-shirt and led her out of the bedroom.

Crystal jumped up and down. "We're having the baby!"

"Yes, sweetie. Call Skeet."

"I did, Papà. I knew Mama screaming had to be Savannah. That baby's already a trouble maker." She giggled.

Skeet ran into the house as if he lived there. "I think Ebony should drive with me. You drive too slow, Smoke."

"Just take care of Crystal, and make the calls for us." He put Ebony's gym shoes on her feet. "Having babies takes hours. I'll call when Savannah arrives."

"Can I call Nonno and tell him?"

Stephanie still had a long way to go, but she had changed notice-ably over the past year. Ebony silently thanked God the family coun-seling was working. "Sure, darling." She knew Nonno would inform Richard's parents.

Richard gently kissed Ebony. "I love you."

He led her to the car. Another contraction attacked. She leaned her head back, biting her lip and praying the contraction would end soon.

"Five minutes, angel." He pulled off.

The pain subsided, and she could breathe again. "I need to focus on something. Anything." She opened the glove compartment and sorted through the papers. She found a packet of photos. "Oh, cool. I can't believe this. You really need to clean out your car." She looked through the pictures. A contraction grabbed her, causing her to almost drop them.

He massaged her leg. "Hang in there with me, angel."

The pain slowly subsided. She saw a picture of Skeet, Richard, and Trae playing pool in the basement of her mother's salon.

She traced Trae's image with her finger. The drive-by shooters were from a rival south side gang. She figured it was probably the same guys who had beaten Richard. She thanked God Skeet left the life before it claimed him, also. Even Meechie cleaned up well. He was now the senior counselor at her non-profit outreach program.

"How you feeling over there?"

"Like I'm having a baby."

He pulled into the lane marked for the emergency room entrance. "Well, let's go have our baby."

She smiled, truly happy. "Yes, let's go have our baby."

DISCUSSION QUESTIONS:

1. Was Richard passing (denying his black blood to be accepted as a white man)?

2. Was Stephanie ashamed of Richard?

3. What was Stephanie afraid of and why?

4. Why didn't Ebony tell Dan or Skeet about Trae's refusal to give her legal custody of Crystal?

5. If you were Ebony, what would you have done about Trae?

6. Had Ebony become tainted?

7. If you were Richard, what would you have done about Trae?

8. Did Richard save Ebony?

9. Was Richard betraying his friendship with Skeet?

10. Why didn't Richard ever tell Ebony he was trying to obtain "proof" of Trae and Skeet's illegal activities?

11. Had Richard become tainted?

12. Was Trae in love with Ebony?

13. What do you think should be done with confiscated drug money/property?

ABOUT THE AUTHOR

Currently a Chicago area resident, Deatri works as an editor. Three children, two dogs, and one husband keep her days pretty full. An avid reader since childhood, Deatri's idea of a great afternoon is a trip to the bookstore, followed by hours curled up on the sofa with her newly purchased novel. Her debut title, *Caught Up* (Feb. 2006), received rave reviews from readers. For more information about Deatri, you may visit her website at **http://www.deewrites.com**. She can be contacted at deatri@deewrites.com.

Excerpt from

CRUSH

BY

CRYSTAL HUBBARD

Coming in March 2007

PROLOGUE

Miranda had one dying thought. *I should have stayed home.*

The words formed within her head, but Miranda couldn't hear them over the ear-splitting music and deafening wall of noise from the crowd. That crowd, that single-minded, ignorant beast that Bernie had so wanted her to be a part of, surged forward, pressing Miranda farther into the unyielding apron of the concert stage and closer to death.

Above the stage in a specially constructed cage of chain link, Lucas Fletcher played the bass solo of "Snatched," his latest American and U.K. Number One hit. He was so involved in the moment, so attuned to his music; he didn't notice security guards rushing from the wings and onto the stage. It would have been a familiar sight. At every concert, security swarmed the stage at least once to remove girls driven temporarily mad by Lucas Fletcher and Karmic Echo's music. Female fans risked possible eviction from the venue and arrest just for the chance to let their fingertips glance off Lucas's denim-wrapped thigh or the scuffed steel toe of his fashionably working-class leather boots.

At the sold-out London opening of Karmic Velocity, the band's current tour, a fan from his hometown of Aberystwyth, Wales incredibly made it onto the stage and threw herself onto Lucas. She ripped off his T-shirt, along with a sizeable length of his chestnut hair. She might have pulled him bald if the Yellow Shirts, his personal security force, hadn't tackled the girl and whisked her into custody. She and the friends that had pitched her onto the stage were later featured on two English talkies, where the girl displayed her coveted prize: the eight-inch long tress of Lucas's hair.

The Boston concert was going well. "Snatched" was one of Lucas's favorite songs, and the fans always responded well to it. Its driving bass solo energized Lucas as much as it electrified the crowd. Only when Arena security, in their heavy green jackets and black caps, joined the Yellow Shirts did Lucas glance down at the stage.

Dear God, it's a crush, he thought. Dread paralyzed him as he stopped playing mid-note. "Bloody hell!" he swore, dropping his bass and leaping out of the cage. He dropped eleven feet to a gigantic speaker, then jumped another eight feet to the stage. The crowd, still pressing forward, thought Lucas's acrobatics were a part of the show, and they cheered and screamed as he raced to the edge of the stage.

Crush, crowd crush, body slams, music mashes–however named, always resulted in tragedy. Everyone dreaded catastrophes like the 1979 Who concert in Cincinnati and Pearl Jam's 2000 concert in Denmark, where fans had been killed while the bands performed. No one had ever been killed at a Karmic Echo concert. Lucas prayed to keep it that way. As security guards lifted unconscious and injured concertgoers to the stage, dozens of other guards worked within the crowd itself, pushing back the frenetic mob. To facilitate the rescue of those being crushed, Len Feast, the lead guitarist, took to a microphone and pleaded with the audience to retreat.

Lucas, the muscles and cords of his well-defined arms and shoulders standing out, worked alongside the Yellow Shirts, pulling his fans to safety. The first five young ladies weren't so bad off that they couldn't find the presence of mind and strength to tear at his clothes and hair.

He was shirtless by the time he grabbed his sixth victim. He kneeled, pulling her dead weight across his lap.

Under the bright wash of the stage lights, her terra cotta skin looked gray. Her full lips, which looked like they'd been built specially for kissing, were a shade of purplish-blue that Revlon hadn't created. Her hazel eyes were half opened and remarkably lovely, despite their glassy sheen. Lucas might have gotten lost in the pool of jade centered within the chocolate brown if he hadn't noticed the cold of her skin as he smoothed her long, molasses-dark hair from her brow.

"Miss?" He gently jostled her in his arms. She didn't respond and he splayed a hand over her chest. "Miss?" He felt no movement, and his panic reached a crescendo.

He curled over her, bringing his cheek to her nose and mouth. Feeling no breath, he laid her flat on her back. All around him, security guards were clearing the stage, his band mates were securing their instruments, and Feast was attempting to calm a somewhat impatient Beantown crowd. Lucas was searching his brain for the right combination of breaths and compressions to revive the cold figure at his knees.

He pinched her nose shut and clapped his mouth over hers, breathing as he'd been taught ages ago while filming a public service spot for the BBC. He tuned out the rhythmic chanting and clapping of a crowd denied a concert they'd paid upwards of $150 a ticket to see. He didn't hear the voices of the security guards restoring order to the venue. Lucas breathed for the fallen woman, compressed her chest, and he vowed to keep doing it until she fully opened her gorgeous eyes and drew breath on her own.

"Come on, lovely," he pleaded as he externally pumped blood through her heart. Fat beads of sweat rolled down the sides of his face. "Open your eyes and tell me to get my bloody paws off you."

"Lucas, the paramedics are here," Feast said, his blue eyes filled with worry. "They'll take care of her."

Lucas hunched over her, and breathed into her.

"Lucas!" Feast clapped a hand on Lucas's shoulder. Lucas shrugged him off to continue his compressions. "Lucas, please, let the professionals at her," Feast begged. Lucas breathed for her, willing her to open her eyes, to move and to fill her lungs on her own.

His wish was granted when a choking gasp escaped her. She coughed, her whole body convulsing from its force. She tried to sit up, and she would have fallen back to the stage if Lucas hadn't caught her up in his arms. He took her chin and aimed her face at his.

Her eyes found his and remained there. With life now sparking within them, her eyes were even lovelier. Large and expressive, they were undoubtedly the most beautiful eyes he had ever fallen into.

She stared at him, too intent on breathing to speak. His collar-length hair, damp with perspiration, gleamed in the bright light as it fell forward to hood his face. He had striking features—a chiseled jaw, perfect cheekbones and a cleft in his chin—that were tense with worry, but his concern was most evident in his eyes, which were the color of a summer sky before a storm. Her breathing settled into a relaxed and comfortable pattern despite the pain in her chest, and she sighed. He shut his eyes in heartfelt relief and folded her into a close embrace. She didn't have the strength, or will, to withdraw from him. She drew comfort from his strong arms and the hard, steady beat of his heart. She had the sense to realize that any woman would be deliriously happy to be exactly where she was now, in the caring and protective embrace of Lucas Fletcher.

But Miranda wasn't any woman.

As paramedics moved in to take her, she drifted off, thinking, *I really should have stayed home...*

EBONY ANGEL

2007 Publication Schedule

January

Corporate Seduction
A.C. Arthur
ISBN-13: 978-1-58571-238-0
ISBN-10: 1-58571-238-8
$9.95

A Taste of Temptation
Reneé Alexis
ISBN-13: 978-1-58571-207-6
ISBN-10: 1-58571-207-8
$9.95

February

The Perfect Frame
Beverly Clark
ISBN-13: 978-1-58571-240-3
ISBN-10: 1-58571-240-X
$9.95

Ebony Angel
Deatri King-Bey
ISBN-13: 978-1-58571-239-7
ISBN-10: 1-58571-239-6
$9.95

March

Sweet Sensations
Gwendolyn Bolton
ISBN-13: 978-1-58571-206-9
ISBN-10: 1-58571-206-X
$9.95

Crush
Crystal Hubbard
ISBN-13: 978-1-58571-243-4
ISBN-10: 1-58571-243-4
$9.95

April

Secret Thunder
Annetta P. Lee
ISBN-13: 978-1-58571-204-5
ISBN-10: 1-58571-204-3
$9.95

Blood Seduction
J.M. Jeffries
ISBN-13: 978-1-58571-237-3
ISBN-10: 1-58571-237-X
$9.95

May

Lies Too Long
Pamela Ridley
ISBN-13: 978-1-58571-246-5
ISBN-10: 1-58571-246-9
$13.95

Two Sides to Every Story
Dyanne Davis
ISBN-13: 978-1-58571-248-9
ISBN-10: 1-58571-248-5
$9.95

June

One of These Days
Michele Sudler
ISBN-13: 978-1-58571-249-6
ISBN-10: 1-58571-249-3
$9.95

Who's That Lady
Andrea Jackson
ISBN-13: 978-1-58571-190-1
ISBN-10: 1-58571-190-X
$9.95

2007 Publication Schedule (continued)

July

Heart of the Phoenix
A.C. Arthur
ISBN-13: 978-1-58571-242-7
ISBN-10: 1-58571-242-6
$9.95

Do Over
Jaci Kenney
ISBN-13: 978-1-58571-241-0
ISBN-10: 1-58571-241-8
$9.95

It's Not Over Yet
J.J. Michael
ISBN-13: 978-1-58571-245-8
ISBN-10: 1-58571-245-0
$9.95

August

The Fires Within
Beverly Clark
ISBN-13: 978-1-58571-244-1
ISBN-10: 1-58571-244-2
$9.95

Stolen Kisses
Dominiqua Douglas
ISBN-13: 978-1-58571-247-2
ISBN-10: 1-58571-247-7
$9.95

September

Small Whispers
Annetta P. Lee
ISBN-13: 978-158571-251-9
ISBN-10: 1-58571-251-5
$6.99

Always You
Crystal Hubbard
ISBN-13: 978-158571-252-6
ISBN-10: 1-58571-252-3
$6.99

October

Not His Type
Chamein Canton
ISBN-13: 978-158571-253-3
ISBN-10: 1-58571-253-1
$6.99

Many Shades of Gray
Dyanne Davis
ISBN-13: 978-158571-254-0
ISBN-10: 1-58571-254-X
$6.99

November

When I'm With You
LaConnie Taylor-Jones
ISBN-13: 978-158571-250-2
ISBN-10: 1-58571-250-7
$6.99

The Mission
Pamela Leigh Starr
ISBN-13: 978-158571-255-7
ISBN-10: 1-58571-255-8
$6.99

December

One in A Million
Barbara Keaton
ISBN-13: 978-158571-257-1
ISBN-10: 1-58571-257-4
$6.99

The Foursome
Celya Bowers
ISBN-13: 978-158571-256-4
ISBN-10: 1-58571-256-6
$6.99

Other Genesis Press, Inc. Titles

A Dangerous Deception	J.M. Jeffries	$8.95
A Dangerous Love	J.M. Jeffries	$8.95
A Dangerous Obsession	J.M. Jeffries	$8.95
A Dangerous Woman	J.M. Jeffries	$9.95
A Dead Man Speaks	Lisa Jones Johnson	$12.95
A Drummer's Beat to Mend	Kei Swanson	$9.95
A Happy Life	Charlotte Harris	$9.95
A Heart's Awakening	Veronica Parker	$9.95
A Lark on the Wing	Phyliss Hamilton	$9.95
A Love of Her Own	Cheris F. Hodges	$9.95
A Love to Cherish	Beverly Clark	$8.95
A Lover's Legacy	Veronica Parker	$9.95
A Pefect Place to Pray	I.L. Goodwin	$12.95
A Risk of Rain	Dar Tomlinson	$8.95
A Twist of Fate	Beverly Clark	$8.95
A Will to Love	Angie Daniels	$9.95
Acquisitions	Kimberley White	$8.95
Across	Carol Payne	$12.95
After the Vows	Leslie Esdaile	$10.95
(Summer Anthology)	T.T. Henderson	
	Jacqueline Thomas	
Again My Love	Kayla Perrin	$10.95
Against the Wind	Gwynne Forster	$8.95
All I Ask	Barbara Keaton	$8.95
Ambrosia	T.T. Henderson	$8.95
An Unfinished Love Affair	Barbara Keaton	$8.95
And Then Came You	Dorothy Elizabeth Love	$8.95
Angel's Paradise	Janice Angelique	$9.95
At Last	Lisa G. Riley	$8.95
Best of Friends	Natalie Dunbar	$8.95
Between Tears	Pamela Ridley	$12.95
Beyond the Rapture	Beverly Clark	$9.95
Blaze	Barbara Keaton	$9.95

Other Genesis Press, Inc. Titles (continued)

Blood Lust	J. M. Jeffries	$9.95
Bodyguard	Andrea Jackson	$9.95
Boss of Me	Diana Nyad	$8.95
Bound by Love	Beverly Clark	$8.95
Breeze	Robin Hampton Allen	$10.95
Broken	Dar Tomlinson	$24.95
The Business of Love	Cheris Hodges	$9.95
By Design	Barbara Keaton	$8.95
Cajun Heat	Charlene Berry	$8.95
Careless Whispers	Rochelle Alers	$8.95
Cats & Other Tales	Marilyn Wagner	$8.95
Caught in a Trap	Andre Michelle	$8.95
Caught Up In the Rapture	Lisa G. Riley	$9.95
Cautious Heart	Cheris F Hodges	$8.95
Caught Up	Deatri King Bey	$12.95
Chances	Pamela Leigh Starr	$8.95
Cherish the Flame	Beverly Clark	$8.95
Class Reunion	Irma Jenkins/John Brown	$12.95
Code Name: Diva	J.M. Jeffries	$9.95
Conquering Dr. Wexler's Heart	Kimberley White	$9.95
Cricket's Serenade	Carolita Blythe	$12.95
Crossing Paths, Tempting Memories	Dorothy Elizabeth Love	$9.95
Cupid	Barbara Keaton	$9.95
Cypress Whisperings	Phyllis Hamilton	$8.95
Dark Embrace	Crystal Wilson Harris	$8.95
Dark Storm Rising	Chinelu Moore	$10.95
Daughter of the Wind	Joan Xian	$8.95
Deadly Sacrifice	Jack Kean	$22.95
Designer Passion	Dar Tomlinson	$8.95
Dreamtective	Liz Swados	$5.95
Ebony Butterfly II	Delilah Dawson	$14.95
Ebony Eyes	Kei Swanson	$9.95

Other Genesis Press, Inc. Titles (continued)

Echoes of Yesterday	Beverly Clark	$9.95
Eden's Garden	Elizabeth Rose	$8.95
Enchanted Desire	Wanda Y. Thomas	$9.95
Everlastin' Love	Gay G. Gunn	$8.95
Everlasting Moments	Dorothy Elizabeth Love	$8.95
Everything and More	Sinclair Lebeau	$8.95
Everything but Love	Natalie Dunbar	$8.95
Eve's Prescription	Edwina Martin Arnold	$8.95
Falling	Natalie Dunbar	$9.95
Fate	Pamela Leigh Starr	$8.95
Finding Isabella	A.J. Garrotto	$8.95
Forbidden Quest	Dar Tomlinson	$10.95
Forever Love	Wanda Thomas	$8.95
From the Ashes	Kathleen Suzanne	$8.95
	Jeanne Sumerix	
Gentle Yearning	Rochelle Alers	$10.95
Glory of Love	Sinclair LeBeau	$10.95
Go Gentle into that Good Night	Malcom Boyd	$12.95
Goldengroove	Mary Beth Craft	$16.95
Groove, Bang, and Jive	Steve Cannon	$8.99
Hand in Glove	Andrea Jackson	$9.95
Hard to Love	Kimberley White	$9.95
Hart & Soul	Angie Daniels	$8.95
Havana Sunrise	Kymberly Hunt	$9.95
Heartbeat	Stephanie Bedwell-Grime	$8.95
Hearts Remember	M. Loui Quezada	$8.95
Hidden Memories	Robin Allen	$10.95
Higher Ground	Leah Latimer	$19.95
Hitler, the War, and the Pope	Ronald Rychiak	$26.95
How to Write a Romance	Kathryn Falk	$18.95
I Married a Reclining Chair	Lisa M. Fuhs	$8.95
I'm Gonna Make You Love Me	Gwyneth Bolton	$9.95
Indigo After Dark Vol. I	Nia Dixon/Angelique	$10.95

Other Genesis Press, Inc. Titles (continued)

Indigo After Dark Vol. II	Dolores Bundy/Cole Riley	$10.95
Indigo After Dark Vol. III	Montana Blue/Coco Morena	$10.95
Indigo After Dark Vol. IV	Cassandra Colt/	$14.95
	Diana Richeaux	
Indigo After Dark Vol. V	Delilah Dawson	$14.95
Icie	Pamela Leigh Starr	$8.95
I'll Be Your Shelter	Giselle Carmichael	$8.95
I'll Paint a Sun	A.J. Garrotto	$9.95
Illusions	Pamela Leigh Starr	$8.95
Indiscretions	Donna Hill	$8.95
Intentional Mistakes	Michele Sudler	$9.95
Interlude	Donna Hill	$8.95
Intimate Intentions	Angie Daniels	$8.95
Ironic	Pamela Leigh Starr	$9.95
Jolie's Surrender	Edwina Martin-Arnold	$8.95
Kiss or Keep	Debra Phillips	$8.95
Lace	Giselle Carmichael	$9.95
Last Train to Memphis	Elsa Cook	$12.95
Lasting Valor	Ken Olsen	$24.95
Let's Get It On	Dyanne Davis	$9.95
Let Us Prey	Hunter Lundy	$25.95
Life Is Never As It Seems	J.J. Michael	$12.95
Lighter Shade of Brown	Vicki Andrews	$8.95
Love Always	Mildred E. Riley	$10.95
Love Doesn't Come Easy	Charlyne Dickerson	$8.95
Love in High Gear	Charlotte Roy	$9.95
Love Lasts Forever	Dominiqua Douglas	$9.95
Love Me Carefully	A.C. Arthur	$9.95
Love Unveiled	Gloria Greene	$10.95
Love's Deception	Charlene Berry	$10.95
Love's Destiny	M. Loui Quezada	$8.95
Mae's Promise	Melody Walcott	$8.95
Magnolia Sunset	Giselle Carmichael	$8.95

Other Genesis Press, Inc. Titles (continued)

Matters of Life and Death	Lesego Malepe, Ph.D.	$15.95
Meant to Be	Jeanne Sumerix	$8.95
Midnight Clear	Leslie Esdaile	$10.95
(Anthology)	Gwynne Forster	
	Carmen Green	
	Monica Jackson	
Midnight Magic	Gwynne Forster	$8.95
Midnight Peril	Vicki Andrews	$10.95
Misconceptions	Pamela Leigh Starr	$9.95
Misty Blue	Dyanne Davis	$9.95
Montgomery's Children	Richard Perry	$14.95
My Buffalo Soldier	Barbara B. K. Reeves	$8.95
Naked Soul	Gwynne Forster	$8.95
Next to Last Chance	Louisa Dixon	$24.95
Nights Over Egypt	Barbara Keaton	$9.95
No Apologies	Seressia Glass	$8.95
No Commitment Required	Seressia Glass	$8.95
No Ordinary Love	Angela Weaver	$9.95
No Regrets	Mildred E. Riley	$8.95
Notes When Summer Ends	Beverly Lauderdale	$12.95
Nowhere to Run	Gay G. Gunn	$10.95
O Bed! O Breakfast!	Rob Kuehnle	$14.95
Object of His Desire	A. C. Arthur	$8.95
Office Policy	A. C. Arthur	$9.95
Once in a Blue Moon	Dorianne Cole	$9.95
One Day at a Time	Bella McFarland	$8.95
Only You	Crystal Hubbard	$9.95
Outside Chance	Louisa Dixon	$24.95
Passion	T.T. Henderson	$10.95
Passion's Blood	Cherif Fortin	$22.95
Passion's Journey	Wanda Thomas	$8.95
Past Promises	Jahmel West	$8.95
Path of Fire	T.T. Henderson	$8.95

Other Genesis Press, Inc. Titles (continued)

Path of Thorns	Annetta P. Lee	$9.95
Peace Be Still	Colette Haywood	$12.95
Picture Perfect	Reon Carter	$8.95
Playing for Keeps	Stephanie Salinas	$8.95
Pride & Joi	Gay G. Gunn	$8.95
Promises to Keep	Alicia Wiggins	$8.95
Quiet Storm	Donna Hill	$10.95
Reckless Surrender	Rochelle Alers	$6.95
Red Polka Dot in a World of Plaid	Varian Johnson	$12.95
Rehoboth Road	Anita Ballard-Jones	$12.95
Reluctant Captive	Joyce Jackson	$8.95
Rendezvous with Fate	Jeanne Sumerix	$8.95
Revelations	Cheris F. Hodges	$8.95
Rise of the Phoenix	Kenneth Whetstone	$12.95
Rivers of the Soul	Leslie Esdaile	$8.95
Rock Star	Rosyln Hardy Holcomb	$9.95
Rocky Mountain Romance	Kathleen Suzanne	$8.95
Rooms of the Heart	Donna Hill	$8.95
Rough on Rats and Tough on Cats	Chris Parker	$12.95
Scent of Rain	Annetta P. Lee	$9.95
Second Chances at Love	Cheris Hodges	$9.95
Secret Library Vol. 1	Nina Sheridan	$18.95
Secret Library Vol. 2	Cassandra Colt	$8.95
Shades of Brown	Denise Becker	$8.95
Shades of Desire	Monica White	$8.95
Shadows in the Moonlight	Jeanne Sumerix	$8.95
Sin	Crystal Rhodes	$8.95
Sin and Surrender	J.M. Jeffries	$9.95
Sinful Intentions	Crystal Rhodes	$12.95
So Amazing	Sinclair LeBeau	$8.95
Somebody's Someone	Sinclair LeBeau	$8.95

Other Genesis Press, Inc. Titles (continued)

Someone to Love	Alicia Wiggins	$8.95
Song in the Park	Martin Brant	$15.95
Soul Eyes	Wayne L. Wilson	$12.95
Soul to Soul	Donna Hill	$8.95
Southern Comfort	J.M. Jeffries	$8.95
Still the Storm	Sharon Robinson	$8.95
Still Waters Run Deep	Leslie Esdaile	$8.95
Stories to Excite You	Anna Forrest/Divine	$14.95
Subtle Secrets	Wanda Y. Thomas	$8.95
Suddenly You	Crystal Hubbard	$9.95
Sweet Repercussions	Kimberley White	$9.95
Sweet Tomorrows	Kimberly White	$8.95
Taken by You	Dorothy Elizabeth Love	$9.95
Tattooed Tears	T. T. Henderson	$8.95
The Color Line	Lizzette Grayson Carter	$9.95
The Color of Trouble	Dyanne Davis	$8.95
The Disappearance of Allison Jones	Kayla Perrin	$5.95
The Honey Dipper's Legacy	Pannell-Allen	$14.95
The Joker's Love Tune	Sidney Rickman	$15.95
The Little Pretender	Barbara Cartland	$10.95
The Love We Had	Natalie Dunbar	$8.95
The Man Who Could Fly	Bob & Milana Beamon	$18.95
The Missing Link	Charlyne Dickerson	$8.95
The Price of Love	Sinclair LeBeau	$8.95
The Smoking Life	Ilene Barth	$29.95
The Words of the Pitcher	Kei Swanson	$8.95
Three Wishes	Seressia Glass	$8.95
Through the Fire	Seressia Glass	$9.95
Ties That Bind	Kathleen Suzanne	$8.95
Tiger Woods	Libby Hughes	$5.95
Time is of the Essence	Angie Daniels	$9.95
Timeless Devotion	Bella McFarland	$9.95
Tomorrow's Promise	Leslie Esdaile	$8.95

Truly Inseparable	Wanda Y. Thomas	$8.95
Unbreak My Heart	Dar Tomlinson	$8.95
Uncommon Prayer	Kenneth Swanson	$9.95
Unconditional	A.C. Arthur	$9.95
Unconditional Love	Alicia Wiggins	$8.95
Under the Cherry Moon	Christal Jordan-Mims	$12.95
Unearthing Passions	Elaine Sims	$9.95
Until Death Do Us Part	Susan Paul	$8.95
Vows of Passion	Bella McFarland	$9.95
Wedding Gown	Dyanne Davis	$8.95
What's Under Benjamin's Bed	Sandra Schaffer	$8.95
When Dreams Float	Dorothy Elizabeth Love	$8.95
Whispers in the Night	Dorothy Elizabeth Love	$8.95
Whispers in the Sand	LaFlorya Gauthier	$10.95
Wild Ravens	Altonya Washington	$9.95
Yesterday Is Gone	Beverly Clark	$10.95
Yesterday's Dreams, Tomorrow's Promises	Reon Laudat	$8.95
Your Precious Love	Sinclair LeBeau	$8.95

Order Form

Mail to: Genesis Press, Inc.
P.O. Box 101
Columbus, MS 39703

Name _____

Address _____

City/State _____ Zip _____

Telephone _____

Ship to (if different from above)

Name _____

Address _____

City/State _____ Zip _____

Telephone _____

Credit Card Information

Credit Card # _____ ☐ Visa   ☐ Mastercard

Expiration Date (mm/yy) _____ ☐ AmEx   ☐ Discover

Qty.	Author	Title	Price	Total

Use this order

form, or call

1-888-INDIGO-1

Total for books _____

Shipping and handling:
  $5 first two books,
  $1 each additional book _____

Total S & H _____

Total amount enclosed _____

Mississippi residents add 7% sales tax